A Passionate Apology

MacHeath moved toward her swiftly, closing the space between them in three paces, and then he captured her hands behind her, holding them against the mast.

"Will you accept the apology of a boneheaded clod?"

Alexa tipped her head up. "You forgot overbearing and insufferable."

Her eyes were still challenging him, but there was a slight smile playing about her lips.

When he kissed her, she was already straining up to meet him. She moaned softly as he tightened his hold, thrusting her back against the mast with his body, leaning into her with all his strength, and nearly lifting her off her feet. Again and again he kissed her, taking her mouth, groaning against it, tasting her until his head swam and his knees trembled. She smelled of open air and heather, and her lips were dappled with sea spray that tasted sweeter than nectar. . . .

The Prodigal Hero

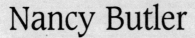

Nancy Butler

A SIGNET BOOK

SIGNET
Published by New American Library, a division of
Penguin Putnam Inc., 375 Hudson Street,
New York, New York 10014, U.S.A.
Penguin Books Ltd, 27 Wrights Lane,
London W8 5TZ, England
Penguin Books Australia Ltd,
Ringwood, Victoria, Australia
Penguin Books Canada Ltd, 10 Alcorn Avenue,
Toronto, Ontario, Canada M4V 3B2
Penguin Books (N.Z.) Ltd, 182–190 Wairau Road,
Auckland 10, New Zealand

Penguin Books Ltd, Registered Offices:
Harmondsworth, Middlesex, England

First published by Signet, an imprint of New American Library, a division of
Penguin Putnam Inc.

First Printing, November 2000
10 9 8 7 6 5 4 3 2 1

Dedicated to Lisa Purcell—
my dear friend, my first reader

And to the members of New Jersey Romance Writers—
a constant wellspring of support and inspiration

Bring quickly the best robe, and put it on him . . .
and bring the fatted calf . . . for this my son was dead,
and is alive again, he was lost, and is found.

Luke 16:22–24

Fancy gloves wears old MacHeath, dear . . .

Bertolt Brecht
The Threepenny Opera

Chapter 1

Christmas is coming, the goose is getting fat . . .

With a muted growl, MacHeath shook off the words of the
old carol that kept repeating inside his head. In the dank,
chilled warrens of London's East End, he doubted if even the
geese were getting fat. If there was one thing the men and
women who loitered on the cracked pavement and straggled
out of the gin shops had in common, it was that they were lean.
Wolfishly lean. Made gaunt by the gnawing, perpetual hunger
of poverty, and worn down by the bleakness of life in this unholy backwater of the thriving metropolis. Even the youngest
of the children who gathered at the street corners, trying to
cadge a penny from every passing stranger, bore haunted ex-
pressions in their pinched faces.

He hiked up the collar of his ragged greatcoat against the
icy dampness, and then fingered the coins in his pocket with
his left hand. He could eat or he could drink. The few
shillings he possessed would not let him do both.

As he passed the entrance to a tavern with the dubious
name of the Doxy's Choice, the decision was made for him.
Alf Connor, and his mate, Bully Finch, were huddled inside
the doorway, well out of the stiff wind that was blowing like
frozen daggers off the nearby Thames. Connor owed him
five pounds, a sum that would be most welcome considering
his current financial situation.

He did a half turn back to the two men and saluted them
with a crooked grin that held little mirth. Connor's narrow
face fell when he recognized MacHeath.

"Mackie," he muttered, ducking his head once in acknowledgment. "You know Bully Finch?"

"Aye," MacHeath said. "We've met in passing."

Finch's broad cheeks tightened into a smile that was more of a grimace. "Haven't seen you in a dog's age," he said, before blowing hard on his fingers to warm them. "Been out of town?"

MacHeath nodded. "I found myself an easy berth as valet to a rich Cornish cub. I passed the spring and summer with him."

Finch chortled, rapping his knuckles on MacHeath's shoulder. "That's a fine joke, Mackie, you as a gentleman's gentleman. Your cub ever notice you was missing one of your paws?"

"It occurred to him eventually," MacHeath drawled. "He wasn't the most wide-awake of fellows."

"Hard to miss that stump, eh?" Finch said. "Even for a gentry cove."

"Not a stump any longer," Connor pronounced with a wink. "Look closer, Bully."

Finch leaned forward, his eyes widening when he beheld MacHeath's right hand. It was gloved, as the left one was, in tan leather. The fingers beneath the glove were set in a relaxed pose, half curled toward the palm. It wouldn't fool anyone upon close examination, but MacHeath knew there were plenty of people who never guessed the glove covered nothing more than a carved wooden facsimile. But in spite of this clever ruse, he usually kept the hand in his pocket or tucked inside his coat front while he walked, fearful always of the despised epithets . . . maimed, crippled, deformed.

"Gor," Finch murmured as he raised the false hand into the spill of light from the tavern's lantern. "It's like a bleedin' miracle."

MacHeath resisted pulling back as the other man examined the hand. Bully Finch was not someone you wanted to wrestle in a doorway. He was six and a half feet of bulging sinew arranged over a big-boned frame that would have done a prizefighter proud. MacHeath was not a small man, nor was he lacking in courage, but he'd think twice about crossing Finch, at least over something as trifling as this. He gritted his teeth and stood still while the man poked and prodded the shaped glove.

"He had it made in Scotland this fall," Connor pronounced with a knowing look. "Some young doctor up there messing about with soldiers who lost their arms and legs in the war. I ran into Mackie directly he got back from there."

"*And lost five pounds to me at cards,*" MacHeath muttered to himself.

Finch whistled in admiration as he released the hand, which MacHeath promptly tucked into his coat front. "Ain't that a pip. My da' lost a leg in a wagon accident. Dragged half a mile, he was, behind his team. Poor old git hobbled around on crutches till the day he died. He sure could have used that Scots doctor."

MacHeath nodded toward the nail-studded door. "You going inside?" The icy needles of wind were having no trouble penetrating his ancient greatcoat.

The two men exchanged a furtive glance, then Connor said, "We be waiting for someone. Business and all."

MacHeath knew better than to inquire after the nature of their business. In this part of London, when two men waited out in the cold to meet someone, chances were pretty fair that any commerce at hand was of the illegal variety. He shrugged and brushed past them. "When you are finished," he said over his shoulder to Connor, "come inside. We have some business of our own to discuss."

Connor winced. His voice rose an octave. "I bin meaning to come to you, Mackie. You know I am good for what I owe. And if this cove ever shows up, why I'll have—"

Bully Finch elbowed him hard in the ribs. Connor's mouth snapped shut, and he looked stricken for an instant. "I'll come inside," he assured MacHeath. "I'll need a dram after waiting out here in this perishing cold."

MacHeath passed into the dark, smoky interior. He studied the layout of the place for a moment before claiming a seat on the high-backed settle beside the fireplace, where he stretched his long legs out toward the hearth with a sigh of relief. He noticed with a sour grin that someone had hung a ragged garland of pine boughs over the mantel in a failed attempt to add a bit of seasonal cheer to the seedy tavern. Christmas *was* coming, but the merriment and gaiety that would spread through the prosperous sections of London would never permeate the mean walls of the Doxy's Choice.

The barmaid, a wraith in faded muslin, brought him a bottle of gin and lingered a moment to smile down at him, displaying her discolored teeth. At least she still had most of them. But he was impervious to the open invitation in her eyes or the brazen posture of her angular body. When he refused to respond to her whispered offer, she took herself off, muttering loudly about men who acted above themselves.

He was just beginning his onslaught on the gin bottle when he heard Finch's gruff baritone come drifting up from over the high back of the settle. "I promise you, we're safe as houses. They know me and Connor here . . . know better than to bother us."

Connor's reedy voice added, "There's no point in us freezing our tails off outside. Just sit yourself down there, against the wall. All cozy and private."

MacHeath shifted on his seat until he was at the end of the settle nearest the wall. Tucking his head back into the corner, he pretended to be asleep.

Another man was speaking now, his voice a sibilant whisper that MacHeath was barely able to make out. When the man raised his voice at one point, the hair on MacHeath's nape stood right on end.

Good God! He'd recognize that voice in the farthest reaches of hell. Even though it had been ten years since he'd heard it, it had been seared into his memory. Darwin Quincy, the only man MacHeath had ever taken the trouble to hate, was sitting behind him with two of the rookery's most unsavory denizens. Like always harkened to like, he knew, so it was no surprise that Quincy was trafficking with Connor and Finch. What did surprise him was that Quincy, who had been a notorious nipfarthing all those years ago, had chosen these two as accomplices. Their services never came cheaply.

He hitched closer to the tiny opening between the wall and the settle, listening intently.

"You have to make sure she's terrified once you've gotten her away from the coach," Quincy was saying emphatically. "Though I don't want her actually harmed. I trust you two know the difference."

"Happens we do," Finch said. "But how can we put the fear o' God into her, if we don't manhandle her a bit?"

Quincy laughed softly. "She is a gently bred young woman, Mr. Finch. I expect the mere sight of you two will be quite enough to send her off into a swoon. She's a plucky chit, but her father's kept her well away from riffraff."

"Plucky, eh?" Connor said, and then asked, "What if she puts up a fight?"

"Can we cosh her?" Finch's tone was almost anticipatory.

Darwin Quincy sighed. "Take whatever measures it requires to frighten her out of her wits. Shoot one of the coachmen, perhaps . . . that should set the proper tone. And then, once you've made off with her, you can tie her up or gag her if you must. But don't mark her. She is to be my wife, after all." He paused and added silkily. "I hope you take my meaning, gentlemen."

Finch guffawed. "You don't want us tumbling her. Now, that's a pity . . . always hankered to bed a lady."

Quincy made a disparaging noise. "Trust me, Mr. Finch, they are never worth the trouble. Though the woman in question is hardly a real lady . . . her father is nothing more than a glorified merchant, a shipbuilder who puffs himself up like a gentleman."

MacHeath's head jerked up slightly in surprise. The shipbuilder had to be Quincy's uncle, Alexander Prescott. MacHeath had worked for him a time back in Exeter. He knew full well that the man only had one child, a rag-tail hoyden of a daughter, who hardly had the makings of a gently bred lady. He'd always suspected she'd end up disguising herself as a boy and sailing off on one of her father's merchant ships. Somehow he doubted the passing years had turned the minx into a paragon of virtue.

She had to be, what . . . twenty-five now. And she'd obviously never married, not if Darwin Quincy was plotting to make her his wife. Or perhaps she'd been widowed. Alexandra Prescott was exactly the sort of female to drive a man to an early grave.

The men behind him let their conversation lag when the barmaid came over to refill their glasses. While Finch bantered with the woman, MacHeath let his mind wander back thirteen years, to the fateful summer's day when he'd first met Alexander Prescott's daughter.

She'd been ambling along one of the piers where her father's tall ships were berthed, a black-and-white spaniel puppy capering beside her. The spaniel kept nipping at her long skirts and making her laugh. MacHeath was testing the lines on one of the new ships, and when he heard a workman call out to her in greeting, he'd gone to the ship's rail to watch her pass by.

Everyone who knew Alexander Prescott had an opinion about his daughter. They swore she was a miracle child, borne to two people both well into their forties. They also proclaimed her a changeling—this being the usual explanation when fair-skinned, towheaded parents brought forth a swarthy, black-haired child. Some whispered that she was the devil's own spawn, reckless and spoiled, and yet as full of impish charm as Old Nick himself.

MacHeath had worked for her father for nearly a month, but had not yet set eyes on the remarkable Alexa. He'd watched her progress down the dock with a dawning smile. There was surely nothing conventionally pretty about her. Her dark curls were tangled into an unruly mop, and her wrinkled white pinafore looked as though she'd had it off a vagrant. But there was a spirit there—in the way she danced along the wooden planking and in the boyish lilt of her voice as she playfully chided the puppy. It showed in the tilt of her head and the bright gleam in her eyes. He felt his heart swell.

In spite of her unkempt appearance, she moved with assurance and grace, a child secure in the knowledge of her own consequence. Neither proud nor arrogant, merely at ease. Since MacHeath rarely felt at ease, he'd found himself envying this girl. Not for her father's wealth or for her bright future, but for her sheer, brimming confidence.

As she drew even with the side of his ship, his pleasure in watching her turned to dismay. The gamboling puppy had finally managed to trip her, and she stumbled onto her knees, perilously near the edge of the pier. When she scrambled to her feet, he saw that the hem of her skirt was still caught beneath her slipper. He leaned forward and called out to warn her. As she spun to look up at him, she staggered. The next instant, she overbalanced backward and tumbled into the water with a startled cry.

MacHeath didn't hesitate. He vaulted over the railing in one fluid motion, aiming his dive for the few feet of clearance between the ship's side and the dock. He hit the water in the exact spot where the girl had gone under, praying he could find her in the murky river water. A pale billow of white floated below him, and he reached for it. His fingers closed tightly over her arm, then he tugged her swiftly to the surface, stroking with his free arm, while she struggled against him.

A small crowd of workmen had gathered at the edge of the dock. Eager hands reached down to draw the pair from the water. MacHeath knelt there on the sun-warmed planking and swiped his wet hair back from his brow. The girl was on her feet now, surrounded by her father's men. In the distance, the commanding figure of Alexander Prescott could be seen hurrying along the dock, his nephew, Darwin Quincy, trailing behind him.

MacHeath rose and took a step toward the girl. "Are ye all right, miss?"

She pushed past the men encircling her, came right up to him, and swung her small fist at his face. The blow connected with his nose hard enough to make his eyes water.

"*Aow!*" he cried, staggering back more in surprise than in pain. "What th' devil was that for?"

"For making me look like a fool," she said between her small white teeth.

He rubbed gingerly at his nose. "What else was I tae do? Ye gave me such a fright, pitchin' into the water like that."

"I gave *you* a fright?" she exclaimed hotly. "How do you think I felt when something grabbed onto me under the water and wouldn't let go?"

"I was trying to save yer life," he muttered, fighting to restrain his temper. As usual it didn't work. "And if ye had better manners," he growled, taking a step toward her, "ye would thank me for not leaving you there tae drown."

"I wasn't drowning," she proclaimed with a scowl.

Prescott now loomed over them, his shaggy white brows bristling with concern. He wrapped an arm around his dripping daughter and tucked her tight against his side. She looked up at him, into eyes that were the same shade of clear, bright blue. "Tell him, Father. Tell him I wasn't drowning."

"She swims like a fish, actually," Prescott said with overt pride. "Learned how three summers ago in Barbados. But I believe you're one of the new lads, so you wouldn't know that. As for her manners . . ." He tugged on one of the girl's wet tendrils. "She is young yet. There's plenty of time before I need to spoil her nature with propriety and such." He smiled at MacHeath then, and held out his hand. "But it's never safe to be in the water so close to a ship, so I will thank you for your efforts, Mr.—"

MacHeath offered his name to the man, the name he had been born with. The one he hadn't dared to use in the past ten years.

Prescott shook his hand enthusiastically. Behind them Darwin Quincy fussed with the watch fobs on his elegant waistcoat and muttered to his uncle that they would miss their luncheon if they tarried.

"You go on to the house without me," Prescott said, motioning to the carriage that waited at the end of the pier. "And take Alexa with you. I'll stay here and get this young fellow cleaned up."

As he turned to follow Prescott, MacHeath didn't miss Quincy's piqued expression. He couldn't resist smiling when Alexa tossed her wet hair over one shoulder, spattering her cousin's pristine coat with a shower of water droplets.

Prescott had taken him back to his office and given him one of his own shirts and a pair of dry breeches, all the while engaging him in conversation about shipbuilding and hull design and rigging. He'd listened calmly while MacHeath spoke of his life with his late father, a shipwright in Clyde, and of his own dreams of designing fast ships.

The old man must have liked what he heard, because from that day on MacHeath had advanced rapidly in the shipyard. Before a year had passed, he found himself working with the old man's select team of shipwrights, designing the fleet merchant ships for which the Prescott name was famous. For the first time in his life, he felt as though he'd found a safe harbor.

In some strange way, his success had been due to that willful child.

He'd tried to befriend her, even brought bones for her spaniel whenever the old man required his presence at the manor house on the hill above the village. But whenever he and Alexa Prescott were face-to-face—and she always seemed to be underfoot after the incident on the dock—she would just glower at him and refuse to say a civil word. Eventually they achieved a sort of truce, but she was likely to dart away from him in a temper at the slightest provocation.

Connor and Finch would have their work cut out for them, he reckoned, if they really planned to carry her off. Especially if she'd retained that pugnacious streak.

Behind the settle, chairs scraped on the oak floor. He heard Quincy utter a few final instructions, and then he watched as the slim blond gentleman crossed the floor of the tavern, holding his arms close to his sides. From the back, Prescott's nephew hadn't changed much, still the delicate tulip of fashion. MacHeath suspected his face would have shown the passage of time—the bland handsomeness now marred by ten years' worth of excessive drinking, Quincy's own particular vice.

MacHeath waited until the blond man was through the door before he moved from his seat. He scuttled away from the fireplace, keeping his head below the raised settle, and found a deserted table near the tavern's back door. He eased into a chair and resumed his onslaught on the gin bottle.

Over the next hour, he watched the barmaid carrying pints of ale to Connor and Finch. He knew it wouldn't be long until they'd need to avail themselves of the privy behind the tavern. When Connor at last came stumbling across the floor toward the back door, MacHeath placed one booted leg in his path. Connor banged up against it and glared at him resentfully. "Let me through, Mackie . . ."

"Not until we settle your account. I gather your, er, business went smoothly."

"Can't say that I'm happy," Connor whined. "Finch set up this rig . . . so he's claiming the larger cut. But I'm one step from the noose, and if I get nabbed for carrying off a lady, I'll swing for sure."

"Desperate times call for desperate measures," MacHeath said, and then added softly to himself. "And these are most desperate times." He cocked his head up at Connor. "So Finch's gentleman is arranging the abduction of a lady. Not my idea of romance, but then I've always had traditional notions in that department. You know . . . flowers, carriage drives, music, and moonlight. But who am I to quibble if abduction is the latest rage in the *ton*?"

"It ain't the latest rage." With a grumbling sigh Connor sank down into the chair beside MacHeath. "Finch's gentleman tried all those other things. The lady wants nothing to do with him."

Smart girl, Alexa, he thought approvingly.

"So he's fixed it that Bully and me will carry her off while she's traveling down to her da's house for Christmas. A few miles outside Reading we'll waylay the coach." He cast a nervous look over his shoulder, but Finch was obscured behind the settle.

"Maybe you shouldn't be telling me this," MacHeath said idly. "None of my concern."

"Aw, I'm not giving you any of the particulars. The thing is, I'm not sure I can trust Bully not to tup the chit. He's always had a weakness where females are concerned. And the gentleman won't pay up if the lady is . . . well, you know."

"Compromised, I believe is the word."

"Right. Because, you see, the gentleman is the one who's goin' to do that. We're to take her to some hedge tavern, where he'll rescue her, pretend to chase us off like a fine, brave lad. Of course, he and the chit will be forced to spend the night together, which will leave her reputation in tatters."

MacHeath caught himself before he blurted out, *But he's her cousin*. Still, it made no sense; a lady traveling with her cousin, however loathsome the individual, was hardly compromised.

In his next breath, Connor offered an explanation. "If she don't throw herself into his arms in gratitude—which I take leave to doubt—I expect he'll have to resort to a bit of coercion. And now Bully's gotten spleenish 'cause he wants to be the first one in."

"Is she such a beauty, then?" he asked, toying with the bottle cork. "That the gentleman can't live without her?"

Connor blew out a breath. "Pull the other one, old sod. Money's the lure here . . . it always is. Chit's father is rolling in the ready, and she's his only get. Finch's gentleman's got hisself in deep with the bloodsuckers . . . so he told them he was betrothed to the girl to keep them from pounding him into the next year."

"Next year's not far off," MacHeath said softly. He quite liked the image of Darwin Quincy being beaten to a pulp by outraged moneylenders. He did not, however, like the image of Alexa Prescott being ravished by her cousin.

Connor pushed back his chair abruptly and stood up. "I better go. . . ."

He took a step toward the back door, and MacHeath's left hand snaked out and grabbed him by the wrist. "Aren't you forgetting something?"

Connor winced. "Lord, Mackie, you got a wicked grip for cripple." He dug around in his breeches pocket and pulled out a pile of sovereigns, tossing them onto the table. "Good thing Finch's gentleman paid us sommat in advance."

As he staggered away toward the door, MacHeath swept

up the coins with his good hand. Connor had paid him something over what he'd owed—in sovereigns *and* in information. Which was fair, considering the debt was over a month old.

He left the tavern before Connor returned. The night air was frigid, but with gin in his belly and gold in his purse, MacHeath hardly noticed. He tucked both hands into the deep pockets of his greatcoat and turned into the wind.

It was chiming midnight when he reached his rooming house; the booming bells of St. Mary-le-Bow echoed across the clear night. At the doorway, he paused to look up at the sky. Orion and his hounds coursed the heavens off to the east. In the northern sky the two Dippers hung suspended, with Polaris visible in the smaller constellation.

Once, in another lifetime, those stars had been his guide, the beacons he followed with as much certainty and awe as those three wise men who had followed a lone star to a stable in Bethlehem. He'd never been a religious man, but that particular story had always appealed to him, the timeless tale of a wondrous light shining down from the night sky, leading weary travelers to their goal. There wasn't a sailor born in any century since, whose heart didn't quicken to that image.

Sailor. He gave a dry laugh. Damned pointless to even think that word.

He avoided, at all costs, any thoughts of the time when the sea had been his life. But seeing Darwin Quincy, being reminded of Alexa Prescott and her father, had brought it all back to him—those three blessed years when he had designed ships for the old man. But that happy time hadn't lasted. Nothing good ever did, he knew that now. He'd been cast out in disgrace, left without the good name he'd been born with.

So he'd taken on another name and another life, as a Channel smuggler. And though the choice had placed him on the far side of the law, he had the solace of a life at sea. Eventually he'd inherited a ship from an aging smuggling captain whose arthritis forced him to retire. The *Siren Song* he'd named her, though she'd been called the *Black Bess* under old Tarlton. He knew it was bad luck to change a ship's name, but by the time he'd finished making modifications on her, she was hardly the same ship. The *Siren* had brought him only good luck. And good profits.

That was before he'd met up with an English spy in a tavern in Dover. The man had gotten him drunk, and had somehow convinced him to work for the British government carrying intelligence officers to France. No one knew the Channel better than he did, the fellow had insisted, no one had a faster ship. MacHeath had been flattered, but there was more to it than that. He'd realized that night—or more truthfully, the next morning when his head cleared—that he wanted more than anything to reclaim the part of himself that he'd lost, his sense of purpose and some small particle of honor.

So he'd agreed to work for the Home Office, though in a most unofficial capacity. For the first time since he'd left the shipyard, he felt he was doing something worthwhile.

But that had ended abruptly two years ago. The *Siren Song* had been waiting off Calais to pick up her usual human cargo, when a French man o' war had appeared around the headland. The French ship had the weather gauge and, after a short chase, she'd blasted the *Siren* from the water. The sea was no longer an option for MacHeath after that, not only because he'd lost his ship. His hand had been crushed by a falling mast, and a French surgeon had been forced to amputate it.

Now there was only pain when he thought of the sea . . . pain and an incredible sense of loss.

And he blamed it all, every wretched course his life had taken, on one man—Darwin Quincy. It was Quincy who had been responsible for his disgrace at the shipyard, and his hatred of the man had festered for all those years since. Now, he realized, he had the means to pay him back. In spades.

Ah, but what was the use of it? It wouldn't regain him his lost hand or the good will of Alexander Prescott, the man he'd once thought of as the best master in the world.

With an oath he pushed the door open and went into the dim hall of the rooming house, still fighting off the strains of the cheerful carol that refused to leave his head.

"Christmas is coming, the goose is getting fat."

Chapter 2

Mrs. Reginald was sniffling every two minutes. And blowing her nose every five minutes. Alexa thought crossly that she could mark the stages of their journey by those noises.

Sniffle . . . sniffle . . . honk.

When she could stand it no longer, she reached over and pushed down the spine of the book her companion was reading. "Reggie," she said, "I love you dearly. Except for my father, you are my favorite person in the world." She took a deep breath. "But I shall go quietly insane if you don't stop sniffling. We have only been on the road two hours, and already my nerves are shattered."

The stout older woman, once her governess and now her hired companion, shook her head. "It's no use, my dear. Your father would insist that the upholstery in his new coach be stuffed with goose down, and you know how I am around feathers."

Alexa's black brows drew down. "You weren't this bad when we traveled to Bath in the summer . . . in this very coach."

"That is because the weather was mild, and we drove with the windows open. Now we are shut up tight in here, not that that is a bad thing. I can't remember a winter this cold in all my years."

"I'd rather be cold than driven to madness," Alexa pronounced under her breath.

Mrs. Reginald gave a weary sigh, and then leaned forward and let down the canvas panel that covered one window. She tried to hide her wince of dismay as a shaft of icy wind shot through it.

"Here," Alexa said as she drew off her thick sable muffler and leaned across the compartment to wrap it around her companion's throat. "This will keep you warm. You know I never feel the cold." She sat back with a satisfied smile.

Mrs. Reginald picked up her book, a collection of poems by William Wordsworth, and tried to make a show of reading. Alexa did not miss the shivers that coursed through her every so often, making the small book tremble in her mittened hands. The sniffling and honking had stopped, which was a relief, but Alexa now felt a lump of guilt somewhere in her middle. There was nothing Reggie would not do for her, and Alexa feared she had once again taken advantage of the woman's good nature.

Half an hour later, after Reggie's nose had gone quite red from the cold, and her lips a tight, pinched blue, Alexa shifted around and drew up the window covering. Her companion's smile of gratitude was hard to decipher in her nearly frozen face.

"Sorry," Alexa muttered. "That wasn't a very sensible plan. But thank you for making the attempt. If you like, I'll have the coachman order us extra hot bricks at the next posting house." She racked her brain to think of some other way to make amends. Alexa often told herself that she didn't possess a cruel nature, only a slightly selfish one. She now pondered where that subtle distinction lay.

She tried to sleep, head canted against one padded corner of the seat, hoping to give herself over to slumber before the sniffles started again. It was a vain hope. Within minutes of the coach's interior being sealed up, Reggie's nose began to misbehave.

Sniffle . . . sniffle . . . honk. Sniffle . . . sniffle . . . honk.

Alexa ground her teeth and gave up any notion of sleep.

"It's a pity your cousin won't be joining us for the holiday," Mrs. Reginald said from behind her book. "We will be sadly lacking in company this year, especially since your aunt again chose not to accompany us."

Alexa chuckled softly. "If you will recall, the last time

Aunt Elizabeth ventured into Papa's house for Christmas, they were at loggerheads the instant she walked through the door. They never got on, even when mama was alive to act as mediator. No, I think she will be much happier spending the holiday with her friends in Norwich."

"Even more reason, then, for your cousin to be there among his family."

"I don't wish to discuss my cousin," she said sharply.

Mrs. Reginald's plump chin took on a decided jut. "I will never understand why you are so severe with Mr. Quincy. He is all that is pleasing in a young gentleman . . . such polished address, such a winning manner. You would do well, as I have told you countless times, to make of him your beau ideal—I wager there is not a gentleman in the *ton* who can match him for looks, breeding, or conversation."

"He is a swine," Alexa said just loud enough for Reggie to hear.

"I am not saying you should marry him, though that would not be beyond thought, since he is your second cousin. I do not hold with first cousins marrying, as you know, but—"

"Enough," Alexa cried softly. "Please, Reggie. I realize Darwin has made a point to win you over. But you must understand that any connection with him is unthinkable. He is vain and idle, among other things."

"And what young man of the *ton* is not? You think I do not note them at the assemblies and balls, with their peacocking ways and their languid airs? It's the fashion for them to appear thus, and none is so fashionable as your cousin."

Alexa bit back her heated response. It would not help to point out Darwin's other, less savory, pursuits to her companion. Reggie would merely humph and reply that her cousin's vices were nothing more than a display of manly character. Alexa could almost hear the words; they'd been down this road many times before.

She retreated back into silence, but her thoughts were no longer easy. Darwin Quincy had taken hold of them, and she could not shake him off.

A week earlier he had come to see her at her Aunt Elizabeth's home, offering his usual tale of woe. It did not surprise her to learn that he was once again sunk deep in debt. She *was* surprised, however, when he mentioned quite casually, that he'd made it known to a few friends that he and Alexa were to be married. She'd been outraged by that startling bit of news, but he'd pleaded with her to acknowledge the betrothal, even in pretense, for just a short while.

"I am bound to come about in time, Alex," he assured her. "I always do."

"What you always do," she proclaimed snidely, "is ride off to Cudbright and blackmail my father into giving you more funds. And no, don't look daggers at me, cousin. Blackmail is the proper word. I've heard you myself, reminding him how poor my matrimonial prospects would be with a cousin in debtor's prison."

"You're a selfish little bitch," he muttered. "You've never had to do without, never had to pinch every farthing as I have. You don't have to watch your friends spending all over town, and know that your own pockets are empty."

Her eyes narrowed. "You gamble and drink to excess. I could find it in my heart to pity you, for I know that such things can take hold of a person. But I've also heard how you attach yourself to young men who are new to the *ton* and take advantage of their inexperience. There was Lord Spence, sent home to Ireland in disgrace, and young Vincent Berringer, who tried to hang himself after you'd ruined him."

He flicked his fingers. "I am not responsible for men who do not know how to go about in Society. If they choose to play at cards with me, and are unlucky enough to lose great sums, how am I responsible?" He gave a dry laugh. "Though better I should relieve them of their blunt, than some well-heeled nob."

When no humor surfaced in her expression after that sally, he changed his tack, becoming coaxing and conciliatory. "Come now, cuz. You don't really want to see old Quincy carried off by the bailiffs, do you? Let the *ton* believe we are to be wed for, say . . . a month. My creditors will give me some breathing space if they think I am about to marry into a fortune. I promise I will stay away from my clubs during that time—"

"Liar," she spat. "You will live at the gaming tables, hoping to recoup your losses. I know how your mind works. At the end of the month, you'd be even deeper in debt."

"Unless my luck changes. I'm due, Alex . . . I can feel it. Why, only last night I—"

"No," she cried. "I will not be part of this charade. I value my good name, Darwin Quincy, a deal more than you do yours. There will be no betrothal . . . you are the last man I would choose to ally myself with, even in pretense."

She'd gone from the room then, left him white-faced and quaking in anger. The memory of it still shook her—the whole encounter had been unpleasant, but what she most recalled was the unveiled hatred she had read in his eyes just before she closed the door. Thank goodness he wouldn't be plaguing them with his presence during the holidays—rumor had it that he was to spend them in Shropshire, with the latest in his long line of gullible young sprigs.

"Think of Christmas instead of your wretched cousin," she muttered. She forced herself to picture her father's house adorned with holly sprigs and evergreen boughs, the mantels bright with red ribbons, the presents beneath them wrapped in tissue paper in a rainbow of colors. It was a heartening image.

His house came alive during the holidays. There would be twelve days of feasting and merriment. Their neighbors would stop by for a visit—she especially looked forward to seeing Mr. Featherbridge, the local vicar. On Christmas Eve her father's workers and their families would come caroling in the great hall. She would prepare the traditional wassail bowl, as her mother had done before her, to welcome their guests.

Her father would be Lord Bountiful, his face beaming as he stood in the midst of his men, a sprig of greenery on the lapel of his finest coat. His generosity to his workers was well-known, but his bounty to Alexa was limited to the twelve days of Christmas. When the holiday merriment ended, when the last morsel of the last plum pudding had been consumed, he would send her away again. Because, dear Papa, in his misguided way, was convinced she would never find a proper husband if she lived under the same roof as a shipbuilder.

Her permanent exile had begun the year she turned seventeen. He'd sent her from his home, first to a hellish lady's academy, and then to while away the spring and fall in her great-aunt Elizabeth's mausoleum of a house in London. Summers were spent with her godmother in Bath. She had been so miserable those first years, missing the sea and the shipyards and the workers. As a child she had made those shipyards her second home, roaming freely among the lumber piles, the drums of nails and the great towering skeletons of the unfinished ships. The carpenters had been her nursemaids, and the skilled shipwrights had been her first tutors.

But that world was now forbidden to her, by a father who realized too late that he'd let his daughter become a wild rover. He'd once used those words as a term of endearment, but after she grew into womanhood and still wanted no part of the social world, they became his lament.

The only time he allowed her to visit him was at Christmas. For two blessed weeks. Every year she pleaded with him to let her stay, and for seven years he had remained adamant. It did no good to point out that she had not taken with the *ton*, that in spite of her expensive gowns and her careful schooling in deportment, in spite of a connection on her mother's side to Lord Ensleigh, she had been overlooked by most of the females in Society and by every eligible male. The numerous fortune hunters who had beaten a path to her aunt's door did not count. Nor did her cousin Darwin, who had begun wooing her long before his most recent descent into debt.

Great-Aunt Elizabeth, who had overseen her come-out— and was sister to the late Baron Ensleigh—had fallen into a decline over Alexa's rejection by Society. It was, she protested to anyone who would listen, unthinkable that Alexa had passed a Season in London without acquiring even one beau. The girl was wealthy, she would remind them, and had more than respectable breeding, at least on one side of her lineage. While it was true she was no beauty, being far too tall for fashion, and inclined to stride about like a hussar captain, she did possess a lovely pair of blue eyes. And though her hair tended to overpower her angular, pointed face, it was a glistening blue-black and would never require a curling iron.

Alexa recalled how, during that first Season, Aunt Elizabeth had insisted she crop her hair. A French hairdresser had been summoned to the house and had ended up swooning on the couch when Alexa threatened her with her own shears. The Prescott curls had remained untouched, her unruly coiffure setting Alexa apart from her peers as much as her tendency to speak her mind on matters political or to utter the occasional nautical oath.

Papa's not going to send me away this year, she now vowed silently. It was time she stood up to him and made him see reason. He was nearing his seventieth year, and though he denied it, age was finally taking its toll on him. She had seen the truth of this last Christmas—he had taken to walking with a cane, though he claimed his lameness was the result of a fall from a nervy young horse. And he insisted his loss of appetite was due to a brief illness he'd suffered in early December. But Alexa saw through his excuses. Her proud, pigheaded father was getting old, and he needed her.

She had spent the past year preparing herself for the task of assisting him at the shipyard. Her charity work with the Chelsea Hospital shifted from looking after the needs of patients to working with the harried director. He gladly taught her some basic accounting, and was amazed that within months she was handling a great deal of the hospital's finances and ordering of supplies.

No, she had not wasted her time in London this past year . . . she had learned to run a business and had honed her skills at managing people. It was her bad luck to have a father and a cousin whom she could not manage at all.

But she had made her decision. Five days after Christmas, she would come into her inheritance. It was another reason the season was so festive, since it encompassed the daughter of the house's birthday. And this year the daughter of the house was determined not to return to London. She would take lodgings in Cudbright if he refused to let her stay with him. Though that was not a happy option. She loved her home, even if it was completely her father's domain—his larger-than-life presence had penetrated every nook and cranny until there was no room for anyone else to lay a claim to the space.

She used to wonder if she would someday have a home of her own. It was the only thing that had ever made her consider marriage—that as a wife she might at last gain a place upon which she could leave her own stamp.

Ah, but that meant she would be required to share it with a husband, most likely a vain, arrogant fribble like her dreadful cousin Darwin, and where was the use of that? Just another male to order her about and squash her spirit. Her father did a topping job in that area, thank you very much.

By the time they reached Reading, it was growing dark. The coachman conferred with her while they changed horses at the White Hart, wondering if he should push on. Alexa was weary, but she was also anxious to close the distance to Devon.

"Do you mind if we travel on a bit farther?" she asked Reggie, still mindful of the older woman's comfort. "There's that pleasant inn near Newbury."

"Perhaps an hour more wouldn't hurt." The woman dabbed at her nose with a delicate square of linen. It was the tenth one she'd gone through since the journey began. Alexa had a notion to buy her some serviceable men's handkerchiefs and present them to her with her other Christmas packages.

"Drive on, then," she ordered, wishing William Coachman didn't look half frozen. He'd probably been hoping she would let them put up at the posting house, where he could thaw out before a taproom fire with a mug of hot cider on his knee. She promised herself that she would ask her father to give both coachmen a bonus.

They passed beyond the outskirts of Reading, across the flatlands that were the beginning of the vast Salisbury Plain.

Alexa had lowered the right-hand window flap to look back at the town—the lights of the city made a pleasant firefly glow against the darkening sky. She was about to fasten up the flap again, when a loud voice called out for the coach to stop. She started back in surprise as the coach drew to an abrupt halt.

Reggie clutched one hand to her bosom. "Highwaymen," she whimpered.

"Nonsense," said Alexa. "We are barely out of the city." She stuck her head out the window again and tried to see who was in the road ahead. She heard hoofbeats and then drew back a little as a caped rider approached her side of the coach. In the darkness of the road, she could make out that he was tall and seemed to be listing to one side.

"Please," he called out hoarsely. "I mean you no harm. I was attacked on the road . . . the ruffians shot me before I could get away."

Alexa could see he was holding his right hand to his shoulder. "Why didn't you just give them your money?" she asked evenly. "Only a fool would try to ride away from armed robbers."

He nudged his horse closer to the coach. "Please, I need a doctor, and I don't know how much longer I can stay in the saddle. If you would take me back to Reading in your coach. . . ."

"We must help him," Reggie hissed at her elbow. "It's the Christian thing to do."

"I suppose," Alexa said irritably. "I don't like it very much, though. He's probably going to bleed all over Papa's new upholstery."

"You are an unnatural child," Reggie pronounced.

"Well, I still don't like it."

Henry, the junior coachman, had climbed down from the box and was attempting to get the injured man off his horse. The rider groaned audibly as he tipped to one side.

"He's too heavy for me, miss," the lad cried, turning back to Alexa. "If he hits the ground, we'll never get him in the coach."

Grumbling in vexation, Alexa swung the door open. She

lifted her skirts, jumped down from the coach, and marched to where the man's horse stood.

"Here," she said to the coachman. "I'll hold him steady while you shift him off the saddle." She stretched up on tiptoes to grasp the man's uninjured shoulder.

Alexa gave a little shriek of alarm when the rider's right arm came swooping down around her waist. He tugged her right off her feet, lifting her up to the saddle. Alexa drew in a deep breath to protest this rough treatment, but the man set his hand firmly over her mouth.

"Get back," he snarled to the young coachman. "I have a pistol and I'll use it."

The lad scrambled away from the horse. Mrs. Reginald, meanwhile, was peering out the window, trying to make sense of what was happening beyond the coach.

"Sorry, ma'am," the rider called out to her. "But this was necessary. You'll find a message at the Lamb in Reading. Go back there now if you value your skins."

Alexa struggled against him as he spun his horse and sent it racing across the open ground. Everything happened so quickly, it took her several seconds to realize she was being carried away from her coach. Twisting her head to one side, she tried to scream out in fury. He again covered her mouth. That was when she bit him, setting her teeth hard into the ball of his thumb.

"Aow . . ." she moaned out loud. Good Lord, his flesh was as hard as granite. She felt along her front teeth with her tongue, sure she had chipped one of them.

The man was laughing against her ear. "Biting won't do you any good, hoyden."

She continued to fight him, drumming her legs against the horse's side, and trying to turn around so she could pummel him with her fists. He clamped his right arm tighter around her, holding her immobile. In the distance she could hear Reggie's staccato screams rising over the plain.

"Be still," he snarled. "I promise you are in no danger."

She growled back at him, through the gloved hand that was still clamped over her mouth. In spite of her red-hot anger, she found herself starting to shiver. The night wind whipped them as they raced across the open terrain, chilling her face and bared throat. She was sure she was trembling from the cold, not with fear. She'd never felt fear a day in her life. Boredom, restlessness, and impatience, but never, ever fear. If she hadn't given her warm fur muffler to Reggie, she knew she would not be quaking in this stranger's arms.

Chapter 3

"They never came . . . we waited near two hours, but the coach never appeared."

"You're sure you had marked the right coach?" Quincy asked brusquely.

Finch nodded. "Me and Connor waited at the White Hart in Reading, just like you told us. We were in the stable yard when your cousin stopped to change horses. I got a good look at the lady when she stepped out to speak to her driver. She was tall and dark-haired, just as you described her. Then we rode on ahead, two miles or so, and waited along the road. But they never came."

"Maybe they decided to stay in Reading," Quincy muttered. "Though I've traveled to Cudbright with my cousin any number of times, and she has never stayed there before. She has a preference for the Eight Bells in Newbury."

Connor nodded. "I heard her tell the driver to keep going. They was changing horses when we rode out."

Darwin Quincy fought down his simmering anger. Somewhere on the road between this hedge tavern and Reading, his uncle's coach had disappeared, and with it, all his prospects.

He stalked around the small parlor, thinking furiously. The two men watched him with anxious eyes. Well, Connor did. Finch looked as angry as Quincy, as though his honor as a hired thug had been compromised.

"Who else knew of our plan?" he said, turning on Finch.

"This is not a coincidence. Someone knew my cousin was traveling this route and got to her first."

"No one knew," Finch protested, shaking his bullet head. "On my mother's life, sir." Then his eyes narrowed. "No, wait a minute. There was a mate of Connor's there that night at the Doxy's Choice. Fellow name of MacHeath. He knew we was there to do some business."

Connor took a step forward, his shoulders sagging. "I just passed some time with him, sir, after you left. He's harmless."

Quincy sighed. "I knew we should have stayed out of that blasted grogshop. Could he have overheard us talking?"

"He was across the room," Connor insisted. "In the corner near the tap."

"Not when we came in, he wasn't," Finch muttered. "There were some fellows playing cards in that corner."

"Who is this MacHeath?"

Finch scratched the side of his shaved head. "He's a clever fellow who makes a living in the rookery working for the landlords—does some carpentry and hauling and such. And he's not above reasoning with tenants what's behind with their rent."

"If he's so clever, what's he doing in the East End?" Quincy asked.

"He used to be a Channel smuggler," Connor said. "There wasn't an excise cutter could catch him, they do say. But he went up against a French warship and lost his right hand in the battle. Had to leave the sea after that." He raised open hands to Quincy. "I promise you, sir, he's not the sort to tread on another fellow's business. You see, he fancies himself something of a gentleman. He's got a code about certain types of work."

"Alf means he won't kill a cove for money," Finch said, and then spat. "And he won't steal, neither. So I doubt he'd take it on himself to abduct a woman."

Quincy weighed this information, and then his face darkened. "Has it occurred to either of you that such a man, one who apes a gentleman's code, might think himself justified in undermining our plan?"

"Don't know," Finch said. "He's Connor's mate, not mine."

"Hard to say what Mackie will do," Connor said with a halfhearted shrug. "Saw him rescue a little boy once. The sprat had climbed out a third-floor window after a lost kite and crawled along a ledge where the wood was all rotten. A piece of it gave way under him, and he was left hanging by his fingers. Everyone in the street just stood there, waiting for him to fall. Old Mackie ran into that building and came through the window. He went right out on that ledge, easy like, talking to that boy the whole time. He got him up off the ledge and carried him back inside."

"Not bad for a man with one hand," Quincy murmured. "So he's brave, if somewhat foolhardy. That's a potent combination. Something in my gut is telling me he's our man."

"But he had no way of knowing which coach to stop," Connor protested again. "He's not a bleedin' mind reader. I never mentioned your name to him, sir. He can't have any idea who you are. He was still in the tavern long after you'd left . . . I swear he didn't follow you."

"Yes," Quincy hissed, "but perhaps he's been following you. You say he knew we had some business that night. Still, I'm damned if I can figure out how he knew we were planning an abduction."

Finch grasped his mate by the wrist. "You didn't tell him, Alf? Tell me you didn't shoot yer bleedin' mouth off to MacHeath."

Connor shook off the viselike grip. "And what if I did?" he cried. "Weren't no harm in it. I just told him we was carrying off a lady for a gent who wanted to marry her. A bit of a laugh, I thought."

"I am not laughing, Mr. Connor," said Quincy in a dangerously quiet voice. "I suspect your mate followed you to the White Hart. He saw my cousin conversing with her driver and, if he is as clever as you say, marked her as the woman you were after. This MacHeath was probably right behind you when you left the posting house. And he carried off the girl before the coach reached your hiding place."

Connor still looked doubtful. "Then, where is the coach?"

Finch cuffed him on the side of the head. "Back in Reading, you clodpole. They wouldn't just keep driving on across Salisbury Plain, now, would they, with the young lady taken? They'd have gone back to rouse the constables."

"Still, there may be a less melodramatic explanation for all this," Quincy said as he lowered himself into a chair. "The coach could have broken down on the outskirts of town . . . one of the horses might have gone lame."

"You better pray that's the case," Finch muttered to his companion.

"But if this MacHeath has taken my cousin, we've got to get her back as quickly as possible. Though it shouldn't be difficult to track down a one-handed man."

Finch shook his head. "Not that easy. He wears a cunning false hand made of wood, with a leather glove over it. Still, he's hard to miss."

"Tell me . . ." Quincy's fingers tapped restlessly on the arm of his chair.

"He's tall, nearly as tall as me. Broad in the shoulder, though he's no heavyweight. Dark hair, a bit of gray at the sides."

"He doesn't sound very remarkable. How would I pick him out in a crowd?"

"Follow the women," Connor stated bluntly. "He's a handsome devil, with a sailor's swagger and dark, knowing eyes."

"Never seen eyes like his," Finch concurred. "Like agate marbles they are, the gray and brown all swirled together."

"Well, if he waylaid my cousin's coach merely to warn her, this would-be gentleman, he would likely send her back to Reading. But if he's carried her off, as I fear, he'll head toward her father's home in Devon." He added with a sneer, "Even an honorable rogue might be tempted to seek a reward from the richest man in the south coast."

He stood up and tugged on his greatcoat. "I'll return to Reading. You two ride west toward Upavon. Check every posting house and inn along the way. But first check any blacksmith in the area, in case the coach had an accident and it turns out this MacHeath fellow had nothing to do with the girl's disappearance. Meet me at tomorrow morning in Up-avon."

He watched as the two men went grumbling from the room. They were doubtless tired and hungry. But they were also greedy, and he trusted their greed to spur them on. He'd pawned everything he could lay his hands on to pay their price, but it would be worth it once he had Alexa at his mercy. His sweet cousin, the shrew who had scorned him from the time she was a child. The upstart merchant's daughter who had too many scruples to aid her own cousin.

That recent humiliation was a keen-edged knife in his gut. But he'd stake his claim to her all the same and tame her in time. Though whether he tamed her or not was immaterial—his uncle's blunt did a lot more for his imagination than that black-haired she-devil.

It was nearing eleven when Quincy arrived at the White Hart. He strode past the nonplused ostler, right into the cavernous carriage shed. His uncle's coach was there, a dark hulk in the shadows. He congratulated himself on this piece of luck—Alexa might still be here after all.

But those hopes were dashed after a short conversation with the ostler, who was waiting for him at the door of the shed.

"What time did that coach arrive here?"

"Just past nine, it were. The lady inside was crying something pitiful. The landlord had to send for the constable. Seems her charge, a young lady traveling down to Devon, was stolen right out of the coach."

Quincy flinched slightly. "Stolen?"

"A highwayman, I reckon," the man said as he swung the double doors closed. "The chief constable said there wasn't nothing he could do until tomorrow."

But Quincy was no longer attending him. He hurried into the inn and asked one of the maids where Mrs. Reginald could be found. As he'd suspected, Alexa's companion was not asleep. She answered his knock, still dressed in her traveling costume, and fell at once into his arms.

"Oh, Mr. Quincy, it's a blessing you are here. Her father is not well these days, you know. A blow like this could send him to his grave."

"Steady on, Mrs. Reginald," he said, coaxing her back into a chair. "I am only come here by chance, thinking I would visit the old gent in Cudbright for the holidays. Imagine my surprise when I discovered you were staying at this inn."

"Then, you don't know? About Alexa?" Tears trembled on her lashes. "We were waylaid by a man on the road. The fiend pretended to be wounded, and when Alexa climbed out to aid him, he carried her off."

"The devil he did!" he cried in patent outrage. "But you're sure it was just one man alone?"

She nodded. "There was no one else nearby . . . I would have seen . . . it is so flat there, out on the plain. William Coachman, bless his heart, took his pistol and rode after him on one of the horses, but he couldn't catch him. Though he followed him far enough to know that the man was heading southwest, away from Reading."

"Damn!" Quincy muttered under his breath. When she recoiled, he smiled at her grimly. "Dear lady, you see how overset I am." He knelt down beside her chair. "But I will find this wretch, upon my honor I will."

Mrs. Reginald clutched his hands. "You are a good man, Mr. Quincy. I know Alexa never liked you, but then she is so harsh in her opinions of most men. I've always thought you were the perfect gentleman."

"I don't wish to distress you further, but I need a description of this fellow. I know it was dark. . . ."

"Yes, I realize now he stayed well back from the carriage lamps and had his muffler pulled up over his chin. He was tall . . . I could tell that much, even if he wasn't sitting upright in the saddle. And strong—he lifted Alexa with one arm."

"Which arm?"

Mrs. Reginald looked puzzled. "His right, I believe, though what that has to do with anything—"

"Which means he was holding the reins with his left hand," Quincy murmured under his breath. It corroborated his suspicions regarding MacHeath. "And how was the fellow dressed?"

"A long black cloak, but no hat. His hair was darkish, definitely not fair. He had the voice of a gentleman, and indeed, you might mistake him for one with his top boots and fine leather gloves."

He rose abruptly and laid a hand over his heart. "Now, please stop worrying, Mrs. Reginald. Stay here at the inn until I send word. I feel certain I can find her. And return her to her father's loving arms."

"You must know that Mr. Prescott will give you anything you ask, if you can bring Alexa home unharmed."

"I know," Quincy said softly. "I know."

The woman began to twist her fingers. Her eyes entreated him. "I must alert her father, but I don't know how to tell him that . . . that—"

He covered her hands and squeezed them gently. "You don't need to write anything, Mrs. Reginald. He won't be expecting Alexa for days yet. There is no need to alarm him." He mustered a quick smile. "I have every faith that she will be recovered. You can write to him after that."

He had one hand on the door latch, when she sprang up from her chair. "Oh, my stars, Mr. Quincy! I just remembered . . . the stranger called out to me before he rode off. I cannot believe I overlooked it. But I have been so very distressed."

"What did he say?" Quincy hissed.

"It was something quite puzzling. Let me think. . . ."

Quincy ground his teeth while Mrs. Reginald's brows knit fretfully. "He said, 'Go back to Reading if you value your skins.' And then he added, 'Look to the Lamb for the message.' " Her brows knit even more. "Some king of religious raving, do you think? Oh, my . . . could it be that Alexa was carried off by a Methodist?"

Quincy shook his head slowly. "I have no idea what the

blackguard meant. Perhaps it will come to me. But I must be off now."

As he made his way down the darkened staircase, his fertile brain was already plotting how to regain his advantage. With Finch and Connor's assistance, he should have little trouble tracking his cousin and her kidnapper. He'd been raised near Salisbury, so he was familiar with most of the small towns between Reading and Devon. He knew that a black-caped rogue with a well-dressed young lady in tow was bound to occasion remark from the villagers.

His major concern was that this MacHeath—and he refused to waste time with any scenario involving another, unknown, kidnapper—had seen him at the tavern. That was bad luck for MacHeath. It meant he'd have to be put out of the way before he could identify Quincy as the man who'd been plotting against Alexa.

Before he left the inn, he ordered the ostler to rouse Prescott's coachmen. The two men came down from the grooms' quarters over the stable, wrapped in horse blankets and in no fine mood.

He grilled them both about the rider who had stopped the coach, and got little more for his troubles than he'd obtained from Mrs. Reginald.

The junior coachman did add one bit of useful information, however. "The fellow was riding a prime goer," he declared. "A strapping bay hunter with a white star. Though, where a common robber got such a fine beast—"

William Coachman jabbed him lightly in the ribs. "He robbed him off some gentleman, Henry, that's where." The man scratched his chin and looked keenly at Quincy. "You aim to go after Miss Alexa, then?"

"Certainly. It's my duty as her cousin."

"That fellow what carried her off . . . he looked to be a man who could handle himself, if you take my meaning, sir."

Quincy bristled noticeably. "Be assured, William, I am skilled in all the gentlemanly arts of self defense."

The coachman squinted. "Been practicing with your pistol, eh, Mr. Q? Last time you shot against Miss Alexa, you didn't fare so—"

"That will be all," Quincy interjected. "I have no further need of you. But I'd like you to remain here and look after Mrs. Reginald while I'm gone. She is understandably distraught."

"Me and Henry had a mind to set out early this morning— see if we couldn't find that fellow's tracks. He might have gone to earth somewhere nearabouts. You never know."

"That will not be necessary," Quincy said emphatically. "I have a number of contacts here in Reading whom I can enlist. Men who are more suited for hunting down ruffians than you two."

"As you like, sir."

He touched his forelock to Quincy, and then both coachmen made their way up the wooden stairs. William stopped at the top and turned to his companion. "I'm not one to disobey an order from a gentleman, Henry my lad, but—"

Henry smiled wickedly and drawled, "But that's assuming it was a gentleman giving the order in the first place. And since Mr. Quincy is, as you and me both know, not quite the gentleman he pretends to be—"

"And since he is not our master, neither, I see no reason why we can't go after Miss Alexa ourselves."

"Besides which, that fribble couldn't find his phiz in a mirror. Bloody lot of hope he has of finding our mistress, even with all his bloomin' contacts. What say we start out now?"

"Done, Henry. We'll go tell Mrs. Reginald what we're about, and then we'll be off."

The landlord at the Lamb and Flag was not at all pleased to be roused from his sleep, especially since the blond gentleman shook him by the shoulders till his bones rattled.

"Dining parlor's closed," he grumbled up from his bench in the hallway. "Eh, what's that you say? A message? No one's left a message here."

"Fetch your wife," Quincy ordered. "Perhaps it was left with her."

"The wife's gone to Bath," the landlord stated as he straightened his tartan waistcoat, which had ridden up over his substantial belly while he dozed. "Her sister has the influenza."

Quincy paced along the hall, sending tiny plumes of dust up from the ancient carpet. "Is there another tavern in Reading called the Lamb? Or a shop of some sort?"

"Can't say that I know it, if there is."

"Was there a man in here earlier tonight . . . tall, dark haired, wearing a black cape and riding a fine bay horse?"

"Aye." The landlord brightened. "Had his tea here. Can't say as I recall his name. Had the look of a sailing man . . . something about his eyes."

"Yes," Quincy said eagerly. "That's sounds like my friend. He was to leave a message here for me. You're sure he didn't leave anything behind."

The landlord pursed his mouth thoughtfully. "He did make a clever drawing for my daughter—of her cat. She left it here somewhere."

He went to the Welsh dresser along the wall, which was strewn with an assortment of papers and handbills.

"Ah, here it is." He took down a sheet of stationery that had been propped up against a hobnail pitcher. Quincy snatched it from him.

"It's a fanciful bit of a thing," said the landlord from over his shoulder. "See, there's words written on the animals and a little poem under each of the pictures."

Quincy's face twisted as he observed the drawing. It was in two panels, the first showing a cat asleep on the hearth, while a long-snouted rat tiptoed toward a large wedge of cheese. The inscription read, "If the cat takes his ease, then the rat takes the cheese." The second panel showed the cat with his paw on the tail of an enraged rat and under it the poem read, "If the cat stays awake, the rat shall he take."

The drawings were skillfully rendered and humorous—if one had a mind to be amused by a rat with the name Quincy spelled out its back, or a cheese with the initials *A. P.* carved into it. Unfortunately for Quincy, there was no name obligingly written upon the sleek, predatory cat.

He cursed under his breath. Somehow this MacHeath fellow had figured out his identity and had left this message for Mrs. Reginald or the coachmen to find. Good thing that lady was too overset to think clearly and the two coachmen were not sharp-witted enough to figure out the rider's message.

"I'll take this," he said, shoving the paper into his coat pocket. When the landlord protested this high-handed behavior, Quincy threw a few coins down onto the dresser. "Buy your daughter a hair ribbon to make up for the loss of it."

He returned to the White Hart and ordered a fresh horse from the ostler—on his uncle's tick—and headed out of the city. Upavon, where he was to rendezvous with his men, was on the main route to Exeter. He'd be there by early morning, and if luck was with him, his cousin and her rescuer would come riding right into his waiting arms.

He didn't like it that his hand had been forced. But it was clear that this blasted MacHeath knew Alexa's own cousin had been behind the plan to abduct her. And Quincy had no doubt the man would tell her that as soon as he had the chance.

He thought furiously while he rode across the barren plains. There didn't seem to be a way he could remove himself from suspicion. Which meant he would have to force himself on the minx—there was no longer any question of earning her gratitude to soften the seduction. By carrying her off, that one-handed rascal had sealed her fate.

Chapter 4

MacHeath pulled his horse up at the edge of a ravine, assessing the landscape below him. Alexa Prescott now lay quiet in his arms, though for the first hour she had battled him almost nonstop. Twice she'd nearly succeeded in throwing herself from the horse's back in her frenzy to get away. But during the past few miles, she'd stopped fighting. He guessed she was exhausted and afraid. One of those things he could remedy . . . the other was up to her.

He sent his horse down the edge of the incline. The beast was a heavyweight hunter that he'd "borrowed" from his former employer's stable in London. He'd left behind a note, explaining his need, and he hoped Roddy would forgive him. If there was one determined do-gooder in London, it was Roddy Kempthorne. Not the brightest fellow he'd ever met, but the one with the largest heart. Who else would have hired a one-handed piece of human wreckage to be his valet? Who else would have sent that valet off to Scotland with the money to coax a brilliant young medical student to make him an artificial hand?

But he'd taken enough of Roddy's charity, and once he'd finished up in Scotland, MacHeath had returned to the place where he felt most at home—the shadowed lanes and alleys of the East End. Somehow his new hand shamed him . . . with all its implications of allowing him a normal life. The only life he craved was the sea, and since that was forever denied him, it didn't matter where he lived or how he earned his bread.

Once he reached the bottom of the ravine, he let the horse pick its way through the rocky debris, until they came to a copse of fir trees. The trees would furnish enough of a windbreak to let him light a fire. He slid off the horse, still cradling the girl in his arms. She was a limp, dead weight. He laid her down beneath the trees, then tugged his cape off and spread it over her.

It took him only a minute or two to pile some fallen branches a little distance from the trees, and to strike a fire with his tinderbox. The resinous pine boughs caught quickly, licking up into a pleasing blaze. Then he took the two blankets that were rolled up behind his saddle and laid them over the hard ground. Not much of a bed, he knew, and certainly not what the lady was used to, but he dared not go near an inn until he'd put more miles between himself and Quincy's men.

He returned to the girl and knelt beside her. The poor creature had tugged his cape up over her face to keep out the cold. He pulled away the edge of the cape, and then sat back on his heels in disbelief. There was nothing under the spill of wool but a pile of pine needles. The little demon had shaped them into a long mound that resembled a body.

With a muffled curse, he rose and gazed along the deep black ravine. She couldn't have gotten far.

He moved away from the soft crackling of the fire and listened intently. Off to his right he heard her, scrabbling along the flinty ground. He went after her swiftly, stopping every twenty feet or so to listen, marking her position before he moved forward again.

She was trying to scale the ice-slicked slope of the ravine when he finally caught up with her. As he loomed out of the darkness below her, she cast a harried look over her shoulder. "Get away from me!" she cried and scrambled a few more feet up the slope.

He continued doggedly in her wake, and when she stood up and turned on him abruptly, he didn't think to duck. Fortunately, the rock she hurled at him went spinning past his head. The next one careened off his shoulder. He lunged toward her before she could pick up another missile. She turned to flee just as his left hand clutched at her skirts. Snarling a stream of curses, she kicked out at him.

"They never did make a lady out of you," he said with relish as he caught her ankle and twisted it upward. She lost her balance and tumbled onto her bottom.

"Back there," he ordered, pointing to the distant fire. "You walk or I carry you."

"Damn your black heart," she groaned hoarsely, as she hugged the nearest boulder, locking her arms tight around it.

He sighed as he pried her fingers away from the half-ton anchor. It was hard work with only one good hand.

Once he'd pulled her off the boulder, he marched her down the slope and along the ravine, a hand on each shoulder. She'd grown up tall, he realized. Tall and slender. Not much in the way of a rounded bosom or curved bottom, just a mass of black hair and two eyes full of simmering rage.

He forced her to sit on the blanket beside the fire, keeping one eye on her while he dug their provisions—a wedge of cheese and two crumbling meat pasties—out of his saddlebag. He offered some to her, but she turned her head away.

"Fine," he said, after taking a bite of his own pasty. "You can starve. I'll cart your carcass home and get the same reward as for returning you alive. Someone there might actually be relieved to be rid of you, you're that much trouble."

"I don't eat pig slop," she said without looking up.

He nearly laughed. She was still the petulant child, sullen and willful. It was a pity her father, who loved her so much, had taken so little care to mold her character. He'd been a good master to his men, guiding them in their work with patience and wisdom. But he'd clearly left his daughter to her own devices, and she'd turned out sour and spiteful.

"You don't know who I am, do you?" he said softly.

She shook her head vehemently in denial. She was too angry to detect the bemused relief in his face. "No, and I don't give a fig who you are. I only care that someone takes the trouble to hang you for this infamy."

"What? For rescuing you?" he asked as he started on her pasty.

Her eyes raised instantly to his. "You're lying. I was in no danger."

"I happen to know differently. But it doesn't matter whether you believe me or not. Frankly, I don't care anything about you, except for what I can gain by getting you safely home."

"I was going home, before you carried me off. Are you holding me for ransom, is that what this is about?"

"You're partly right . . . ransom being just another word for blackmail."

"I am happily unfamiliar with the subtleties of such things."

He leaned toward her. "It's quite simple . . . I expect even you can understand it. A wealthy young woman is abducted, compromised by a money-hungry toad, and then blackmailed into marrying that toad . . . or else she risks breaking her father's heart."

She jumped to her feet, her hands fisted at her sides. "And are you knave enough to do that?"

MacHeath rolled his eyes toward the heavens. The chit had clearly seen too many bad theatrical productions.

"I warn you, you'd better not come near me," she said with venom.

"You're not in any position to be giving orders," he said placidly as he returned to his meat pie.

"Promise me," she insisted, taking a step closer.

He looked up at her from over his dinner. "No."

Her eyes grew wild, and in desperation she plucked a burning branch from the edge of the fire and flung it at him in a shower of sparks.

"Damn!" MacHeath cried as he scrambled away from the branch, dropping the better part of his pasty. He batted furiously at the glowing embers that had landed on his coat, and then groaned in frustration when he realized she had run off again.

When he caught up with her, she was attempting to climb onto the horse's back—she had both hands on the saddle and one foot in the stirrup—but since he'd loosened the girth, the saddle had slipped around to the horse's ribs. She was hopping awkwardly on one foot, trying to regain her balance.

"You are more trouble than a sack of wet cats," he muttered as he wrestled her away from the horse. She spun around in his hold and tried to kick him in the shins, and he was forced to wrap his arms around her to keep himself from bodily harm.

"Don't you touch me!" she spat out, thrusting away from him. She put her head up and, with icy disdain, walked back to the fire.

He removed the saddle from the agitated horse and spared a moment to calm him before he followed her.

"Sit down," he ordered as he kicked the burning branch back into the fire. "First of all, I'd need to have my brain box examined if I ever went anywhere near you. I was speaking hypothetically just now. I would hardly refer to myself as a toad."

She cast him a resentful glare before she settled onto her blanket opposite him. "Your coat is still burning," she said conversationally.

He looked down in alarm and quickly tamped out the few smoldering patches. "Thank you," he said.

She sat silent for a time, her eyes wary. Finally she put her chin up and said, "I insist that you explain yourself."

"I've told you what I know."

"Yes, that someone was going to compromise me. I would like to know who."

He had a feeling that when he gave her an answer, her mood was not going to improve noticeably. "I am going to sleep now," he said with a wide yawn. "It's been a long day, what with abductions and attempts to set me afire, and such. I will tell you what I know in the morning."

He reached toward her with his boot and poked her meaningfully in the foot. "And if you run off again while I sleep, you might like to know that there are two ugly customers after you. If they manage to find you, I think you will be very sorry. Not unless you fancy East End ruffians. Though, from what I know of you, there is always that possibility."

"How can I sleep? You have given me no reason to trust you."

He cocked his head thoughtfully for a moment. "Will it help if I tell you that I have an old connection to your family?"

"I know all my father's acquaintances," she said with a skeptical frown.

"I didn't say it was your father," he replied. "Now, try to sleep. You'll make better sense of things in the morning."

Alexa felt a wave of relief as she watched him roll over in his blanket, his back toward the fire. She knew she was still in shock, still quaking on the inside at this distressing turn of events. Nothing in her life had prepared her for this. Even in her more daring escapades as a child—exploring the old tin mines on Dartmoor or climbing the cliffs that overlooked the Channel to hunt for bird's nests—she had always been in control of the situation.

But now she was at the mercy of this stranger, and it ate at her to feel so helpless. It was too bad she had left her reticule behind in the coach when she went to help the stranger. She never, ever, traveled the roads unarmed. The rascal would not have carried her very far with a pistol ball in his belly.

Still, she was clever and resourceful, certainly a match for this paltry fellow with his tattered greatcoat and worn boots. She didn't believe for a minute his trumped-up tale of rescuing her. It was more likely he was going to ransom her; it was well-known in London that she was a considerable heiress.

Her gaze shifted from the fire to where the stranger lay sleeping, and she pondered just how a man fell so low that he was reduced to preying on women. His dark hair reflected the red gleam of the flames. Several strands caught the light and shone a bright chestnut. The image jarred her, and she immediately shut her eyes.

When she was a girl she'd known a young man with hair like that, a deep brown with hidden highlights. She used to watch him working in the sun, just to see those rare sparks appear. Though she was careful that he never caught her at it. She also recalled sneaking into her father's workrooms to watch him sketching or making models of his designs. His deft hands could carve miraculous miniature ships from blocks of wood. He was a true artist, Papa always said.

She made a pretense of being cross with him all the time, because she was so wary of him. Wary of how much he drew her to him. Like a lodestone. She would daydream, though, that when she was older, once she had outgrown her awkward, inconvenient childhood, he would be waiting for her.

That dream had been shattered when the young man did something deceitful and was taken away to jail. Her child's mind had not been able to comprehend this, why the man who was her father's favorite—perhaps even his chosen successor, some whispered—had betrayed him.

For months they talked of nothing else in the shipyard, but the workmen shared few of the details with her. She learned more of his crime when she was older and could understand such wicked things. After that, she determined to put him out of her mind, and so she had grown up and the memories had faded, but somehow she'd never forgotten how the sun gleamed off his wind-tossed hair.

She shivered fiercely. Even in this sheltered place the cold was insidious, making her bones ache. She crawled off to the stand of pines and returned with the stranger's cape, wrapping it around herself like a chrysalis before she snuggled again into her blanket. The wool of the cape smelled of heather and horses. A comforting scent, redolent with memories of running free on the moors beyond her father's home, astride a pony as untamed as she was.

A few hours later, after she'd drifted into a restless sleep, a sound woke her. Someone was singing softly.

"Christmas is coming, the goose is getting fat."

She opened her eyes and saw the stranger sitting up on the other side of the fire, feeding twigs into the flames. There was something oddly reassuring about a kidnapper who hummed Christmas songs. Still, she reminded herself, he was holding her against her will.

"It was dying," he said when he noticed her looking at him. "I didn't want you to get cold."

"It is difficult to sleep with you caterwauling," she said bluntly.

"The blasted song just keeps running through my head," he said with a slight smile. "Though I've been told I have a rather pleasant voice."

"There is nothing pleasant about you," she said, leaning up on one elbow so he could observe her sneer.

He studied her intently, his eyes dark and probing. When he spoke again, his tone was that of a stern parent. "I know you think this show of defiance is necessary. That I will be impressed by your spirit and your grit. But the truth is, I find you extremely tiresome. I have no patience with spoiled children, which is exactly how you are behaving. Now, I know this is not what you are used to—"

"That is a gross understatement," she muttered loudly.

"—but it is how things are at present. I had a very sound reason for taking you, and whether you believe me or not, the threat still exists. And I cannot guarantee your safety if you defy me at every turn."

"Take me back to Reading, then," she entreated. "I will come to no harm there."

He shook his head slowly. "The only place I know you will come to no harm is with me."

"Then I demand you tell me who you are saving me from."

His eyes darted to her face. "See? You are in no mood to be reasonable. Still issuing orders as though I were one of your father's lackeys." He looked down at the twig he held and snapped it in two against his thigh.

She opened her mouth to protest, and then shut it again without uttering a word. He was right. There was no arguing his harsh and distressingly accurate observation. She *had* been acting like a child in the throes of a tantrum instead of a grown woman displaying fortitude and courage. For one thing, she might try displaying a little dignity. Somewhere in her past, the ability to behave with ladylike decorum had been drummed into her. She summoned up her most gracious voice and said, "It was not my intention to—"

"Go to sleep," he interrupted her gruffly.

He ignored her after that, his eyes drawn down to the fire, his face taut with displeasure. She studied him covertly, needing to distract herself from the thousand questions that were circling inside her head.

The flames danced against the planes of his face, lighting the high cheekbones and the lean jut of his nose. His eyes were in shadow, but the lashes were dark and long enough to touch his cheeks. His mouth, now formed into a melancholy half smile as he gazed into the fire, was wide and distinctly etched over a strong, determined chin.

It was not the face of a polished town beau, there were too many lines around his eyes, too much weathering on his tanned skin for ideal masculine beauty. He'd been marked by time and experience and, she suspected, by some terrible sadness. But those marks only added to his appeal. She was dismayed to discover that she found his harsh, rugged countenance compelling, even attractive.

His gaze shifted and he caught her examining him. She fought down her blush of embarrassment.

"You've been to sea," she said softly. "You've got sailor's eyes."

"You're wrong," he said with a tight frown. "I never go near the sea."

Alexa sighed. "Neither do I . . . not any longer."

"What?" he said. "I thought you were on your way to Exeter. Last time I looked, it was right there on the coast."

"My father does not allow me near the water when I am there. And when I am gone from his home, I spend my time inland."

"So you are under his thumb, then, eh? That surprises me."

"Why? Because I fought back when you carried me off?" Her dark brows drew together. "Let me tell you, then, why I don't fight him. He is a shipbuilder, as you doubtless know. He believes it is his fault that I am unwed, that he raised a female wharf rat, to use his own words. It makes him very unhappy—he fears for my future—and so I must stay away from the sea and from the river where he builds his ships, from all the places where I learned such wild habits."

"Why don't you wed, then, if that's all it would take to please him?"

She gave him a tiny, wry smile. "Because that would make me unhappy."

"You are an unnatural female," he said under his breath.

"Yes, I believe I've heard that before. But I have little use for men in general. I find them bossy, belittling, and full of opinions about what is best for me. The few I have esteemed have inevitably disappointed me."

"Including your father?"

"Most especially my father. He turned his back on me once I was grown."

"And yet you care about him and obey him."

"I do. . . ." Her voice drifted off.

He threw the last of his branches into the flames, and then moved closer to her before he stretched out on the ground. Alexa wished he'd stayed on the far side of the fire—now that she'd noticed how attractive he was, she was having trouble keeping her eyes off his face. He would surely notice her scrutiny.

"Has it ever occurred to you," he said, propping his head on his hand, "that one of those belittling, bossy men might also inspire affection in you? Most women find men aggravating and troublesome, but they still agree to marry them and have children with them. I believe some women are actually quite fond of their husbands."

She wrinkled her nose. "In my experience, women only marry to gain security. As Mr. Franklin once said, if you barter your independence for security, you deserve neither."

"Ho," he crowed. "She quotes Benjamin Franklin. Now, that is rare in a female." He added with a wicked grin, "You know, he also said that all cats are gray in the dark."

Her cheeks drew in. "I am aware that that phrase has some bawdy meaning, and I think it's very unfair of you to say such a thing, when I have no means of responding intelligently."

"You like sparring, don't you?" he said as an aside. "But I wasn't baiting you. I meant that . . . when you are in the dark with a man, you might find yourself overlooking his faults and discovering a few of his virtues."

She made a tortured face. "Please. I am not some schoolroom miss. I know what transpires between a man and a woman in the dark—"

"Do you?" he asked softly.

"And I do not think those . . . relations . . . could possibly change my view of men. In fact, I expect they would cement my bad opinion." She pointed a finger at him. "Can you deny that a man who is overbearing and smug in his daily life would be any different during . . . intimate moments with his wife?"

The stranger rolled onto his stomach and set his chin on his crossed arms. He stared at her for several seconds, his eyes narrowed. "I bet you've never even been kissed," he said at last.

Alexa puffed out a quick breath. "Only by my odious cousin Darwin, when I was fifteen. I had to hit him with a tennis racquet to make him stop."

"Well, that explains your distaste."

"Why?" she asked sharply. "Do you know my cousin?"

"It's the name . . . I can't imagine any woman wanting to be kissed by a Darwin."

"What is your name," she asked, before she realized he might take that as a leading question.

He hesitated only an instant. "MacHeath."

"That's not your real name, is it?"

"No." He smiled and rubbed one finger along his lip. "Where I come from, it's best not to know a man's real name."

"Are you a Scot?"

"My father was. I was born in Glasgow, but I came here to England when he died."

"Where did you live?"

He shook his head. "Enough questions. We need to be away early . . . you'd better go back to sleep."

She lay down, wriggling to make a hollow in the pine

needles before she pulled the cloak up to her chin. "Mr. MacHeath, will you tell me one thing?"

"Mmm . . ." His eyes were closed, but she saw him nod.

"You said to me earlier, 'You don't know who I am, do you?' And then you implied you had a connection with my family. The truth is, I have no idea who you are. Should I recognize you?"

He opened one eye. "I am Madman MacHeath, the notorious highwayman. Does that ease your mind?"

She grinned at him. "You are not a very good liar."

"I am also not a very good highwayman . . . I keep carrying off the women instead of their jewels."

She was still chuckling when he rolled over and went to sleep.

Chapter 5

MacHeath roused her gently with a hand on her shoulder. She was so soundly asleep, he feared she might have frozen to death during the night. He'd definitely have to find them proper lodgings for the balance of their journey.

He was relieved that some sort of truce had been achieved between them last night. She had actually spoken to him with civility before she'd fallen asleep. He didn't blame her for being upset with him, but he had no taste for being tongue-whipped by a stripling girl. Especially one he had taken the trouble to aid.

He thought back to that fateful night when he'd overheard Quincy making his plans in the tavern. He'd barely slept for thinking about Alexa, and the life she would lead if she was leg-shackled to her pimple of a cousin.

It occurred to him that the easiest course would have been to track Quincy down in London and cosh him over the head to keep him from his wicked rendezvous with Alexa. But MacHeath knew that if he merely put Quincy out of the way for a few days—leaving Alexa to go blithely on her way to Exeter—she certainly wouldn't learn of it the next time her cousin cooked up some plot to compromise her.

It also crossed his mind that if Alexa were no longer in the picture, as in deceased, Quincy might very will be next in line for Prescott's money. This troubling notion chewed at him. What if Quincy had misled Connor and Finch about his intentions? What if instead of saving her from those ruffians and bedding her, he intended to murder her. How easy it would be to plead his case with her grieving father—"But, sir . . . before I could remove her from their clutches, one of her abductors shot her. She died in my arms, dear uncle, telling me of her love for you."

A shiver of disgust racked him. He wondered if Quincy had it in him to be quite that bloodthirsty. His usual style was back-stabbing inference and malicious slander.

MacHeath had looked across the room then, to the small pile of gold coins scattered on the rickety table. Beside them lay the last vestiges of his life at sea . . . his copper spyglass and a brace of pistols. Not much there to pawn . . . and he would need funds if he was to carry out this enterprise.

He'd made a bargain with himself. He would take the money Connor had given him and sit down to a card game at his favorite haunt, where the occasional lordling kept the stakes relatively high. If fate favored him, he would set out after Alexa. If not, she would be at her cousin's mercy.

The next night he'd come away from the table in the early hours of morning with more than twenty pounds in his pocket and the beginnings of a plan to not only thwart Darwin Quincy, but to thumb his nose at him, as well.

The only thing he hadn't counted on was how the sight of Alexa Prescott would affect him. She'd been only the faintest of memories, a gangling girl of fourteen the last time he'd seen her, one who showed no more promise of classical beauty than she had the first day he'd met her.

But something had happened to her in the intervening ten years. For one thing, she had finally learned how to dress. The royal-blue pelisse she wore was the perfect complement to her blue eyes. The rich sable trim on her velvet bonnet set off the blue-black gleam of her hair in a delightful manner. It was a pity she now wore it up, as was the fashion. Even back in Cudbright, it had been her one real claim to beauty.

But if she'd still been dressed in a wrinkled pinafore, with her petticoats all spattered with mud, this Alexa Prescott would have caught a man's eye. Her father's Roman nose, which had always seemed ridiculous on her otherwise gamine face, now gave her a profile that was distinguished and elegant. Her rosy mouth was still petulant, but he knew few men were proof against a woman who could exhibit a pretty pout.

Furthermore, she was gloriously tall. And perhaps not so lacking in curves as he'd first thought. Their tussle beside the horse had given him a very gratifying sense of firm breasts and nicely rounded hips.

He stifled these thoughts before they could take hold. No sense in assessing an object you could never afford to buy.

He shook Alexa again until she stirred. When she finally sat up, she was cranky and disoriented. He squatted beside her and passed her his tin mug, which he had refilled with weak tea.

"This tastes like ditch water," she complained. "And it needs sugar."

"At least it's hot ditchwater," he said as he rose and began to kick apart the sputtering fire.

"I can't get very far on tea. Don't you have any scones or honey buns?"

"Fresh out," he said. Then he recalled that she hadn't eaten anything last night, that both the cheese and the pasties had ended up inside him. He went to his pack and took a strip of dried beef from a roll of butcher paper.

He thought she would refuse his offering, but instead she took hold of it and began to chew it with vigor. "I am surprised you would have this," she informed him. "It is what sailors eat at sea."

"Sailors and men too poor to buy fresh meat," he said as he led the horse from the tree where he'd tethered it.

"Are you poor, Mr. MacHeath?" she inquired between bites. "Is that why you carried me off? This farce would all make sense if that were the case. You needn't continue this ludicrous pretense that other men are after me."

MacHeath slung the saddle forcefully over the hunter's back. It landed with a loud thud, which made the horse dance in place.

"It is not a pretense," he bit out, not bothering to hide his irritation. "I don't possess the imagination to have made up such a tangled tale. One that is worthy of Mrs. Edgeworth, I might add, since it is your odious cousin Darwin Quincy who is plotting against you."

"Darwin?" Her expression held only disbelief.

"Precisely. He hired two men from the East End to abduct you."

"The ugly customers?"

"Mmm. He was going to rescue you from them at a hedge tavern beyond Reading. Some nonsense about earning your gratitude. I overheard them in a London tavern planning it out, and I overheard the whole—Dash it all, stop that. This is nothing to laugh about."

She tried to school her face into sober lines. "I'm sorry," she said. "But if you'd ever met Darwin, you would know why I find it amusing. He is the most idle creature on the planet. He is wearied by strolling across St. James Park, for heaven's sake. Hardly a man of action."

"Which is why he hired my friend Connor and his mate, Finch. They don't come cheaply, but if you want action without conscience, there are none better."

"I knew Darwin was angry with me," she muttered, almost to herself. "I saw that look of rage in his eyes. But I never thought . . . to hire such men to come after me." Her head shot up. "Did you just say you are friends with them, with men who abduct people for a living?"

"Among other things," he drawled. "I don't think you want to know what else they will do for money."

"You really do know such men? But you are . . . I mean, you speak as though you were—"

"A gentleman?" he finished for her. "I suppose I should be flattered. I've been many things in my life, Miss Prescott, but that was never one of them."

"I don't mind that you're not a gentleman," she said as she crawled out from under the cloak and got to her feet with a groan. "My father's father was a cockle monger." She was bending forward, stretching her back, when she looked up at him and gave him a wide smile.

It lanced through him like lightning. He'd been waiting thirteen years for Alexa Prescott to smile at him, and he still wasn't prepared for the effect. Her pointed face softened,

her blue eyes gleamed, and her mouth, so easily provoked to
a scowl, took on a warmth that was astonishing.

"You should do that more often," he said gruffly as he
tightened the horse's girth. She cocked her head in uncertainty. "Smile," he said. "You should smile."

"I could smile until my jaw cracked," she said, swinging
her arms in a wide circle at her sides. "And it still wouldn't
give me any claim to beauty."

"Well, you may not be a nonpareil, but you do have
some—What the devil are you doing, Alexa?"

She was now jumping up and down in place.

"Trying to work out the stiffness," she huffed breathlessly. "I am all cramped muscles and knotted joints this
morning. And I did not give you leave to use my name."

"Sorry, Miss Prescott. I thought maybe this was some
sort of morning ritual you performed. It wouldn't have
boded well for the husband hunt, I can tell you that."

She stopped jumping and folded her arms across her
chest. "Well, good. I shall keep that in mind. If anyone attempts to court me, I will commence my exercises immediately."

"Totally unnatural," he muttered as he packed up his
saddlebag.

They set out several minutes later, Alexa perched behind
the saddle, one arm set primly around MacHeath's waist.
She had argued with him over this arrangement and had pre-
vailed. It was one thing to be carried off in the arms of a
stranger, it was quite another to voluntarily place oneself in
those arms. Especially since she now knew how extraordi-
narily good-looking he was, and tall and lean and graceful,
to boot.

The sun was shining over the Salisbury Plain, melting the
hoarfrost that had settled in the night on both grass and
gorse. Large, muddy puddles had accumulated from the
runoff, and MacHeath was kept busy guiding his horse
around them.

"You ride very well for a sailor," she remarked, after he'd
managed to keep the horse from bolting when a flock of

grouse exploded out of a gooseberry bush directly in front of them.

"I told you, I am not a sailor."

"Maybe not now, but you were once. I've got an instinct about things like that."

"Too bad you didn't have an instinct about your cousin Darwin. The wretch was planning to do more than merely keep you overnight in a hedge tavern."

"Darwin? You think he was going to force himself on me? That is ridiculous. He is most definitely not in the petticoat line."

MacHeath twisted around in the saddle to glare at her. "You are either hopelessly naive or incredibly stupid. I don't know which is worse. Maybe I should just set you free . . . if you meet up with Connor and Finch, you will see firsthand what sort of rogues they are, and they in turn will deliver you to your cousin, who will ravish you in a seedy room in an equally seedy inn."

"I'd like to see him try," she declared stoutly. "Maybe your two friends would be able to overpower me, but Darwin is a lily-livered whelp. I used to beat him at everything—archery, quoits, footraces—and he is eight years my senior."

"That is a pathetic record. I can see now why he needs to even the score with you. And I suppose you flaunted your victories?"

She squirmed a little. "He was always so full of himself, with his superior airs and looking down his bony nose at everyone. But I knew the truth of it, that his parents had very little money, for all their good breeding, which is why he came to stay with us so often. My mother originally felt sorry for him, and then, after she died, my father kept inviting him out of respect for her wishes."

"So where does he get his blunt from now? He looks prosperous enough."

"One of his aunts died and left him some money a few years ago," she said, pleased that she'd known what blunt meant. "But I doubt there is very much of it left."

"Which is why," MacHeath said patiently, "he needs to

marry you. He is in debt up to his patrician eyebrows. With London moneylenders, who are not known for their excessive charity. And since you've refused his suit in the past, he's taking extreme measures to make sure you won't refuse him again."

She thumped him softly on the back. "You needn't speak to me as though I am a lackwit, Mr. MacHeath. I am neither naive nor stupid. Only totally incredulous that Darwin has finally found something worth striving for. A pity it's turned out to be me."

They rode for hours, well past noon, until the growling in Alexa's stomach grew louder than the clip-clop of the horse's hooves. They stopped at a farm, where the farmwife was happy to sell them a basket of honey buns and a portion of ham hock. They sat side by side in the shelter of a wide oak that was canted over a small brook, and MacHeath watched Alexa toss crumbs to the minnows that skittered below the bank.

"I've been thinking," she said, licking the honey from her fingers before drawing on her gloves, "are you planning to take me all the way back to Exeter?"

"That is my intent," he said evenly just before he bit into his portion of ham. "As I've said, I have business with your father."

She squirmed restlessly beside him. "If I travel with you all that way, I will be as surely compromised as I would have been with my cousin. I wish you had just stopped my coach and warned me what was afoot."

He stopped chewing. "Oh, and you would have believed me?"

"If you'd been reasonable I might have. You could have said there was trouble in the road ahead, and insisted we go back to Reading to spend the night."

He sighed. "And do you think Quincy would have given up so easily? No, he'd have carried out his plan the next day—sent his bullies on ahead to waylay you once it was dark. You don't seem to understand the caliber of men we are talking bout. They are ruthless, dogged, and without conscience. Hell, for all I know, they might have dragged you from your bed in Reading and carried you off."

Alexa shivered. "I knew Darwin was in a bad way . . . but I still can't credit he would go to such lengths to get his hands on my money."

"But you do believe me?"

"It seems I have no choice. Unless you are a consummate liar and intend to ransom me yourself, I can think of no other reason why you would trouble to take me from my coach. It must be as you say." With a tight smile she turned to him. "I suppose I should thank you."

He got to his feet abruptly. "Stow that," he muttered. "I'm not doing this for you. As I told you last night, I am only after one thing . . . a fine, fat purse when we get to your father's home."

She tipped her head back to gaze up at him. "He will have to believe you, before he will pay you. I'm sure my cousin will deny everything."

"I'm sure he will . . . that's his usual style. But I saw him with my friends—"

"I thought you didn't know him . . . I don't understand. You said last night that you'd never met him."

"No, I just sidestepped answering you, if you will recall."

An expression of awareness spread across her face. "You also said you were a connection of my family's—you're connected to Darwin somehow, aren't you?"

"Inextricably linked," he said darkly.

"You're not one of his friends from London—"

"Friendship hardly enters into it, Miss Prescott."

"Well, that's a relief," she pronounced. "I don't much care for any of my cousin's friends. They are a rackety bunch."

"Especially the ones he hires in the East End. And I don't think we're shed of those fellows, either. Which is why I'm keeping you with me and not just putting you on a coach to Exeter."

"My reputation will be in ruins," she said as she got to her feet.

"Not if you keep this little episode to yourself. I doubt

your companion will be eager to spread the word that her charge was carried off by a stranger."

"Oh, dear," she cried softly. "I'd forgotten all about Mrs. Reginald. She will be beside herself with worry. And I know she will write to my father, and then he will be frantic. He might just shoot you for your trouble, you know."

"Hmm, I suppose there is that possibility. Tell you what, if it will ease your mind, you can write to them tonight. I intend to find us lodgings in Dagshott."

"And what should I tell them? That a strange man spouting nonsense about my cousin has carried me off, but means me no harm?"

"That'll do in a pinch," he said with a swift grin as he untied the horse from the farm's rail fence.

"I meant to be home by Christmas," she said forlornly. "I don't suppose we can manage that riding doubled up."

"I'm sorry, but my finances didn't allow me the use of two horses."

Alexa hung her head. She was feeling a bit more charitable toward her abductor, though she still had trouble crediting his charges against her cousin. But she was sorely disappointed that she would miss the one special day she and her father had always shared.

"Does it mean that much to you?" he asked gently.

"I only ever get to visit him at Christmas, you see." She reminded MacHeath of her father's nonsensical notion that he was bad for her matrimonial chances, which had led to her being kept away from his home during the year. "He's always been stubborn," she added.

"Good thing you didn't inherit that trait," he said with a straight face.

She put up her chin. "I know my own shortcomings, Mr. MacHeath. But I've been a dutiful daughter these seven years, stubborn or not. This year, however, I am determined not to go back to London. I belong with him, but I will need every minute I can get to convince him of it."

He looked into the distance, where the plain rolled away to the west. "I estimated it would take us at least five days to reach Exeter on horseback."

Her face fell. "Christmas Eve is but three days off. Isn't there a quicker way?"

"I'm afraid not," he said.

Dagshott was a middle-sized village, proud of its Norman Abbey and less proud of the fact that it had been reduced to an empty hulk in the sixteenth century by the soldiers of Henry VIII. It now lay in picturesque ruin, just beyond the village.

Alexa made several admiring comments as they passed the monolith in the dusky light, but then protested vehemently when MacHeath drew up his horse in front of a rundown inn just past the abbey. "There has to be a better place than this."

"If there is, we can't afford it. I must remind you, Miss Prescott, that we are on a strict budget."

"I won't stay here," she declared. "It is . . . disgusting."

"It is this place, or spending the night under the stars."

Sleeping out-of-doors again was unthinkable. She still had a crick in her neck from last night. And she was sure she was developing a sniffle worthy of Mrs. Reginald's.

"I have jewelry you could pawn," she suggested. "Then we could stay in a decent place, and you could hire me a horse to ride."

"I will not take money from a woman," he said emphatically. "It's out of the question."

She nearly bucked off the horse's rump in frustration. "Ooh, that is exactly the kind of vexing thing men always say. What matter where the money comes from? You will be spending it on me, after all." She plucked off her ear bobs and her two rings and reached around him. "Take them," she ordered, thrusting her fist against his ribs. "Or I will pitch them into the road."

She heard his sigh as his left hand closed over hers.

"You should get a good sum for the ruby ring—it's Elizabethan. That should hold us for a time, though I still can't believe you carried me off with your pockets to let."

"That is precisely why I did it. For the reward. And when I get the money from your father—"

"*If* you get the money."

"When I get the money, I will make sure these items are redeemed."

"My father can see to that."

He spun to her and his eyes were bright with anger. "Unlike your cousin, I take care of my own debts, Miss Prescott."

They continued on through the town until they came to a prosperous-looking inn called the Crusader, which was situated in a commercial row on the town's high street. He set her down at the doorway, and she watched him ride off in search of a pawnshop.

It was rising seven o'clock, and quite dark out, and she felt a creeping sensation of fear now that she was alone. He might have been a very wicked man, this MacHeath, with his unsavory ruffian friends, but she had quickly gotten used to being under his protection. In truth, he'd not done her any harm, and had actually behaved toward her in a relatively gentlemanly manner. Well, except for spending the night sleeping beside her. Tonight he would sleep in the stables, he'd assured her. And a good thing, too. One did not want to get used to having such a robust, attractive man in close proximity.

She went into the inn and, following MacHeath's instructions, gave the landlord a false name and said that she had suffered an accident while out in her pony cart.

"My groom has gone off to the farrier," she lied blithely. "And I have decided to overnight here, instead of returning to my aunt's home."

Fortunately, the landlord did not ask her where her aunt's home might be. He showed her into a small private parlor and promised to send in evening tea.

She shed her pelisse and bonnet, and settled wearily onto a padded chair before the fire, shifting uncomfortably on her stiff haunches. Riding pillion with only a folded blanket beneath her had taken its toll on her posterior. She had a feeling that when this adventure was over, she'd be as crabbed and contorted as a crone.

Tea came in, a tray of sliced meats and buttered dark

bread accompanied by a mug of hot cider. She attacked the
food voraciously; all that fresh air had given her a keen appetite. She was drowsing over the cider, when she realized
she ought to order something for MacHeath. He had to be as
peckish as she was, especially since he'd made sure she had
the larger portion of their luncheon.

She cracked the door and looked down the dim hallway
for the landlord. He was near the front entrance conversing
with two men. She was about to call out to him, when one
of the men, a brawny fellow with a shaved head, said, "The
lady is tall and dark-haired, and is wearin' a blue carriage
dress. She's run off with a sorry rogue."

The landlord made some muttered comment, and the
brawny man exploded. "A' course we got a right to ask
about your patrons. We're from Bow Street, me and Mr.
Connor. Doing the King's business."

Alexa instantly drew back into the room, muffling her
gasp. She shut the door as softly as she could and then reeled
back against it. The man had distinctly said "me and Connor." They weren't from Bow Street—they were Quincy's
ugly customers. Dash it all, MacHeath hadn't been making
it up.

She had no way of knowing whether the innkeeper would
give her away to the two men, but she was not going to stay
here and find out.

She ran across the room and swiftly tugged on her pelisse
and her bonnet, before she darted to the window. Fortunately, it let out into a side alley rather than the street. The
casement resisted opening at first, but she put her back into
it and managed to gain enough clearance to slip out. She
pushed it closed behind her and stumbled down the littered
alley, away from the light.

Ten feet from the window, she stopped, hugging the wall
in the darkness, listening for the sounds of pursuit and waiting for her heart to stop pounding. She'd been furious last
night when MacHeath had carried her off, and then made
her sleep on the hard ground, but she'd never felt afraid.
Angry, yes, and frustrated by her inability to escape him, but
not really frightened. She knew that now, because for the

first time in her life she felt the cold, clammy grip of true panic. She was unable to think clearly, unable to move, her limbs trembling and weak. It was all she could do to stand upright with her face pressed against the rough bricks.

"MacHeath," she whimpered. She had to get to MacHeath before those men found her. If he came back to the inn any time soon, he'd walk right into them. And then she'd be alone.

Mustering all her courage, she took one step toward the street. And then another. It seemed an age before she was able to peek around the corner of the building. There was no sign of the two men. They'd either given up on her, which she doubted, or the landlord was letting them conduct their search of his inn.

She erupted from her hiding place as though all the fiends of hell were on her tail and flew down the street in the direction that MacHeath had ridden. She nearly catapulted into him as she rounded a corner. He was on foot, leading the horse, and her forward motion drove him back against the beast's chest.

"Good God! What is it?"

She dragged them both, man and horse, into a nearby alley.

"They're here!" she gasped. "Right here! Oh, I'm sorry I doubted you. Sorry I laughed."

His hands held her steady, fingers tight on her shoulders. "Slow down, Alexa. Take a breath."

"There's no time for a breath . . . we must be away from this place at once. They are searching for me . . . don't you understand?"

"Who?"

"The ugly customers . . . Connor and . . . what was his name, the great huge one with the shaved head—"

"Finch, Bully Finch."

"Oh, by all that is wonderful," she groaned softly. "There is a man named Bully chasing after me."

"So they've run us to earth," he muttered. His voice was grim. "How did you manage to get away?"

"I climbed out the window of the inn after I heard them

talking in the hall. The landlord was not happy about letting them inside . . . but I fear they convinced him."

He wrapped the horse's reins tight around his fist and coaxed the animal deeper into the shadows. "We'll wait," he said as he leaned back against the wattled wall.

She grabbed him by the lapels of his greatcoat and shook him. "Are you insane?"

With his left hand he gently disengaged her fingers. "Think, Alexa," he whispered into the darkness. "What will they do? Once they've discovered you've bolted, they will ride in pursuit. Away from here. So, by all rights, this is the safest place to be."

"You are quite mad."

He shrugged. "I've no mind to sleep in a hedgerow tonight. Which is where we'll end up if we leave Dagshott. In a hedgerow without a fire, I might add, because we dare not light one with those rogues nearby." He cocked his head toward her. "Of course, we could always return to that little hedge tavern."

"That is out of the question. Not to mention, those wretches surely sought us there, as well." No place was safe, she realized with dismay. Her teeth began to chatter, and she set her jaw so that he would not hear.

"Come here," he said as he reached out and tugged her beside him. "You're cold."

"I'm not cold," she said faintly. "I am f-frightened."

If he had any idea what it cost her to make such an admission, he did not voice it. Instead he drew one arm around her, so that his long cloak enveloped her.

"Listen to me, Alexa," he said in a soft, deep whisper. "I won't let anyone harm you."

"I'm so ashamed," she said against the soft wool of his coat. "I cowered there by the inn like a rabbit in the dark. I could barely breathe."

"Mmm, but you got your legs under you again, which is what counts in the end. A person doesn't develop a cool head overnight, you know. But it sounds like you made a pretty fair start."

His arm tightened around her for an instant, and she savored the comforting pressure. No one had comforted her since her mother died, though she suspected that was her own fault. She put on such a display of independence and self-sufficiency, that it was no wonder her family and friends never saw any need to reach out to her. Oh, she had been cosseted and spoiled, her every want had been met, but no one, not even her father, had so much as hugged her since she'd put up her hair. As though adulthood meant the loss of all human contact.

Eventually, the warm width of MacHeath's chest and the secure weight of his arm across her shoulders lulled her into a near sleep. She relaxed against him, letting her body mold itself to his, clinging to his coat like a little child, her head tucked beneath his chin.

She lost all awareness of her surroundings, except for the sensation of her bonnet being pushed back and a hand stroking over her hair. Time passed, but she was not aware of it. There was a haven here in this man's arms, a haven against ruffians named Bully, and odious cousins with designs on her money, and pigheaded fathers who sent their daughters into exile.

Eventually MacHeath's soft voice shook her back to reality. "I think it will be safe to go back to the inn now."

He set her away from him, and she felt the cold immediately. "But what if Finch and Connor come back to the Crusader when they can't find our trail? What then?"

"I have thought of that. The solution is quite simple."

"What are you planning?"

"Just follow my lead," he said.

She could have sworn he was grinning.

The landlord of the Crusader was beaming at them. "Ah, a runaway couple. There's no need to fret, sir. Those fellows won't hear a peep from me if they come back here. Didn't like the cut of them one bit—trying to threaten me in my own establishment." He made a disparaging noise. "Bow Street Runners, my aunt Fanny."

"They were hired by my wife's cousin," MacHeath explained in a low, conspiratorial voice. "The man she was being forced to wed. But it's too late for him," he added, pulling Alexa up against his side. "I've made her my own now, and no other shall have her."

She did her best to offer the landlord a simpering smile, which was difficult with her teeth grinding in annoyance. It was just like MacHeath to turn this into a May game. Still, the ruse seemed to have worked on the landlord. He promised to keep their secret and insisted that MacHeath join him in the taproom for a celebratory glass of his best claret while his lady got settled in their chamber.

"You're going to sleep in the stable, right?" she hissed to MacHeath after the landlord had gone to fetch the wine.

"What? On my honeymoon night?"

She prayed she could detect a hint of laughter behind his words.

She went up to the room they had been assigned, and paced restlessly for nearly three quarters of an hour before MacHeath returned.

"Sorry," he said as he came in, holding an open bottle of claret in the crook of his arm and carrying two glasses. He set them down on the low dresser by the door. "I thought it would be best to humor him. I barely got away, though— once our host had launched into a tirade against the excise duties on brandy, he looked to go on all night. I . . . had to remind him that my new wife was doubtless missing me sorely." He poured some wine into one of the glasses and offered it to her with a crooked grin. "Well, are you?"

Alexa ignored both the proffered glass and his attempt at humor. "I am ruined for all time," she wailed. "Even if we did use false names—and I take leave to tell you, I don't think Mr. And Mrs. Broadbeam was a very inspired choice—my cousin will know from his hired bullies that I was here with you. Have you not thought of that? He can use that circumstance to make me marry him. He won't have to even lay a hand on me to force me into it.

"Pheh . . ." MacHeath flicked his fingers in the air. "His men didn't see me here with you. For all they know, you escaped from me outside Reading and have traveled here alone. And as for all these protestations about being ruined . . . you yourself told me you have no intention of marrying."

"Yes, but I also have every intention of keeping my good name intact. Not marrying is my choice, but I don't wish to become a pariah in Society. Which is just where this is all heading."

"You'll weather it," he said evenly as he crossed the room and pushed open the window, letting in an icy draft. The roof of a small shed lay four feet below the sill.

She put up her chin. "You make very free with my reputation, sir."

He turned back to her, and his face bore a look of amused commiseration. "If it's any solace, I'll marry you myself before I let that wretch have you."

"Oh, that's reassuring," she huffed. "I told Quincy that he was the last man on earth I would wed, but I see now I have to revise my ranking."

"I'm not such a bad bargain, Mrs. Broadbeam. A little tattered, perhaps. But I had the feeling back there in the alley that you were rather pleased to have me around." He set his left hand on her chin.

"Stop that," she said with annoyance as she tried to pull back. How wretchedly smug of him to remind her of that brief moment of weakness.

"What, sweetheart?" he teased. "It's our wedding night."

Her eyes flashed a warning as she shifted away from his touch. "This is no longer amusing. I was growing to like you until two minutes ago. But I see you are no better than Darwin or his bullies."

He laughed softly. "I expect I am a deal better than any of them. You know, I've a mind to correct your bad opinion of men. I admit Darwin's kisses would be enough to put most women off the male species, but you are hardly most women—"

"I told you, I have no interest in such things."

He gave her a closemouthed smile. "And *I* have a great deal of interest. And therein lies the problem."

"If you are trying to destroy my trust in you, you are succeeding admirably."

"On the contrary," he said as he closed the gap between them, "I am trying to determine just how much you will trust me." He slid one arm around her and lowered his head until his mouth hovered over hers. Alexa's eyes narrowed ominously.

And then, as she felt him lean into her, a strange, not unwelcomed warmth suffused her. She knew he was merely baiting her—it was something he seemed to enjoy—but she had a sudden, wistful longing for him to be in earnest. As he had been when he'd comforted her. She saw that, earnest or not, the expression in his dark eyes now held little comfort and a great deal of heat.

"MacHeath," she murmured. She'd meant it to come out as a warning snarl, but it sounded more like an endearment. She tried again. "You forget yourself, sir."

"No," he said in a quiet, musing voice, "I think perhaps I am finding myself." He again cupped her chin with his hand, tracing the ball of his thumb along the line of her jaw. Back and forth it moved, leaving behind a whisper trail of heat.

"See?" he said gently, lowering his head another inch. "All men are not cut from the same cloth."

She could feel his warm breath on her cheek, stirring the tendrils of hair that had loosened from her chignon. A shiver ran along her spine, where his hand was clasped tight against her gown.

"Trust me," he said in the softest voice imaginable.

She shivered again, almost violently this time. Without conscious thought, she closed her eyes and tipped her head back.

"This is for you, Alexa," he murmured.

She waited breathlessly for him to complete the connection between them. She could not have moved away from him if her life depended on it.

When he stepped back from her abruptly, her eyes flew open in shock. His own eyes were dancing with mirth as he set a small canvas bag into her hand. She glared up at him, thinking it would serve him right if she slapped that sly grin off his face.

"It's the money I got for your jewels, Mrs. B.," he said with a wink as he slipped out the open window. "Lock up now," he cautioned just before he scrambled down the roof of the shed.

Alexa stood there at the open window, clutching the bag of coins, and wishing for something more substantial to heave at him. What a shame the bottle of wine was on the other side of the room.

She had a difficult time falling asleep, fearful that the ugly customers would return and that the landlord would forget his promise to protect them. When she did at last settle into a fitful doze, her dreams were of little comfort. Great hulking men with shaved heads carrying flaming torches chased her around the ruined abbey, while a man who looked very much like MacHeath cheered her on from the battlements. He had at last come to her rescue by pouring what appeared to be boiling porridge on her attackers.

As dreams went, it was distinctly unsatisfying. Far better to drowse in bed the next morning and remember what it felt like to be held in MacHeath's arms. Even Darwin had never dared overstep the bounds of propriety by laying his hands on her. But then, Darwin did not possess such broad shoulders or such finely muscled legs. It had been quite a revelation to her that a man's body could feel so . . . well, pleasant, when pressed against hers. It was enough to shake the foundation of her many prejudices against men. That little smattering of desire she had felt—actually not so little, if truth be told—had awakened her to a thrilling new awareness, and she teetered on the threshold of understanding for the first time in her adult life.

It was as MacHeath had told her—even the most vexatious man might offer something rare to a woman.

She stopped herself from these rosy meanderings when she realized she was beginning to sound suspiciously like a besotted schoolgirl. MacHeath had been toying with her, teaching her a lesson. She had boasted that she found the attentions of men uninspiring, and he—doubtless made bold by the wine he had consumed—had been determined to prove her wrong. There was nothing more to it than that. She was sure that he could never be interested in her in that way.

He might not have been a true gentleman, and he certainly hadn't a feather to fly with, but she didn't doubt that with his roguish face and lean, graceful body, women would flock to him, ladies and light skirts both. This thought so depressed her that she had little appetite for her breakfast. But she forced herself to eat it; MacHeath was probably doing with a lot less down there in the stable.

She'd chosen to dine in her room, since she didn't want to field any awkward questions about her bridegroom's absence. Fortunately, MacHeath scratched on the door just as she was finishing the last of her cocoa.

"My dear Mrs. Broadbeam," he said with a wry grin when she let him in.

She went striding away from him and sat on the bed with her hands folded across her chest. "Don't you dare call me that," she snapped. "And I believe an apology is in order."

He leaned back against the door and shrugged. "Very well." He cleared his throat theatrically. "I am sorry I didn't kiss you, Miss Prescott."

She practically growled at him. "That is not what I meant, and you know it."

"Then, I'm all at sea here."

"Never mind. It clearly entertains you to be obtuse."

"I was rather hoping it would entertain you, but I see you are determined to start another day full of crotchets. It's well that you never intend to wed . . . you are not very stimulating company first thing in the morning."

"As if that has anything to do with anything," she said primly and was surprised when he laughed outright.

"Enough," he said, once he had recovered himself. "I will get over being startled by your incredible innocence soon enough. And that's a pity, because you are quite a rarity, Alexa." He choked back another chuckle.

"I assume you have come here for something other than making jokes at my expense," she said in her most quelling voice.

He nodded and, after pouring a spill of their nuptial wine

into a glass, took a seat near the fire. "First off, I had a look around the village this morning. No sign of our pursuers, I'm happy to say. Unfortunately, I was unable to locate a horse for you. Dagshott is sadly lacking in livestock. I've also rethought our travel plans. Quincy's men believe we are heading overland to Exeter. So it would be wise, I think, to head south . . . we'll pass through Rumpley late this morning, where I have a notion we can find you a horse. Then we'll make for Bournemouth. I've an old friend there who can take us up the coast by boat."

"Aha," she cried, pointing a finger at him. "I knew you were a sailor."

"Just because I am acquainted with a sailor, Miss Prescott, does not make me one. I get quite bilious on a ship, if you must know. But I will put my infirmity aside for the sake of getting you to Exeter in time to share Christmas with your father."

"Very magnanimous," she stated. "Especially since I'd be more than halfway home by now if you'd left me alone."

He looked at her from over the rim of his glass. "You'd be tucked up between the sheets of Quincy's bed, you mean."

"What a repellant thing to consider," she groaned. "Now you've made *me* feel bilious."

While they were settling their account with the landlord, he remarked that they were turning out to be a most popular young couple. "Had another two fellows here late last night, asking after the young lady."

Alexa clutched MacHeath's sleeve before she could stop herself.

"Easy, ma'am," their host said. "They looked a lot less threatening than the first two, just a gray-haired man with a ruddy face and a bright young fellow with gapped teeth. They told me a different tale, however. Said you'd been carried off from your coach at gunpoint." He tipped his head back and appraised Alexa. "You're sure this fellow isn't forcing you to stay with him? You say the word, and my lads will come running."

MacHeath shot a glance at her, and she felt the muscles in his arm tense beneath her fingers. With a wicked gleam in her eyes, she leaned up and kissed him smartly on the cheek. "Why, sir, I am with Mr. Broadbeam of my own free will. There's absolutely no question of force."

There, she thought, *that's paid him back for last night.*

They were several miles outside the village before MacHeath spoke what was on his mind. "I keep wondering about those other two men who were asking about us. They don't sound like Quincy's type of hireling."

"Perhaps Mrs. Reginald sent some men from Reading to come after me."

"It's certainly possible. Speaking of your companion, did you post your letters last night?"

"I didn't write to my father. . . . I thought we'd have another horse this morning. If we rode hard to Salisbury and got on a mail coach, there was every chance we would have arrived in Cudbright tomorrow night. My father's expecting me tomorrow, so I thought there was no need to alarm him."

"We might still make it," he said thoughtfully. "We'll be in Rumpley by noon at the latest, and I promise I'll find a horse for you. If we ride straight on to Bournemouth and catch a fair wind across Lyme Bay, you'll be in Cudbright before dark tomorrow."

Catch a fair wind, she echoed silently with a secret smile. And he claimed he was no sailor.

"And so you didn't write to Mrs. Reginald, either?"

"Mmm. I sent her a message at the White Hart—I assume she went back there. I told her not to worry, that I was in good hands, and that she should travel on to my father's house, that I'd explain everything when I got home. With any luck, she won't get there before us and upset Papa."

"But wouldn't she have written to him after you were taken?"

"I don't think so. She is very timid, and he puts her in a quake over the least little thing. Just to make sure, though, I asked her not to write to him if she hadn't already. Her nerves are so easily overset . . . I'm sure this whole thing has rattled her enormously, but I tried to sound reassuring. It was difficult . . . I am not feeling very reassured myself."

MacHeath halted the horse at once and turned around in the saddle.

"I swear I won't let anything happen to you, Alexa. These may be rough, hardened rogues who are after you, but I've lived among them long enough to become hardened myself. I'm not afraid of them, and with such men, that is more than half the battle."

She set her hand upon his shoulder. "That almost makes me sad. I suspect you were meant for finer things than rubbing elbows with hired thugs."

He shrugged carelessly before he turned away from her. "There's nothing I was meant for," he said in a low voice. "Not any longer."

Alexa wisely chose not to pursue this line of conversation. She knew when a door had been firmly shut in her face. But that didn't stop her from conjecturing on why such an intelligent, compelling man lived on the edges of society. She eventually decided that he had suffered a Great Tragedy somewhere in his past and determined to ferret it out before their journey was ended.

Chapter 6

❧

Quincy was not at all pleased. "I can't believe you let her get away!"

Finch and Connor both scraped at the threadbare carpet with their boot toes. It seemed they were bound always to be on the defensive with their employer, standing cowed and abject while he raked them down in the parlors of shabby little inns.

Finch finally raised his head. "But we did get close, sir. She was there at the Crusader—the landlord admitted she was, once we put a healthy bit o' fear into him. But she must have heard us come in, and she run off. We searched the whole village, and then scoured the next two towns before we come here. No one saw any sight of the woman or MacHeath. It's like they dropped off the bleedin' planet."

Quincy thought a moment. "If she ran off, then she knew she was discovered. Which means, if MacHeath has even half a brain, he will change direction. They'd be too easy to follow if they kept on toward Salisbury. It's my guess they've gone south now. MacHeath was a smuggler, as you say, he knows the sea. That's where he'll take her. My cousin is a handful on a good day, and by now she's likely driven him to distraction. He'll want to be rid of her as soon as may be, which means he'll take her to the coast. He can get her to Devon faster by ship than on horseback."

"Would they make for Portsmouth?" Connor asked.

In his head Quincy pictured a map of the coast. "That

would mean backtracking. I'd think Bournemouth. It's a straight course to Exeter from there by boat."

"They'll be wary now," Finch pointed out. "Less likely to stop off in any inns along the way. We'll have the devil of a time tracking them if that's the case."

"Yes, but they'll need to stop for food. He can't be carrying much in the way of provisions, not with my cousin up behind him."

"Last we heard they had but one horse between them," Connor said, "but there's a chance he's gotten a beast for her to ride. 'Specially now that he knows we're right behind them."

"Good point. Check all the liveries around Dagshott. And then drop south from there. He's heading for the Channel, I swear it." In spite of the confidence in his voice, he rubbed the side of his face fretfully with one manicured finger.

Connor's brow was gnarled in perplexity. "Then, you're not going to help us with the search, Mr. Quincy?"

The blond man made a hissing noise of displeasure. "I've told you, don't ever use my name. Even between yourselves." He waited until they nodded. "At any rate, I think I can do more for my cause by attending my uncle. We are running out of time, unfortunately. If you haven't caught up with them before Bournemouth, I want you to take a mail coach to Exeter." He scribbled the direction of his uncle's home and handed the paper to Finch. "I'll need you in Cudbright to keep watch on the house. I don't want Alexa slipping through the net. She mustn't get to her father. Do you understand?"

"Aye," said Finch with a quick nod of his head.

"When you do find my cousin, send me word at my uncle's. We'll work out some sort of plan then. Meanwhile, I'll be holding the old gent's hand and being the very best of caring nephews."

Quincy smiled to himself; this would be the role of a lifetime. There was much he could gain by offering his solicitude to the old man in his time of distress. He would place himself at his uncle's disposal, and force himself to bow and scrape if that was what was required. Anything was worth earning Prescott's gratitude.

He'd spent most of his life trying to curry his wealthy uncle's favor, but the man had always treated him with aloof disregard. Prescott was never actually rude to him, but neither had he taken him to his bosom. That special place had been reserved for his wife, who had been the center of Prescott's universe. And then Alexa had been born, and Quincy saw any hopes of gaining the man's approval vanish. The little upstart had eclipsed him, and as he grew older and understood that, for all his good birth, he was in reality the impecunious relation, he began to hate her . . . her father's darling, her father's favorite, her father's only heir.

As if he'd read his thoughts, Finch said, "I was wonderin', sir, who gets the old man's gelt if the girl dies?"

"I believe I would. My cousin has no siblings, and my uncle has no other relations. I am not blood kin to him—my mother was his wife's cousin. But I've run tame in that house since I was in leading strings—I am the closest thing to a son he's got."

"So why don't you just put the chit out of the way?"

"Because," he said with great forbearance, "I am a gentleman, and such low behavior is repugnant to me."

"Phaw," Finch said in disgust. "Pull t'other one."

"Anyway, I need the money now. Not when the old man finally turns up his toes."

"We could help him along, as well," Finch said matter-of-factly.

"Yes, but I expect a killing spree along the Devon coast might raise some suspicions. Just do as I say and find the damned girl. If you feel the urge to murder someone, MacHeath is a prime candidate."

It was nearing noon when MacHeath and Alexa rode into a bustling market town. He settled her in the parlor of an inn, the Squire's Hat, and went off to hire a horse. Alexa grew fretful while she waited. Even though MacHeath had assured her that it was unlikely they were being followed, sitting there alone in the parlor reminded her too much of the previous evening at the Crusader. She started at every strange noise and nearly leaped from her chair when the maid came through the door with her luncheon.

When she could stand the waiting no longer, she left her meal half finished and went in search of her missing companion. She walked quickly along the main street of the town, past a chemist shop, a tidy bakery, and a dry goods store. A group of laborers touched their caps to her as she went past them, and a farm girl in a pony trap slowed down to admire Alexa's pelisse in a very obvious manner. It was reassuring; she felt she could be in little danger in such a public place.

The row of shops eventually gave way to a grassy field; beyond it the street curved to the right at a stone bridge. There appeared to be more shops on the other side.

She was crossing the bridge, wondering where in blazes MacHeath had gone, when she heard two horses come up behind her. Only one rider went past her, however, which she thought curious. He wore a wide-brimmed hat and was mounted on a large gray horse. She was about to give him good day, when he swung his beast around sideways, blocking the end of the bridge. He sat there then, leering at her.

When she spun around, she saw that the other rider, a weedy fellow on a yellow mare, had likewise barricaded the entrance to the bridge.

"This is rare luck, Alf," the man on the gray called out. "There we was, all set to give up the search, and she walks right by us."

"Let me pass," she said in her most imperious voice, meanwhile looking desperately in either direction for assistance. She cautioned herself not to panic as she'd done last night. But then she had not been face-to-face with the ugly customers as she was now. "My father is a magistrate here in . . . St. Nicholas," she declared boldly. "And I assure you, he will learn of your insolence."

The weedy man guffawed. "An' I thought this town was called Rumpley. My mistake, I guess." He nudged his horse closer.

She edged away from him, but the brawny man had also

brought his horse closer to the center of the span, boxing her in.

"It's a pleasant day for a stroll, ma'am," he said. "But it's an even better day for a nice, long ride." He licked his lips as he took off his hat. The watery winter sun gleamed down on his bare skull. "If you take my meaning."

Alexa's heart began to pound furiously. She again looked past the men for someone to aid her. The street behind her was obscured by a large thicket of laurels—it was unlikely anyone could even see the bridge through them. The street beyond her appeared to be deserted.

She watched in terror as Finch began to dismount. Once that Goliath had his hands on her, she would never get away. As she opened her mouth to scream, he plucked out his pistol and leveled it at her. "Not a peep," he growled. There was no mistaking the menace in his voice.

Without conscious thought, she hiked up her skirts and scrambled onto the stone railing of the bridge. "Stay back or I will jump!" she warned them. She cast a quick look over her shoulder. The river below looked deep enough that she wouldn't brain herself if she leaped into it.

"Now, sweetheart," Finch crooned as he approached her. "We don't mean you any harm. We just want to take you someplace warm and safe."

"Like a hedge tavern?" she challenged him. "Where my devoted cousin is waiting to ravish me?"

"That's not what we have in mind for you. What lying bastard told you that?"

"I did."

Both men's eyes swung instantly to the far end of the bridge, where MacHeath stood holding a raised pistol in his left hand; a second one was tucked into his waistcoat. The taut expression on his face boded neither of them any good.

"Aw, Mackie," Alf called in a wheedling tone. "You wouldn't use your popper on an old friend. Tell you what? We'll let you in on the deal . . . right, Bully?"

MacHeath took a step closer. "That has some possibilities. Why don't you two ride off and let me think it over."

"Weren't born yesterday," Finch growled, his deep frown

making his bulbous forehead look like a melon gone bad. "That's not how this is going to play out."

Alexa saw that he was edging the barrel of his pistol up along his horse's withers; the animal was blocking MacHeath's view of it.

"He's got a gun!" she shouted from her perch.

MacHeath instantly straightened his arm and shot Bully Finch in the side of the neck, right over his horse's saddle.

Alf squawked in surprise and fumbled for his own weapon, but his horse had commenced to dancing. Finch roared in pain and rage as he staggered sideways, one hand clasped over the long, bloody gash on his neck. Darting a swift, vicious look at MacHeath, he raised his shaking pistol and aimed it at Alexa.

What she read in his face stopped her heart. Without a second's hesitation she stepped backward off the ledge and plummeted straight down to the water below.

Just before she hit the surface, she heard the echo of Finch's shot.

The river was deeper than it had appeared from the bridge, deeper and swifter. She pushed up from the bottom, where the water weeds tangled in her skirts, and sputtered to the surface. The shock of the icy water stole all her breath. Paddling furiously, she tried making for the reed-covered bank, but the current was too strong, and she found herself being swept under the bridge.

She looked up frantically as she cleared the archway. A number of people were gathered up there now, but the two riders had disappeared. She thought she saw MacHeath leaning over the stone railing.

Suddenly she experienced a shimmering, fantastical vision of a tall man leaping over the side of the bridge in a perfect arcing dive.

Something jolted inside her. A memory from long ago—one she had never quite forgotten—slammed into her. Simeon Hasting . . . her dear, disgraced Simeon . . . slicing down into the water to save her.

But no one had dived from the bridge, and that ancient memory was torn away from her abruptly when a sideways eddy propelled her into a pile of jagged rocks. She fought the current until she was drawn back to midstream.

"*Alexa-a-a*!" MacHeath shouted her name from the bank, running to keep pace with her. "There's a landing farther down," he called out. "Just stay with me, sweetheart."

She saw the pale shingle up ahead, thrusting out into the water, and she stroked toward it with all her strength. Her body was completely numb below her neck, but she somehow managed to keep kicking.

At the landing MacHeath was already waiting for her, thigh deep in the water. He clasped her arm with his left hand as she swept by, and then clamped his right arm around her waist, tugging her into shallow water.

Once they were out of the river, she collapsed on the pebbled beach.

"Get blankets!" MacHeath roared in what she swore was a captain's quarterdeck voice. He was standing over her, feet spread, and she had no trouble at all picturing him on a ship. She tried to tell him this, but her teeth were chattering so badly she could only stutter out his name.

He crouched beside her. "Sit up, if you can. You'll breathe easier that way."

"I'm . . . all . . . right," she managed to get out.

He laid a hand against the back of her neck. It was so warm. "Good," he said, "but I'll feel easier when I've gotten you out of the cold."

She raised herself onto her elbows and stared up at him. "I just had the strangest vision," she whispered hoarsely.

He set his fingers on her lips. "Shssh, don't fret yourself, Alexa."

"It seemed so real," she added in a wavery voice.

But he'd turned his attention to the tall, lanky man who was hurriedly approaching with a pile of blankets. MacHeath quickly wrapped two of them around her.

They were horse blankets, she realized. The pungent odor of the stable steamed up from her wet body.

"We need to get her inside immediately," he said to the liveryman. Then he hesitated. "If you have a spare room. Even the barn would be better than remaining out here."

"I'll hear none of that," said a dark-haired woman, who had come up beside the liveryman. "Of course we have a room for you. It's Christmas, after all . . . it wouldn't be fitting to make you stay in the barn."

But that's what Christmas is all about, Alexa remarked to herself. She nearly grinned. At least her sense of irony hadn't deserted her. Only all her other senses.

"Shall I carry you?" MacHeath asked, one arm still around her shoulders.

"I think you'd better. I am so numb, I fear my limbs are going to crack right off." She looked up and saw that his face had gone dark and remote.

"What is it, MacHeath?" She gripped his arm. "Those men are gone, aren't they?"

"For the moment. The villagers came rushing out into the street when they heard the shots, and the two of them fled."

"And where did *you* come from?" she asked as he swung her up into his arms. "I could have sworn there was no one near the bridge."

"I was speaking to Mr. Gable in the doorway of the livery barn when I saw you'd gotten into trouble. Dash it all, Alexa, I would have killed Finch outright if I'd known he was going to turn his pistol on you. Thank God you fell off that bridge when you did."

"I didn't fall," she said in a subdued voice. "I knew he was going to shoot me—I saw it in his eyes—so I jumped. I didn't panic this time . . . I remembered what you'd said about keeping a cool head."

He stopped walking and looked down at her with no little awe. "You amaze me beyond words. That was the most coolheaded thing I've ever seen."

She felt the warm blush rise up from her chest.

Mr. Gable and his wife led them over the bridge, through the thinning crowd of villagers, to a neat brick house just beyond the span. They went through a hallway to a small parlor hung with garlands of pine, where MacHeath set her down.

"The attic room's not very fancy," said Mr. Gable, holding open a narrow door, which gave on to a narrow, winding staircase. "My wife's brother sleeps up there when he is home from the navy. But there is a small fireplace."

"I'll bring you up some dry clothes," Mrs. Gable added.

"Thank you," MacHeath said with feeling.

"You just take your lady upstairs and get her warmed up."

Alexa preceded him up the steep stairs, stumbling a little at the top step. He reached up and encircled her waist, propping her against the wall. "I hope," he said softly, "that you have learned to stay where I put you, Miss Prescott."

She lowered her eyes. "I know. It was a foolish thing to do. I just wondered what was taking you so long."

He made no response to that, but leaned past her and opened the door. "Come on, you're dripping all over Mrs. Gable's stairs."

The walls of the attic room sloped down precariously above a narrow bed and a scuffed washstand. MacHeath went immediately to the fireplace, where several half-burned logs lay in the hearth. "You need to take off everything you are wearing," he said without turning around. "Everything."

Alexa was peeling herself out of her sodden, clinging, pelisse when Mrs. Gable came into the room, carrying a stack of clothing. She dropped her bundle on the bed and quickly turned to assist Alexa.

MacHeath stood up from the fireplace, where the logs were now burning nicely, and, again without turning, muttered that he would get himself dried off in the barn. Alexa realized that he was nearly as wet as she was—his boots, his breeches, and the bottom half of his greatcoat were soaked.

"Nonsense," Mrs. Gable said briskly. "You'll do no such thing."

"But the lady and I are not—"

"There's no fire in the barn," she said. "You both need to stay here and get warm."

She crossed the small space and handed him some clothing. "These should do until your things dry out."

After she finished undoing the buttons at the back of Alexa's gown, she slipped from the room. Alexa's ears still burned from the words the woman had whispered over her shoulder before she left. "Mr. Gable and I passed the occasional time together before we were wed," she'd said. "I am not one to judge others. And by the look of your man, he knows his way around keeping a lady warm."

Alexa put this thought from her mind as she quickly drew off her sopping outerwear. Her stockings and petticoat followed. She dried herself with the length of flannel Mrs. Gable had left behind and slipped into the dry chemise, before drawing on a red woolen dress, which had faded to a pleasing shade of rose. Whisking up the quilted comforter, she wrapped it around herself and hunkered down on the bed.

"You can undress now," she called to MacHeath. "I have my eyes closed, so your modesty will not be offended."

"Keep them closed," he growled. She heard his greatcoat rustle as he drew it off.

She waited five minutes and then opened one eye. He was standing by the fire facing away from her, clad only in a pair of corduroy breeches and woolen stockings. As she watched, he struggled to pull a homespun shirt down over his head. His naked back was smooth, a tawny color that was several shades lighter than his face.

At the shipyards she had grown used to seeing the workmen without their shirts—in the heat of summer they often wore nothing more than canvas breeches—so she reckoned herself a fair judge of a man's back. MacHeath's was in no way disappointing—well-muscled and sleek, it tapered dramatically from his broad shoulders to his narrow waist.

She stifled a sigh of discontent as he finally managed to tug the shirt over his torso, obscuring her view of that intriguing expanse.

"Can I look now?"

He turned and saw that she was already watching him. "As if you ever awaited my permission for anything."

He began draping their wet clothing over a low bench beside the fire. He was still wearing his gloves, and she thought that an odd thing. It occurred to her that she had never seen him without them, though that was not surprising, since they'd spent most of their time together out-of-doors. But he had even kept them on last night at the inn.

She wondered what his hands would look like. Long and elegant, she guessed, strong and supple. Not so very different from his tawny back.

He did not seem disposed to make conversation, but paced restlessly along the narrow confines of the little chamber. Alexa picked up the flannel and began to rub her hair. Though it curled out of control, its texture was fine and it dried fairly quickly.

She was watching him idly, while she blotted at a long tendril that she had pulled over one shoulder, when he halted before the fireplace and took down a small carved ship from the mantelshelf. The handiwork of Mrs. Gable's nautical brother, no doubt.

He held it in his left hand, letting his fingers trace over the curve of the hull. Alexa was about to remark that it was not a bad replica, when she heard his low, shuddering sigh. She didn't need to see his face to comprehend the pain behind that sound.

Something about his posture, the dark head bent over the small ship, the fingers lovingly skimming over the smooth wood, sent her rocketing back in time . . .

A young man sat at a drafting table, leaning intently over the ship model he was carving, while the sunlight beamed in from a window, finding the fire in his deep-brown hair.

"Oh . . . my . . . God." Alexa stood up slowly, as if in a trance, the flannel and comforter both falling away, unnoticed, to the floor.

MacHeath spun around, his eyes narrowed with instant concern. "Alexa?"

"Go," she said in a voice quivering with distress. "Please go."

He took a step closer, one hand raised toward her, and she shrank back.

"No." She shook her head so violently that her wet hair lashed both sides of her face. "It's just the aftershock," she whispered raggedly. "I . . . I need to be alone. Please leave me."

Whatever emotion he read in her countenance, it was enough to send him to the door. "I'll be down in the barn," he said. "If you need me, just tell—"

"Go," she said again, and he ducked his head once and went out.

The instant the door closed, she sank down to her knees, her fisted hands held tight over her face.

It is not possible . . . she cried silently.

And yet it had been right in front of her, almost from the start. The unusual color of his hair, the Scots father, his mention of a connection to her family. Good heavens, he had even asked her if she recognized him.

She had to have been blind not to see it. Not to have known him—the one man who had possessed her thoughts from the time she was twelve years old.

Simeon Hastings.

She leaned against the bed, clutching the comforter to her chest. *Had he ever planned to tell her?* Her father would have recognized him, she was sure of that. And so would half the workmen in Cudbright. It was only she, with her idealized, childhood image of Simeon Hastings—preserved, unchanging, like a portrait in a locket—who had not been able to recognize the open-faced, idealistic youth in the weathered, caustic man he had become.

"Oh, and Quincy would surely have known him," she muttered with a frown. After all, it was Quincy who had been struck down when he discovered Simeon stealing from her father's safe. It was Quincy who had vowed to testify against him at the assizes in Exeter. It was Quincy who had feared for his safety when Simeon escaped from jail a week before he was to stand trial.

No wonder the man had made such a point of denying any cordiality between her cousin and himself. *Friendship hardly enters into it.*

And what, then, was her role in this melodrama? The answer, coming rapidly upon her silent question, was all too obvious.

Revenge.

Oh, and foolish creature that she was, she had softened

her heart to him, believing he was decent and kind, and that, even if he'd been thinking only of a reward at the beginning, he'd come to care for her.

She shuddered now at her naïveté, her complete ignorance of the depths of human deceit. She was nothing more than a pawn to him, the means to make Darwin Quincy suffer. The man who called himself MacHeath had no concern for her, other than her usefulness in his game of retribution.

Her heart throbbed with a hollow, wrenching pain. Any excuses she had earlier manufactured to explain Simeon Hastings's crime—that he'd been forced into stealing by some unknown family need, or that somehow Quincy had mistaken his actions and accused him in error—were now swept away by MacHeath's callous duplicity.

She trembled at the thought of what her fate might have been if she'd stayed with him. That he would never have returned her to her father was a certainty. One did not do favors for old enemies.

They were heading for the sea . . . such an easy place to dispose of a body. Though her death would not trouble Quincy nearly as much as the loss of her money, it would strike a blow, perhaps a deadly one, against her father.

It didn't matter, though, who he was aiming his vengeance at—her cousin or her father or herself. Her illusions had been shattered, and the last vestige of her childhood dreams vanished.

She knew she was safe for the moment. He could hardly do her bodily harm under this roof. There had to be a constable or a magistrate here in Rumpley, someone who would be interested to learn that her companion was a wanted man. She was halfway to the door, determined to warn her host, when something stopped her.

It was the piercing memory of MacHeath's arms holding her tenderly against him in a dark alley, while his hand stroked over her hair. It was the stirring sensation of his body, strong and muscular, molded to hers in the bedroom of an inn, and the sound of his husky voice as he'd whispered, "Trust me, Alexa."

If he'd wanted to harm Quincy, then taking her virtue

would have been a very good first step. Even a man as desperate for funds as her cousin, would balk at taking another man's leavings. Last night MacHeath could have bedded her, if that was his intention—he had so beguiled her, she didn't know if she'd have fought back. But he hadn't taken advantage of her, he hadn't even kissed her, though she'd nearly thrown herself at him. No, he had done nothing more than grin at her in his infuriatingly roughish manner and climb out the window.

She pounded her fists softly against the door. The icy river water must have shrunken her brain, to make her believe that Simeon Hastings could ever hurt her. And even though, as MacHeath, he had fallen into low company, she didn't think his character could have altered so greatly, even in ten years. What more proof did she need, her insistent heart whispered, than that he had just now put his own life in peril to rescue her?

But then, what did it all mean? Would he intentionally risk prison by returning her to Cudbright, where he was sure to be recognized? Was he that foolish? That noble?

Was it, as he claimed, that he was only after a purse from her father? But Papa would not blithely give money to the man who had betrayed him. He was more likely to have him clapped in irons.

I have business with your father.

The words he had spoken yesterday with such portent echoed back to her. Was it possible that he was after more than just a monetary reward? Was he going back to plead his case, using her as leverage to get a fair hearing from his former master?

The questions shifted and darted inside her head. She weighed what she knew of the man against these new perplexities. Nothing made any sense. She needed someone else's counsel, she realized. Her own scrambled wits had failed to give her an answer.

She crept down the stairs and found Mrs. Gable seated in the parlor.

"Feeling better?" she said from over her knitting, when she noticed Alexa hovering in the doorway. "Mr.

MacHeath's gone into the barn to look at one of the horses."
She tipped her head to one side and grinned. "Ah, he is a
bonny man."

Alexa opened her mouth to protest that there was nothing
bonny about a man who had kept her in the dark about so
many things, but she never got the words out. A boy of five
or so came pelting into the room from the front hall and
went straight to his mother's knee.

"Look, Mummy," he cried, holding up a ragged piece of
paper. "The man made me a picture of Towser chasing his
tail."

Alexa nearly wept. In the old days Simeon Hastings had
often made drawings for her, pictures of her spaniel or her
moor pony. He would leave them by the kitchen door,
tucked under an old wooden buoy her father had salvaged.
The days she found one of those drawings in that secret
place were always full of bright promise.

She sank down into the chair beside Mrs. Gable, her eyes
bleak.

The child ran to her, holding out the drawing. "See," he
said. "Isn't Towser a funny fellow?"

She nodded and swallowed a sob. Mrs. Gable shot her a
swift look of comprehension and told the boy to run off outside.

"What's happened?" she asked. "You didn't look this bad
after nearly drowning in the river."

Alexa's voice was barely audible. "I . . . I just discovered
something very . . . disturbing." She held the back of her
hand to her mouth. "I don't know what to do."

"Do you want to talk about it?" the woman asked gently.

"I don't know if I can. You are a stranger, and yet you've
been so very kind to me and Mr. MacHeath." She stifled another sob. "But you see, that's the problem, he isn't . . . he
isn't—"

"He isn't named MacHeath," Mr. Gable said from the
hall doorway.

Alexa's head reared up in surprise.

"Though I don't know what his real name is," he added
as he came into the parlor. "When he was our captain, we all

assumed he was using a false name. It was common among smugglers. Most of us had something in our past we wanted forgotten."

"Smugglers?" Alexa repeated in a tiny voice.

"I expect he'll have my head for telling you, miss, but it's old news. I used to sail under your Mr. MacHeath. Till I discovered I had more aptitude for four-legged beasts than four-masted ships. So I left the coast and came inland. That's why he tarried so long with me that you had to come looking for him. We were talking over old times."

She took a few seconds to process this spate of startling information.

"He knew I was here in Rumpley," Mr. Gable continued, "and figured I might be of some help to him. We bein' old mates and all."

Her eyes flashed. "He never told me any of this . . . about you or about his real identity or about having been a smuggler."

"A man who keeps secrets most often has good reason," he stated evenly. "He told me that until he carried you off two days ago, he hadn't set eyes on you in ten years." He looked at her assessingly. "You couldn't have been more than a gangly girl at the time . . . it's no wonder you didn't recognize him now. I last saw him five years ago—he came here for the boy's christening—and I barely made him out today, he's changed that much."

"Did he happen to tell you," she asked archly, "that he was caught stealing from my father?"

Mr. Gable folded his arms over his chest and refused to look abashed. "From what I know of him, that's a mite hard to swallow. I've seen the captain wade into a tavern brawl to save one of his crew, and I've seen him lift a spar off a man during a storm, when any second the whole tangle of wood and rigging might come tumbling down on them. He even gave me the money to make a new start here." He tipped his head toward her. "If there is one thing I know about MacHeath, it's that he doesn't have the makings of a thief."

"Only of a smuggler," Alexa retorted.

Mrs. Gable quickly interjected, "The Brethren have their

own code, most of them. My husband is as honest as a parson, miss."

"The fact remains, MacHeath was caught robbing my father's safe. He struck my cousin and bloodied his head. Fortunately, Quincy was able to knock him out, and then call for help."

Mr. Gable spat, earning a look of reproof from his wife. "Might that be the same cousin MacHeath told me about, the one who set those ruffians on you? Begging your pardon, miss, he's hardly someone whose word I would take on face value."

Alexa chewed at her lower lip. Mr. Gable's testimony echoed her own instincts about Simeon Hastings. "If MacHeath is so honest, so upright," she said at last, "why, then, hasn't he revealed his true identity to me?"

"I suggest you ask him that yourself," Mr. Gable replied. "I would guess it tickled him that you didn't recognize him. He always had a rare humor and was not above a joke or two in the old days."

Alexa got to her feet and stood there wavering with indecision. Mrs. Gable spied Alexa's bare toes beneath her gown and quickly fetched her a pair of clogs.

"You go off into the barn now and have it out with him," she said, wrapping her own woolen shawl over Alexa's shoulders. "That's always the best way with men." She cast a pointed look at her husband. "You'll never get a straight answer unless you ask a straight question. Trust me."

Chapter 7

MacHeath felt a blessed relief the instant he unstrapped the damned contraption from his arm. This was the longest he'd gone without removing it since the doctor in Edinburgh had fitted it on him. He rubbed at the red marks the leather harness had left on his arm and kept his eyes averted from the stump where wrist and hand should have been. At least there was no one here but the horses to observe this pitiful lack.

He set about rubbing the false hand with the neat's-foot oil he kept in his saddlebag. It had gotten wet when he pulled Alexa out of the river, and he knew the delicate joints that allowed the fingers to flex would rust if they were not well oiled. While he worked, he chewed over Alexa's behavior just now, the strange start she'd taken. Her eyes had stared at him in blank shock, as though she were seeing a ghost.

The possibility that she had finally determined his real identity occurred to him. And was then immediately discarded. If she hadn't placed him that first morning, when she saw him in full daylight, she was never going to. Not that it had surprised him when she hadn't—the face that looked back at him in his shaving mirror bore little resemblance to the young man he'd been ten years ago. Gone were the smooth brow, the relaxed mouth, and the unsullied complexion of his youth; they'd been replaced by a gaunt, weathered facade.

No, it was unlikely she'd have a revelation this late in the game. Still, something had shaken her composure. Perhaps it was, as she'd said, merely the aftershock of her encounter with Quincy's men. But then why the devil had she sent him away? Had he so frightened her last night, with his pretense of seduction, that she feared to seek comfort from him now? The notion disturbed him. It also disturbed him, looking back to their encounter at the inn, that his pretense had lasted all of ten seconds. As soon as he'd taken her in his arms, the instant he'd breathed in her sweet, heady scent, a hunger for her had risen up unbidden and completely overwhelmed him.

He couldn't imagine why he had let himself touch her. Maybe it had been the wine he'd drunk, or the spark of desire he'd felt and instantly tamped down when he'd held her in the alley. Or maybe it was the notion that they were playing at honeymooning, and he knew with bitter certainty that he'd never again be with a woman like Alexa.

That he'd been able to move away from her, leave her with her own fledgling hunger written on her lovely face, had been a miracle. Somehow he had been able to muster a grin and a quip even though his body had been screaming with need.

Such a convincing performance was surely worthy of the London stage.

He put Alexa, with her indomitable spirit and her ripe, untried body, out of his mind, and set his thoughts to outwitting their adversaries. They were still out there, he knew, and not far away. They'd need time to clean up Finch's wound and to regroup.

And then they would be back.

He had a thought to take Eb Gable and ride out in search of them, let the hunters become the hunted for a change. But he had no way of knowing in which direction they'd ridden. He and Eb could be away from the house when the two men came back for Alexa, leaving the women and the little boy at their mercy.

What he really needed was time, enough time to get a decent head start. If Alexa hadn't been nearly frozen by the river water, they could ride off right now, while the coast was relatively clear. But he'd seen the toll the episode on the bridge had taken on her; she wouldn't be fit to ride for hours, not until nightfall at least.

Another plan began to form in his head. If it worked, it

would guarantee that he and Alexa would have an hour or more to get clear of Rumpley. They'd each be riding their own horses for a change—Eb had offered him a lanky chestnut mare for Alexa to ride, one he swore could keep up with the big hunter.

He smiled grimly as he focused on oiling his false hand and muttered, "Desperate times, indeed."

Alexa went quietly through the door that connected the hallway to the side entrance of the livery barn. It was dark inside the cavernous structure—except for where a lantern hung near the end of the center aisle—and it was surprisingly warm. Most of the stalls were occupied; the curious horses gazed at her benignly over their slatted doors as she went toward the light.

The sound of her clogs on the wooden floor must have alerted MacHeath—he looked up abruptly from the grain bin, where he'd been occupied at some task, and took a step back. As she continued toward him, he retreated farther into the shadows.

"Go back to the house," he called in a voice she had never before heard him use.

She stopped walking and said, "Simeon?"

He breathed a deep sigh. "So it's out at last. I must say it took you long enough."

"Weren't you ever going to tell me?" she said with a catch in her voice. "I feel like the worst sort of fool. I imagine you were laughing at me the whole time for not knowing you were Simeon Hastings."

"Simeon Hastings is dead," he said in a monotone. "He died in Exeter jail. There is only MacHeath now. But none of that matters . . . you must go back to the house."

"I don't know what to do," she cried softly to his shadowy form. "I trusted you, and now I find that you have deceived and misled me . . . oh, about so many things. I dare not leave here alone, but if I am to continue on with you, I must know what it is you are planning once you get to Cudbright. Please, Simeon, tell me what you intend."

"I haven't thought that far ahead," he said with a shrug. The movement called attention to his right arm, which he was holding behind himself. She spared a moment to wonder if he'd been injured by one of Quincy's men.

"What's wrong with your arm?" she asked sharply.

Instead of answering, he backed even closer to the wall, where the darkness all but obscured him. "For the love of God, Alexa, I beg you to go back inside."

She stood there in the aisle, unable to move forward, for such was the urgency in his voice that she dared not approach him, and yet that same urgency compelled her to stay and discover what had put such fear into his tone.

On the surface of the grain bin before her, there lay an opened tin of neat's-foot oil and a cotton cloth. Something was hidden beneath the cloth. She assumed he'd been cleaning his pistol, but when she moved up to the bin, MacHeath let out a soft curse.

She twitched the cloth aside and thought at first that the object beneath it was some sort of toy. It was a life-size wooden hand with a leather harness attached to one end, the narrow straps lined with lamb's wool. It was too finely wrought to be a plaything, however. Whatever could he want with—

Her puzzlement quickly turned to anguish when the truth dawned.

Aware that his eyes were intently focused on her, she carefully replaced the cloth, willing her fingers not to tremble. She had not dared to touch the object. That would have been a gross invasion of his privacy, now that she knew what it signified. Again, she should have seen the signs right from the start.

For such a graceful man, he'd been awkward at certain tasks, such as tightening the saddle girth. He'd never even removed the horse's bridle—replacing it would have been nearly impossible with only one serviceable hand. He also had never sat down to a proper meal with her, had never opened a bottle or done anything that required two good hands.

The recollections that flooded her, however, were no more than an excuse to keep from facing a horrific conclusion—Simeon Hasting, that vital, athletic young man who had possessed such an amazing ability as a draftsman, was now terribly maimed.

She cast him one brief look that was fraught with misery before she turned and scurried away down the stable aisle. She was nearly at the side door, before the inner voice she so rarely heeded made itself known to her in no uncertain terms.

What did it matter that he had lost a hand? He was still strong and brave and so very capable. He'd shot that wretched Bully Finch in the neck, and she doubted there was another man in the kingdom who could have made such a clean shot over the saddle of a fretful horse. It shouldn't matter to her that he was less than whole.

But it did matter, if only because she knew instinctively that such an injury would leave a man feeling set apart, rejected. She was beginning to understand why he had taken refuge in the East End, where the detritus of London mingled in a territory free from Society's harsh judgments.

The Simeon she had known all those years ago had been so proud—it would have destroyed him to be an object of pity or scorn. Or worst of all, of ridicule. Which explained why he had gone to great lengths to disguise his infirmity.

But did it really matter to her? She wrestled with the question. She had come here to confront him about his past, and now realized she was more concerned with his future . . . and whether she might have a place in it. The thought shocked her. Did she really believe she could have any sort of life with a tattered rogue like MacHeath?

She might have shared her life with Simeon Hastings, had things gone differently. Her father would not have stood in her way; there was every chance he would have encouraged her. He'd seen in the young man the bright future of Prescott Shipyard and had voiced that sentiment to her more than once.

Ah, but there was little of Simeon Hastings left in MacHeath. She could almost believe what he'd said just now, that Simeon was dead. All that spark of eagerness, that passion to conquer new worlds, was gone. MacHeath was jaded, doubtless corrupt, and full of bitter humors. The events that had shaped his life from the time he escaped Exeter jail, combined with the injury that had cost him his hand, had conspired to make him an outcast from the world she dwelled in.

Outcast . . .

And what was she, then? Exiled from her own home, living a half-life in London with an elderly relative too self-involved to notice Alexa's discontent, forced to be part of a Society she scorned and who scorned her in return. She was barely a shadow of the free-spirited Alexa Prescott that Simeon had known. Until these past days, she amended, when her fettered soul had once again been set free.

They had both changed greatly, she realized. His alterations were simply more noticeable. But if he had been able to reanimate her to the point where she felt the wild, adventurous aspects of her nature returning, who was to say she was not having a similar effect on him? What had he said to her last night? *I believe I am finding myself.*

A wellspring of joy erupted inside her suddenly, and her complex, confusing doubts evaporated. Somehow, by some miracle, this man had been returned to her—it might very well have been from the dead, as he'd said, since he'd felt that lost to her for ten long years. She was an idiot to wonder over his motives or to lament his injury.

She spun around and began walking toward him. She was running full out by the time she reached his dark sanctuary.

"No!" he cried as she pitched into him, knocking him back against the wall.

"I will not turn away from you!" she cried, her fingers seeking for purchase on his shirtfront. "I will not. I cannot."

He fought her, trying to pull away, but she was determined not to let him go.

"I don't want your blasted pity," he said between his teeth.

She forced him to turn in a half circle so that the diffused lantern light shone on her, and then she threw her head back. "Look at me! Is this pity you see in my face?"

But his eyes were closed tight, his own face taut with restrained emotion. "I can't look at you, Alexa," he said raggedly.

"Coward," she taunted him gently. "What are you afraid

you will see? A friend who trusts you, an advocate who believes in you?"

MacHeath could not articulate what he feared. It would destroy him to discover even the tiniest trace of maudlin sympathy in her blue eyes. Or worse yet, a stinging look of horrified revulsion.

"Simeon," she murmured, laying her head against his chest. "I know I ran away from you just now, when I realized what was wrong. This has been an afternoon full of tumult and upsetting discoveries. I no sooner learn your true identity, than I am forced to cope with this unexpected tragedy. So spare me a little consideration, please. And some time to become accustomed to this."

She ran her hand down his right arm, which was again tucked behind him, and he gasped loudly as her fingers encircled what remained of his wrist.

"Does it pain you?"

Like blazes, he longed to reply. He wondered how she would react if he told her that some nights his missing hand ached so intensely that he would awaken in a cold sweat. Ah, but then she would think he was addled as well as crippled.

"You must go now," he said. "I will see that you have a proper escort. Gable will take you to Exeter on the mail coach if I ask it of him."

"Ah, Mr. Gable, your old smuggling mate."

"He was not to tell you any of that."

"It doesn't matter. I have no intention of returning home with anyone but you."

"There is no point in arguing," he said as he finally managed to thrust away from her. "You know who I am now . . . you know absolutely that my reasons for taking you were less than noble, that I was more concerned with harming Quincy than with aiding you."

"Yes, I did come to that exact conclusion. See, I do have some ability to reason. I even thought you might do away with me to hurt my father."

"Your father? Why would I wish him ill? He was kind to me in every instance."

"Yes, but he also stood by while they carted you off to jail. I was angry at him over that for a long, long time."

He eyed her with evident surprise. "You believed in my innocence?"

She shook her head. "It was hard to refute what my cousin told us, especially after they found more money hidden in your rooms. But I begged my father to spare you. He could have just let you slip away, and none the wiser."

MacHeath leaned his head back against the wall and laughed softly to himself. "I wanted to stand trial," he said. "You might not believe that, but it is true. I still had some notion that justice would prevail. But once I was inside the jail, I met a great many rogues who also insisted on their innocence. I saw that my voice was not going to carry much weight against a gentleman like Darwin Quincy. So when one of the other prisoners took the opportunity to escape, I was right on his heels."

She touched his sleeve. "And so MacHeath was born."

"It was my mother's family name, I chose it on a whim." He added grimly, "And I brought dishonor to it."

"Oh, bosh," she said. "Names are fleeting things, like a slate that can be wiped clean. My grandfather was Smelly Ned Prescott, the cockle monger. Papa never let that get in the way—he made the name Prescott one to be proud of."

He gave her a halfhearted grin. "Smelly Ned, eh?"

Her eyes danced. "Worse than the River Exe at low tide, I swear it."

"Oh, Alexa," he said with a throb. He couldn't stop himself from sliding his left arm around her. She stepped into his embrace, wrapping both arms tight around his neck.

"Tell me nothing's altered between us," she pleaded softly. "That we can go on from here."

He said nothing, just gazed at her without trying to disguise the doubt he felt.

"We *can* go on," she insisted. "Now that I know who you are . . . and what you were. I understand that you suffered a terrible injury, but you seem to have made a good recovery. And how apparent is your loss, really, if I didn't notice it after three days in your company? How greatly does it impede you if you were able to protect me from two ruthless men?"

"It impedes me enough," he said gruffly.

He could not begin to convey to her how the loss had affected him. That knowing he could never again go to sea was a blight on his whole existence. Though, in fairness, she was perhaps the one woman who might understand. But he would not tell her. He could not reveal that after he and his crew had been ransomed from the French, he'd gone aboard several merchant ships in London looking for work, and that each time his application had been laughed off as a kind of joke.

And he certainly would not admit that he hadn't been with a woman since that fateful encounter with the French ship. Even the false hand had not given him any confidence that he would not be laughed at or shunned, even by a whore.

He was about to tell her that he had absolutely no intention of discussing his blasted hand, when he realized she was prodding him toward the grain bin.

"I am curious about how this works," she said as she lifted the cloth from the wooden facsimile. "Would you show me?"

He was incoherent. She must be mad to think he would reveal his most private shame to her, but Alexa had already lifted the false hand and was examining it.

"It's a very clever device." Her fingers stroked over each curled finger. "Lighter than it appears, and nicely balanced."

He wanted to wrench it away from her, to shout at her to put it down and leave him the bloody hell alone. Instead he stood there unmoving, barely breathing, as she lifted his right arm and tugged his short cuff away from the scarred stump.

"Am I doing this properly?" she asked as she fitted the base of the lamb's wool wrist up against his own.

"Yes," he managed to gasp. He looked straight ahead, trying not to shudder, while she fastened the harness that reached to the middle of his forearm.

"Not too tight?"

"No," he said. It was practically a whimper.

"Good." She refastened his cuff, smoothed down his sleeve, and than stood back. "You can breathe now," she said, not trying to hide the fond amusement in her voice.

"No one . . ." he said haltingly, "no one has . . . ever done that before."

She smiled wistfully. "Was it so terrible? I didn't muss you about or anything, did I? I'm used to tending the soldiers at the Chelsea Hospital. I have a light touch, they all told me. With a bit of practice, I daresay, I could become rather good at this."

What the devil did she mean by that?

He looked down at her and saw everything that was in her heart shining in her bright, indigo gaze. Hope warring with uncertainty, admiration mixed with caution. And the one thing he'd never expected to see in another person's eyes—a fierce, protective concern. Not pity, not revulsion, but rather an expression that promised, *I will never let anything hurt you.* It made his own heart twist into a knot of longing.

If he could choose a moment to think back on in his old age, one that held only relief and the surcease of pain, this would surely have been it.

"Come inside," she said gently, placing her hand on his shoulder. "We have enemies we need to outwit. We need to make a plan."

"You're sure you wouldn't rather go on without me?"

She said a very rude word. "As if I would entrust myself to anyone but you. And, besides, you need to go to Cudbright. It's time my father discovered the truth about that night, don't you think?"

"The truth? And what do you think the truth is, Miss Prescott?"

She wrinkled her long, elegant nose. "Something that has my cousin at the bottom of it, I'm sure."

Chapter 8

❧

Finch didn't stop roaring for a good two miles. By the time he and Connor finally drew up their horses, Finch's coat front was covered with blood, but the neck wound had nearly stopped bleeding.

Connor doctored him the best he could, which was difficult, since he spent most of the time avoiding Finch's flailing fists. He soaked his neck cloth in some brandy from his hip flask, and wrapped it around the other man's throat.

"It's not so bad," he pronounced. "Just a long gash." He thought it wise not to tell Finch that a bit of his earlobe was missing. His friend was hardly in the mood for any more bad news.

Connor hesitantly brought up the notion of abandoning their pursuit, but Finch had his dander up now. He swore he would kill MacHeath the next time they met. "And that bitch of his, too, with her high-and-mighty airs. I don't care about Quincy's money any longer."

"Well, you should," Connor protested. "We done a lot more for him than we agreed on. Days and nights on the road, asking after his cousin at every blasted inn and tavern. I swear, when this is over, I never want to see another landlord. We deserve to get our fair cut, Bully, and now that you been shot, we should double our fee. So no more losing your temper and tryin' to shoot the chit. Save your anger for MacHeath."

Finch agreed with a surly grunt.

Connor fidgeted with his flask. "So what do we do now? You think he's gone to earth in Rumpley?"

"Mmm. Probably waiting there in that inn for cover of darkness before he tries to leave." He hunkered down against a wide tree trunk. "Plus, the chit'll need time to recover from being dunked in the river."

"What if she drowned?"

"Then, I say good riddance to her. But *he'll* still be there," he muttered as he reached up and snatched the flask from Connor. After a long swallow, he swiped his sleeve across his mouth. "And then he'll regret the day he ever crossed our path, Alf. By God, he will."

It was twilight when their quarry came strolling along the high street. Finch watched from a shadowed alley opposite the inn as the man in the black cape and the woman in the blue pelisse made their leisurely way toward the Squire's Hat. Several times they stopped to peer into a shop window or to nod at one of the numerous passersby.

Finch growled to himself—there were too many people out there on the street for him to risk a shot at MacHeath. For such a small town, the pavement seemed to be awash with humanity.

Once the couple had entered the inn, Finch gave a sharp, high whistle. Connor's head popped out of the alleyway directly across from him, and he nodded once before his head disappeared. Two minutes later Finch saw him flit across the road at the far end of the village. When Connor finally crept up behind him, he was breathless.

"You spotted 'em, Bully?"

"Mmm. No use you minding the back door of the inn— they weren't staying there after all. They just came down the street from the direction of the bridge, arm in arm and bold as brass."

"Where are they now?"

"Look," Finch said with glee as he pointed to the front of the Squire's Hat. The couple was just settling themselves at the table nearest the inn's bow window, their profiles backlit by the candles in the dining parlor. "Couldn't ask for more than that," he proclaimed softly. "We'll follow them when they leave. If they don't use the front door, then we'll run around to the back and surprise them as they come out."

The two waited for over an hour, and still the couple seemed intent on their meal. After another half hour, Connor began to squirm. "What're they doin', Bully? Samplin' every bleedin' thing in the kitchen?"

Finch watched as the man and woman in the window touched their glasses together in an obvious toast. He chuckled. "I fancy they be congratulatin' each other on gettin' shed of us." He added softly, "That's right, MacHeath, drink to Bully Finch. And I'll drink to you when you're in hell."

Finally the couple rose from the table. Less than a minute later, they came out onto the pavement and set out in the direction of the bridge. They had only gone a few feet when the man bent to the lady and whispered something into her ear. She erupted in a peal of loud, cackling laughter.

"Ooh, Ebbie," she shrieked. "You have a wicked, wicked tongue on you . . . and I should know."

Finch immediately lowered his gun and swore. "Something's amiss."

"That don't sound like Quincy's cousin," his companion concurred.

The couple resumed walking, and the tall man started to sing in a braying voice. "The ladies down in Hades wear garters made in France, and if you're willing to pay a shilling, the devil makes them dance. . . ."

The woman began to giggle loudly, while punching her partner playfully in the ribs.

"We been duped," Finch snarled. "C'mon, let's see if those two jugbit fools know anything."

Connor was halfway into the street, when Finch caught his arm and yanked him back. "No, we best go around and catch them at the bridge. We're less likely to get interrupted there."

They headed down the alley at a run, Connor a little in front of his mate, who had to move gingerly because of his neck wound. By the time Finch reached the field behind the shop, Connor was stomping around and cursing.

"Our horses are gone!" he cried, pointing to a leafless lilac thicket. "And I tied them good and tight."

"Maybe some pranking boys set them loose. But we ain't got time to look for them now. Come on . . ."

They hurried along through the unlit yards that lay behind the shop row, stumbling over refuse barrels and piles of cord wood, and then assumed a more leisurely pace once they were on the street. The tipsy couple was just crossing the bridge when they caught up with them.

"'Scuse me, ma'am," Finch called out. "If I might speak with you. Me and my friend are from Bow Street."

"Ooh, Bow Street," she crowed to the man beside her. "Fancy that, Ebbie."

Finch felt his bile rise. He took a deep breath before he continued. "We be looking for a woman with a blue coat exactly like the one you are wearing. I was wondering how you came by it."

"I gave it to her," the man said proudly. "Foun' it behind the tailor's shop this afternoon. Soaking wet, it were. Wetter than an old wet hen." He began to giggle softly.

"What time was that?"

The man shrugged. "Sommat past two."

The woman preened and ran her hand over the embroidered sleeve. "Fine, ain't it? I dried it by the fire, and bless me if it didn't fit just right."

"You didn't see anyone suspicious around?"

"You mean strangers?" As the man spoke, he listed so far to one side that he nearly obscured his companion. "None but you and yon little scrap of a fellow."

Finch touched his forelock to the couple and quickly retraced his steps to Connor. "MacHeath's scarpered," he said with a scowl. "And those two don't know nothing about it. We'd better find our horses and get after the girl."

After an hour of fruitless searching, they concluded that their horses had not merely wandered off, but had been stolen.

"Imagine that," Connor mused as they trudged along the dark street to the livery stable, which had been pointed out to them by a young man lounging near the inn.

"Imagine what?"

"Someone having the bleedin' gall to steal *our* horses."

They hammered repeatedly on the door to the livery-man's house, but there was no answer. Which should not have surprised them, since there were no lights showing in any of the windows.

"Looks like we have to help ourselves," said Finch with a guttural whisper.

He tried to force the front door of the barn, but it was latched from the inside. A window on the far side of the building appeared more promising. Unfortunately, he had barely begun to jimmy it open, when Towser—who was a terrier of uncertain ancestry, but with no lack of terrier tenacity—came racing around the corner of the building. He catapulted into Finch and sank his teeth into the back of his thigh.

Finch screamed and tried to shake the animal off.

"Shoot the blasted dog!" he cried, dancing around the stable yard like a man possessed by six devils. But when Connor drew his pistol and started to take aim, Finch realized his backside was in as much danger as the determined dog. "No, don't shoot!" he wailed. "Run!"

Towser did not let go until the men had crossed the bridge at a brisk gallop. With his honor satisfied and his territory safe once more, he shook himself from snout to tail and went off to inspect a barrel of refuse that had been overturned behind the butcher shop.

A good dog's work was never done.

Mr. and Mrs. Gable waited another hour before they relit the candles in their parlor. "You think we've seen the last of them?" she asked.

"They'll be away after the real MacHeath by now," her husband replied. "But thanks to us, he and his lady have a decent lead on them."

"Well, then, Ebbie," she said, aping the accent she'd used in the street, "I'm thinkin' we deserves another little toast."

"You were a treat to do this for my friend," he said as he poured them each a glass of brandy. "Especially since the big, ugly one came right up to us. MacHeath and I never thought he'd do that when we planned this out. I wouldn't have let you be part of the masquerade otherwise."

"I wasn't afraid." She clinked her glass against his, and her eyes danced. "You had your pistol with you, after all. That's one advantage of marrying an ex-smuggler—you know your man can handle a rough customer or two."

She winked at him roguishly, and gave him a teasing smile. They might as well make a night of it, she reckoned; she'd sent their boy off to a neighbor's earlier, to keep him out of harm's way, so they had the house to themselves for a change.

Her musing was abruptly interrupted by a loud knock on the door. Mrs. Gable nearly dropped her glass. Her husband quickly extinguished the candles and went to look out the front window.

"It's two men," he said over his shoulder. "No, my love, don't tremble so. It's not those two rogues. Looks to be an older man and a young fellow."

"Should we see what they want?"

"Mmm. Might be they're just looking for horses to let."

Mrs. Gable rallied slightly. "Then, let them in, Eb. But keep your pistol handy."

Gambling was in Darwin Quincy's blood. The turn of a card or the outcome of a horse race quickened his pulse and made his brain hum. So it was the most natural thing that he should venture into Alexander Prescott's office without knowing whether Alexa had yet written to alert her father about his own part in the abduction plot.

He found Prescott at his desk, his back to the large window that overlooked the riverfront and the shipyard. The older man looked up as he came through the door. Quincy hesitated, awaiting some sign of accusation, and when nothing more than a surprised, "Best of the season to you, nephew," was forthcoming, he tossed his hat onto a bench with a silent sigh of relief.

"I didn't look for you this year," Prescott said as he pinched his half glasses off his nose and set aside the papers he'd been reading.

Quincy schooled his face into somber lines. "I am come here to share your sorrow, Uncle."

He was gratified when Prescott's face paled. "My sorrow? Good Lord, what has happened?"

"I thought you must know by now," he said softly. "Else I would not have sprung it on you so abruptly. I assumed Mrs. Reginald had written to you the night it happened. Ah, but she was so overset, and perhaps feared your anger . . . because, after all, she allowed such a thing to occur while your daughter was in her care."

Prescott set his hands on the desk and leaned forward. "Is it Alexa? Quick now, don't drag it out."

"She has been abducted, sir."

Prescott started back in his chair. "What's that?"

"Outside Reading, a rogue lured her from the coach and carried her off." He paused a moment, watching as his uncle's eyes narrowed. "I instantly enlisted several men to search for her . . . I led them myself for two days, and then thought that I could be of more service here. I was sure you would need someone beside you in your time of distress. It . . . it never occurred to me that you had not been notified or I'd have sent word myself."

Prescott got up slowly, like Zeus arising from his Olympian throne. His white brows quivered in barely contained fury as his fist crashed down on the desk. "Who had the blasted impudence to carry off my daughter?"

"I . . . I have no idea, Uncle. I assumed the man was holding her for ransom. But I gather you have received no message from him. That is most strange."

"If I know my girl, she coshed the fellow on the head the instant his back was turned and ran off. That would be just like Alexa."

Quincy sniffed. "She is a gallant girl, certainly, but perhaps you give her too much credit."

"Nonsense, she is my daughter, and more of a trouper, even as a cub, than you ever were." Prescott drew in a steadying breath. "But that's old business. You are here now, and I thank you for it. I never figured you for a man to come through in a crisis. Looks like I have to rethink things a mite."

He moved to the window, and Quincy saw that his hands were trembling as he plucked at the heavy draperies. "My poor girl," he murmured. "My poor little Lexie."

Quincy went to his side and laid a comforting hand on his broad shoulder.

"Let me support you, sir. Because I care for you, and because it is the least I can do to repay you for all your kindnesses to me."

Prescott turned to him, his usually robust face now gaunt and gray.

"She's everything to me," he said raggedly. "If I were to lose her . . ."

"Come." Quincy motioned him back to his chair. "I will tell you what I have learned so far, and then we'll put our heads together and determine the best way to get her back."

"Yes, together we will get her back," Prescott said with some of his former vigor. "I never doubted you were a clever lad, Darwin. Never for a minute."

Quincy slid into the chair opposite the desk and crossed his legs. The smug, satisfied smile that curled his thin mouth lingered there only an instant.

Chapter 9

MacHeath and Alexa kept up a punishing pace as they traveled across the rolling countryside of south Hampshire. They were making excellent time for a change. The horse Mr. Gable gave Alexa had lived up to her reputation, easily keeping abreast of MacHeath's hunter. Alexa had insisted on riding astride, and neither MacHeath nor Mr. Gable had tried to dissuade her. Over cross-country terrain, they knew, it would be far safer than using a sidesaddle.

They had waited until dusk to slip out of the barn, praying that the Gables' ruse would keep Finch and Connor from following them. Every five miles or so during their flight, MacHeath had scanned the horizon behind them with his spyglass, but, so far, there had been no signs of pursuit.

They kept on through the night and into the next day. Few noted them since they stayed away from any towns. They barely spoke, barely acknowledged each other, but when their eyes happened to meet, they both smiled. And then looked away.

After their confrontation in the barn, MacHeath had convinced Alexa to sleep for a few hours. She'd insisted that he remain with her in the attic room, and he had ended up kneeling beside the bed, his arms crossed on the counterpane. They had done nothing more intimate than gaze at each other, and once or twice, MacHeath had stroked a tendril of hair away from her face. They did not speak of what had transpired in the barn, but it was clear that something almost miraculous was growing between them. Alexa had seen tenderness in his expression and what she hoped was a sweet reciprocation of her own budding feelings.

At one point she touched his false hand, again obscured by its leather glove, and then drifted her fingers up his arm. "Will you tell me about this?"

He lowered his gaze. "There's little to tell. My ship met up with a French man-o'-war off Calais and was blasted out of the water. Before the ship went down, a falling spar crushed my hand. A French surgeon took it off, and a Scottish doctor up in Edinburgh put it back—in a less fleshly form."

She pinched his arm gently. "Why do I get the feeling you are leaving out a great deal?"

His dark eyes, for once unobscured by their long lashes, gazed intently into hers. "Because there's no use talking about it, Alexa."

"I understand," she said. "But thank you for telling me anyway."

He hesitated, and then said in a gruff whisper, "Thank you for understanding."

As it happened, it was MacHeath who had dozed off first, his head cradled in his arms, and Alexa was able to trace her fingers over his face for the first time. She felt the rough stubble on his chin, where three day's worth of beard was showing, and the smooth line of his cheekbone. She caressed the creases beside his eyes and the delicate filigree of his long eyelashes. As though he was aware of her touch, he sighed in his sleep, and she leaned forward and brushed her lips over his mouth.

And then she slept, with one hand twined in his hair.

Alexa turned to him now as they pulled up at a river ford and smiled at the memory of his lean face beneath her hands. She wondered if he would ever feel such a strong compulsion to touch her. Considering the way she looked at this moment, she somehow doubted it.

Her hair had been twisted back into an untidy tail and tied with a bit of twine. Over Mrs. Gable's rose-colored dress, she wore a man's woolen jacket and a heavy cloak. The gown's cut was too narrow for sitting astride comfortably, and it had ridden up over her half boots and heavy woolen stockings. She tried to tug the hem down into a more modest arrangement and caught MacHeath looking at her legs.

"You've a neat ankle, ma'am," he said with a crooked grin.

"Yes, and these stockings are so flattering," she responded tartly.

"I'm not complaining."

His grin widened to a smile that showed off his white teeth and softened his weathered face. Their rousing ride had whipped his dark hair into unruly waves, and the bright sunlight had turned his dark-gray eyes to shining silver. He'd traded his black cape for one of deepest brown, courtesy of Mr. Gable. Its edges lifted and danced around him in the wind as he sat, relaxed and graceful, in the saddle, and she thought that if there was a more stirring vision in the whole of the land, she had yet to see it.

"What are *you* looking at, hoyden?"

"I am enjoying the prospect," she replied.

"So am I," he said softly with a look of barely contained hunger. She realized with relief that her mismatched attire had not put him off her. Not by a long shot.

They crossed the water without mishap, and then raced to the top of the hill on the river's far side. The winter-bare downs rolled away from them to the south. "Smell that?" he asked, drawing up his horse.

She raised her head and tested the air. "We're near the Channel, aren't we?"

He drew his spyglass from his pocket and held it out to her. Alexa could see the city of Bournemouth in the distance, the towers of Corfe Castle straight ahead; to the east lay the shadowy presence of the Isle of Wight, looking like a great gray whale basking in the paler blue of the Channel.

"We're less than an hour from the sea, I would guess."

She handed him the glass, and then touched his sleeve. "We've both been away too long, Simeon."

He pulled back from her, his face now somber. "I won't ever go back to the sea, Alexa. There's nothing for me there any longer."

She understood then, and felt like a fool for not having figured it out sooner. This was his Great Tragedy. Not the loss of his hand, but of his livelihood, of his only true vocation. Men who went to sea, she knew full well, were spoiled for life on land. They chafed and fretted when they were not on board a ship.

"Surely other men who have lost a hand were able to remain at sea." She had a moment of inspiration. "What of Nelson? He lost both an eye and a limb."

"Nelson was a blasted admiral. I doubt he ever went anywhere near a line or a rigging." He sighed, and added, "I tried, Alexa. I tried more than once to get another berth."

He didn't have to tell her the result; the misery in his face was answer enough.

"There are other roads, surely."

"Not for me. I was born to work on a ship. Life is an empty cask without that."

She wanted to protest, to plead with him to let her be the special thing that replaced the sea in his heart. But it was too soon—the feelings that were growing between them were too new, too delicate, to bear such a burden.

They rode on again in silence, but this time their journey was no longer leavened by shared smiles.

Just outside Bournemouth, MacHeath turned down a narrow track that cut to the west. The village where MacHeath's friend lived lay so close to the water that the main street was practically part of the beach. They dismounted and led their horses along the waterfront, past a group of men who were sharing a smoke beside the sheltering hull of a rotted fishing boat. Just beyond a chandler's warehouse, they followed a winding path to a small cottage. When MacHeath hailed him, his friend, Nat Tarlton, came hobbling out his front door. Alexa guessed his age to be something near sixty. He was bent and gnarled, but with the deep-water tan and piercing eyes of a lifelong sailor.

When he recognized his visitor, the man's craggy face split into a broad smile.

"MacHeath, by all that is unholy! You rascally son of a sea dog." The old man began to thump him repeatedly on the back. "I heard you lost the *Bess* some years back. That was a sad day. Heard about this, too—" He raised MacHeath's right hand, and then pushed his cap back in wonder. "But I didn't know you'd gone and found yourself a false hand. It's good to see you didn't let a paltry injury get you down."

MacHeath gritted his teeth slightly, then tugged Alexa forward. "Nat, this is Miss Prescott. Alexa, my good friend, Nat Tarlton."

He took up Alexa's hand and patted it. "A pleasure, miss."

When he ushered them into his cottage, and lit a lantern against the darkening afternoon, Alexa saw that the main room was filled with wooden crates.

"Still in the trade?" MacHeath asked with some surprise.

"Naw, this ain't contree-band. I am holding onto some inventory for my nephew. He lost his tackle shop in the last big storm."

MacHeath fidgeted with his cuff, and then looked up. "I need a favor, Nat."

"Anything, you know that."

"We need a boat to get us to Cudbright, and someone to captain it."

Nat's watery eyes crinkled. "Ho, that's a good one, Mackie. You needin' a captain." He turned to Alexa with a wink. "This here's the best natural sailor I ever come across in all my days. Got a nose for the wind and an eye for the sky. He understands the sea . . . I wouldn't of given him the *Black Bess* otherwise."

MacHeath was wearing a scowl, and Alexa feared what he might say to the old man. "Can't you take us there, Mr. Tarlton? Mr. MacHeath has not sailed for a very long time and—"

"What's that to do with anything? It's in his blood, by God." He spun to MacHeath. "You ain't turned scared, have you? No, that's not what's happened. You weren't never scared of nothing."

With a resigned sigh, MacHeath shrugged back the edge of his cape and slowly held up his right hand.

"So?" Tarlton asked scornfully.

"I can't hold a line, I can't raise a sail. I certainly can't climb a rigging."

"The lady can help with the lines and the sails."

"Yes, I can," Alexa said. She'd been sailing with her father since she'd learned to walk, and could crew a ship as well as any man.

"I want you to take us," MacHeath insisted.

"Can't, lad. My arthritics come along bad this past year. I can barely get down the path into town some days. Still have my ketch, though. My nephew takes it out now and again."

"Then, perhaps he can sail us to Exeter."

" 'Fraid not. He's gone off to Bournemouth with his wife—lookin' for a new place to set up shop."

Alexa pulled MacHeath aside, with an apologetic glance at Nat.

"We don't have time to stand here arguing," she whispered forcefully. "If he will let us use his boat, there's an end to it. Between us, I'm sure we can manage."

He shook his head. "After the last time I was turned down for work, I vowed I would never set foot on another ship. Isn't it enough that for your sake I am forgetting that promise, without you asking me to sail the blasted boat?"

"That was an idiotic promise," she said between her teeth. "And *I* will sail the blasted boat. All you have to do is steer."

"Oh, so you will navigate as well?" he drawled.

"No," she practically shouted. "But I would imagine a man who'd lost his hand would still have the ability to navigate. Or have you lost your wits, as well?"

"I lost my wits when I decided to rescue you. And see where it's gotten me?"

"It's gotten you back to sea, you overbearing, insufferable, boneheaded clot!"

Nat Tarlton seemed to be enjoying their mutual display of temper; he rocked back and forth on his thick brogues, grinning widely. But when MacHeath spun to him and asked gruffly where he might find someone who could take him to

Devon, Nat instantly wiped the grin off his face and pointed to a cove beyond the end of the village.

"You might want to take a gander at my little ketch," he added. "She be named the *Bluebird*. Blue hull with a red stripe."

MacHeath went striding out the door, muttering to himself. Nat watched him go and then turned to Alexa. "Always thought he'd make sommat of hisself. He warn't cut out for the smuggling trade, though he did well by it, for a time." He scratched his balding head and gave her a long look. "There was a wee girl he used to talk about back then . . . when he was in his cups mostly. I allus hoped he'd find her again someday and carry her off. Wonder what happened to her. He used to call her a black-haired she-devil."

Alexa tried not to grin. "I believe that was me."

Nat Tarlton whistled softly. "So, did he do it? Did he finally carry you off?"

She leaned over and whispered against his weathered cheek. "Mr. Tarlton, you have no idea."

Nat decided to go after MacHeath, so he could, as he put it, "knock some sense into him." He left Alexa with instructions to pack up whatever she and MacHeath might need in the way of supplies. She scouted around and found an old sack behind one of the crates. Nat Tarlton's larder was not overflowing, but she managed to locate a tin of biscuits and some salted beef. She also unearthed a small crock of cider. She removed a biscuit from the tin before she stowed it in the sack, and munched on it while she examined the interior of the small cottage.

There was no doubt that its owner was of nautical inclinations. Yellowed maritime charts decorated the walls, and ship's lanterns hung from the rafters. The window ledge was decorated with oddly shaped seashells, and on a narrow table littered with the paraphernalia of a pipe smoker, she saw a framed pencil sketch of a brigantine. She recognized MacHeath's handiwork. This must be Tarlton's ship, the *Black Bess*. She bent to examine the drawing, and out of the corner of her eye she noticed two men peering into the window at the side of the cottage.

Her heart skipped a beat.

Without giving any sign that she'd seen them, she set the drawing down and picked up a large cowry shell, pretending to study it while she sneaked glances at the window. Her heart eased its thudding when she realized that it was not the ugly customers—there was not enough disparity in their sizes, for one thing. However, the overhang of the roof set the two men in shadow, so she was unable to make out anything else, especially since they both had their mufflers pulled up to their noses.

She wondered how it was that the instant she was out of MacHeath's sight, two pursuers invariably appeared. And here she was, trapped in a cottage that had only one door. An unlocked door, she observed from across the room. Just as she moved toward it with the intention of sliding the bolt, the faces disappeared from the window.

She flung herself against the door and grappled with the lock. There was a good sturdy bolt on the door itself but no corresponding pin for it to slide into on the frame. She cursed people living in safe, little villages who never felt the need to keep their door locks in good repair.

Snatching the sack of provisions off the table, she quickly doused the lantern above her, and then darted behind a stack of wooden boxes. Hiding was not very productive, she knew, since those men had certainly seen her moving about in here. But she wasn't going to make it easy for them. In the small space of the cottage, crowded as it was with furniture and crates, there was a chance she could elude them and get away to her horse. It was a slight hope, but the only one she could think of to keep her courage up.

The door creaked open, and she heard footsteps on the plank floor.

"Miss Alexa?"

She didn't recognize the voice, but that hardly surprised her, since it was muffled behind a woolen scarf. With a wild shriek, she overturned the topmost box on the stack, and its contents—about a thousand fishhooks—spilled out onto the floor. She jumped up, swinging the sack around her head like a shepherd's sling. It struck the slighter of the two men, making him cry out as the crock connected with the side of his head. He skidded on the fishhooks, trying to right himself and cursing loudly, while the larger man danced back from her makeshift weapon and found himself also entangled in the hooks.

The door had been left open, and she darted toward it.

Her mare was tethered at the back of the cottage, and she flung herself into the saddle, still only half seated as the horse skittered forward. She snatched up the reins of MacHeath's hunter, and then headed toward two horses that were tethered farther up the narrow lane. She keened like a banshee as she raced toward them. Both horses reared back onto their haunches, snapping their reins. Then they were gone, clattering up the hillside away from the village. She drove her heels into the mare's side and turned her toward the cove. Behind her she heard the cries of the two men as they went charging after their horses.

She raced along the rocky path toward the water, relieved to see MacHeath and Nat Tarlton below her on the beach. MacHeath was speaking to another man, while Nat hovered in the background, an unlit pipe in his mouth. They all looked up as she came galloping toward them, leaving a wake of splattering gravel and sand.

"Two men . . . at the cottage!" she cried breathlessly as she tumbled down from the horse. "I managed to get away . . . but they'll be right behind me."

Nat stepped forward and thrust past the fisherman with whom MacHeath had been negotiating. "Take the *Bluebird*," he growled. "Get the girl away."

MacHeath pulled out one of his pistols, his eyes intent on the beach path. The two men, still on foot, had just appeared over the rise.

"No," she said, pushing down the barrel. "It's not Finch and Connor. It might be those men from Dagshott. But I don't think we should wait around to find out."

He nodded once and slipped the weapon back into his pocket. Crossing quickly to his horse, he tugged his saddlebag and the bedroll from its back. Nat was already beside his beached ketch, untying the line that held it to a piling. He handed Alexa over the side, and then he and MacHeath shoved it into the water.

"Pole out past the shallows," Nat said. "You'll catch a fair wind beyond the breakers."

MacHeath drew out his pistol again and tossed it to Nat before he leaped into the boat. "In case those fellows turn ugly," he said. "I'll be back for the horses within the week."

Alexa was already hoisting the sail. It rippled a few times, and then, as the ketch moved into deeper water, it belled out and the ketch began to pick up speed. She cast a quick look over her shoulder to the beach; Nat had backed off from her two pursuers, who were now dancing around on the shingle, waving their arms and shouting to her. Fortunately the wind was carrying their cries away from the small boat.

She glanced at MacHeath, who was sitting on the stern seat minding the tiller, and gave a guilty sigh. As soon as the men had entered the cottage, she'd known who they were. For one thing, a ruffian wouldn't have addressed her as "Miss Alexa." Once she recognized them, she nearly laughed that she had been so frightened. But that they meant no harm didn't matter—she had no mind to be rescued. Things were progressing in a most interesting manner with MacHeath, and furthermore, she had an overriding instinct that he needed to get back to sea. That wouldn't happen if she'd let those men apprehend her. They'd likely send MacHeath on his way and take her back to Cudbright with them, and then nothing would be sorted out. Quincy would deny anything to do with her abduction. And MacHeath would have no chance to plead his case with her father. No, going home without him was not an option.

But thank heavens she'd convinced him not to shoot at the two men. Her father would never forgive her if—

The wind shifted slightly, and Alexa returned her attention to the lines.

Once they were free of the headland, the sail swelled, and the *Bluebird* showed her mettle, cutting cleanly through the water like a cruising shark. Though the Channel was running to a fair chop, the breeze was steady from the southeast, which meant Alexa would not have to tack unless it changed direction. It looked to be a straight shot across Lyme Bay to the mouth of the River Exe. Twelve hours, maybe fifteen, if the wind gave them any trouble. They'd be sailing through the night, which bothered her a little. She'd never been out at night in such a small boat. Though she imagined they would never lose sight of land, where the lights in the coastal towns would help keep them on course.

When she and her parents had sailed to Barbados the year she was nine, the voyage had lasted over a month. The nights at sea had been her favorite part of the trip. But that had been during the warm, summer months. Now the wind cut across the Channel in icy needles, and she knew it would only get colder as it got darker.

The ship was now heading into the first rays of the sunset; the sky at the horizon, with its jagged aurora of fiery orange spikes, looked like Rome on one of Nero's bad days.

MacHeath had not spoken to her since their spat in Nat's cottage, except to issue a few curt instructions once they were on board the *Bluebird*. She'd heard his hurried farewell to the old smuggler, and her heart had sunk when he'd told Nat he'd be returning in a week's time. She wanted desperately to believe that once he got to Cudbright, he would remain there with her.

Although, if he couldn't convince her father of his innocence, there was every possibility he would have no choice about remaining in Devon—not if he was taken off to Exeter jail in chains.

When they'd awakened in the attic bedroom yesterday, he'd offered to tell her about what had transpired in her father's office ten years ago. She knew that the morning after the theft, the constables had carted him off, still barely conscious, before he had had a chance to plead his case. But she'd told him she would wait. She needed him to understand that she believed in his innocence *without* hearing his tale.

MacHeath adjusted the tiller with his left hand, keeping

the ketch on a course parallel to the shoreline. Nat's *Blue-bird* was a tidy, nimble little ship, swift over the water and quick to respond. She practically sailed herself. He occupied himself by watching Alexa, who was making constant adjustments to the sail to take maximum advantage of the stiff breeze. But he kept forgetting to admire her seamanship, lost instead in the wild beauty of her hair, which scudded around her face in a dark tangle. The wind had brushed a rosy blush over her cheeks that was entrancing. At the moment she was backlit by a breathtaking sunset, and he had to strain his memory to recall viewing anything even half as lovely.

She hadn't said a word to him since they'd fled the cove, just nodded or grunted when he told her what to do. Not that he could blame her for her starchy silence—he'd acted like a nodcock back there at Nat's, whining about his infirmity, and horrified that she might guess that he was afraid to set foot in a boat.

There, he'd finally admitted it. He was afraid.

It wasn't so much the loss of his hand that had kept him from pursuing work on a ship. That had been an all-too-convenient excuse. It was true the first few captains he'd spoken to had dismissed him. But there were hundreds of captains, hundreds of ship owners, who could use a seasoned sailor, however impaired, with the ability to read the stars and plot a sure course.

But he'd grown strangely disoriented the two times he'd gone aboard a ship for those interviews. His stomach had churned, his brow had beaded with sweat. After the second time, he had staggered onto the dock, ill and dizzy, and had sworn he would never try again, never even set foot on another ship. When he'd told Alexa that ships made him bilious, it wasn't exactly a lie.

It was easy enough to know where the sweaty, dizzying fear came from—the memories of that last sea battle, coupled with the trauma of losing his hand had never really left him. The screams of his drowning men as the water surged around them still haunted him. They had been followed by his own screams a scant half hour later, when the French surgeon, coolly disregarding his urgent pleas, had lopped off his hand. At least the fellow had done a neat job of stitching him up, but that didn't occur to MacHeath until much later, once he and his surviving crewmen had been traded back to the British. By then, the neatly mended wound was of little matter. There were other, deeper scars that were still tender to the touch.

Or so he thought.

He'd now discovered, almost immediately, that he was able to slip back into this, his true habitat, with great ease. His concern for getting Alexa safely away had completely overridden his fear. He felt no dizziness, no panic. The ketch rose and sank beneath him, the rhythmic cadence as soothing to him as a mother's caress. The sail thudded as a gust filled it, and the lines creaked and chattered. There was no music on earth more welcome than those humble sounds.

He owed Alexa for getting him out here. Who knew how many years he would have avoided the sea, or even if he'd have ever come back? And that would have been a sorry waste.

His heart filled with pure, exhilarating pleasure for the first time in two years. He had all he needed—a ship and the sea and the sky. And the woman. It was the first time he'd added that particular item to his equation of perfection. For this short while, he would have a bounty of the things he valued most.

Alexa was leaning against the mast, her arms angled behind her. The boat was making way smoothly now, and she no longer needed to tend the sails so closely. She was gazing at him from under her brows, a challenge in her blue eyes, her chin at a determined angle. Throwing her victory right in his face, no doubt.

Something inside him started to simmer in response to that look.

This was a woman who backed down from very little, and the thought intrigued him. She could muster up passion aplenty when it came to wrangling and arguing. He wondered—and felt his belly tighten at the image—just how must passion she could muster in a more appropriate venue.

He reached for the docking line that trailed behind him in

the water, and wrapped its sodden length around the tiller to hold it in place. They had the whole width of the Channel around them if they veered off course, and he had more pressing business now than steering the boat.

He rose from the plank seat, relieved to find his legs steady under him, as though he'd trod a deck only days before. He moved toward her swiftly, closing the space between them in three paces, and then he captured her hands behind her, holding them against the mast.

"Will you accept the apology of a boneheaded clot?"

She tipped her head up. "You forgot overbearing and insufferable."

Her eyes were still challenging him, but there was a slight smile playing over her mouth.

When he kissed her, she was already straining up to meet him. She moaned softly as he tightened his hold, thrusting her back against the mast with his body, leaning into her with all his strength, nearly lifting her off her feet. Again and again he kissed her, taking her mouth, groaning against it, tasting her until his head swam and his knees trembled. She smelled of open air and heather, and her lips were dappled with sea spray that tasted sweeter than nectar.

He released her hands and felt them immediately tangle in his hair, tugging at the long strands that brushed his collar. He breathed her name over and over against her cheek, while his hands moved to her hips and began an intent, sensuous slide up her body. His chest tightened—he swore he could feel her with both hands . . . the swell of her hips, the sweet indentation of her waist, the breath-stealing rise of her breasts. She'd slipped her hands beneath his coat, her curled fingers clawed their way up his back and then down again.

He thought he might go mad.

The wind was chill and blowing strong, but the fire in the pit of his stomach was an inferno, heating him, consuming him. Alexa had opened to him like a rose, all her beauty and all her passion displayed to him without restraint.

"Simeon!" she cried, arching against him, hip and thigh and belly pressing into him with a canny innocence that made his blood roar through his veins. She was so delight-

ful to touch, to caress, to kiss. Not delicate, not hesitant, but
lusty and hungry and as driven by desire as he was.

He lowered his head again, thinking that he would make
a lifelong habit of kissing her, when the wind shifted
abruptly and the sail started to swing around.

"Blast it, we're coming about!" he cried as he dragged
her away from the mast. The spar came bearing down on
them, and they both ducked as the canvas whooshed overhead. The boat heeled over acutely and picked up speed.

Alexa was laughing as she scrambled to loosen the line.
MacHeath came up behind her and took it from her.

"Mind the tiller," he said, nodding toward the stern. He
put his whole body weight behind the rope before he tugged
on it to secure the sail. "Wind's shifted. It seems we're going
to have to tack now."

"Aye, Captain," she drawled as she undid the rope holding the tiller. "Can you manage?"

"I seem to be." He had the line in his left hand, the trailing end wrapped around his right wrist. She watched as he
pulled it taut, and then looped the end over a brass cleat in
an inverted figure eight. Any sailor could do that knot one-
handed, but he'd done it instinctively, without thinking.

"Yes," she said with a silent sigh of relief. "Yes, you do."

Chapter 10

MacHeath was heartily glad of the small crisis that had torn him away from Alexa's arms. Things might have gotten out of hand in a very short time if that sail hadn't come swinging toward them—he'd been nearly mindless with desire. Thank God he'd gotten some control back now.

That she was willing, he had no doubt. Willing to kiss him, willing to be his advocate, perhaps even willing to share her life with him. In the precipitate manner of females since the dawn of time, she was probably already planning their future together.

All because of that foolish infatuation she felt for him. It was clear that as a child, she'd made him into a sort of demigod. It was equally clear she had carried that childlike hero worship into her adult life.

Ah, but there had been nothing childlike in the way she'd faced him in Gable's barn. She'd confronted him and his wretched infirmity like a woman of maturity and compassion. It had taken more than just pluck to do that, to overwhelm the enormous barrier of his shame. He now realized he had to rethink the depth of her feelings for him. The notion that she might truly be in love with him made him feel something akin to elation.

Which he promptly squelched.

He reminded himself that his own feelings for Alexa were strictly superficial. Which was a damned difficult thing to do, considering the way his heart had been misbehaving

ever since she'd put her arms around him in the barn, with
an expression of such promise in her eyes.

He thought back to that precious interlude they'd shared
in the attic bedroom. He'd never felt so contented, leaning
there on her bed. He hadn't even wanted to touch her; just
watching her, seeing the emotions play over her face, had
been utterly satisfying. He hadn't ever felt like that before,
not with any woman. It almost frightened him.

Yet, the plain truth was, his feelings for her were immaterial. Even if he was able to convince her father of his innocence, even if he managed to regain his honor, he had
nothing to bestow on a wife. No home, no status or rank, not
even his own name. He could never go back to being
Simeon Hastings—the name was sullied in his mind. He'd
spent most of his adult life as MacHeath, and so he would
remain, but it was not a name worthy of Alexa Prescott.

He had never before considered taking a wife, even when
he prospered in the smuggler's trade. His life then was too
full of risks, and too much of his time was spent at sea. He'd
had as many women as his appetites required whenever he
was in port—on either side of the Channel.

But now he found himself wishing for more than a female to warm his bed. He wanted a companion, someone to
share his days as well as his nights, who would soothe him
and challenge him and make him laugh. A woman whose
eyes promised to protect him from all hurt and scorn. A
woman exactly like Alexa Prescott.

The trouble was, he needed to protect her in return, keep
her safe from the buffeting of life's storms. His masculine
pride made that imperative. And how the devil was he to do
that? He had no wealth or possessions to bring to her, nothing but a world-weary heart and a very questionable past.

He could hear her protests over this vast catalog of his
faults. She had more money than she could ever require, she
would proclaim. She wouldn't care if he was sunk below reproach in the eyes of the world. She would insist that his
feelings for her were the only offering she required.

If life were only that uncomplicated.

He knew he had to set her away from him. Kissing her,

he realized, had been a very bad idea. The incredible connection that had leaped between them would only fuel her conviction that they were meant to be together. It was difficult enough for him to talk himself out of that same conclusion. Still, he had to do something, say something to make her draw away. The more she looked at him with a dazzle of stars in her eyes, the harder it was for him to think clearly. If he dared to kiss her again, his resolve might just shatter completely.

And then he'd find himself married to an heiress and heir presumptive to a prosperous shipyard . . . and called fortune hunter and parasite behind his back by everyone he met. Better to return to the East End, where at least the names they called him were tolerable. He'd revert to Mackie the Cripple before he ever became MacHeath the Kept Man.

Eventually the wind grew too strong for the small boat. MacHeath suggested they find somewhere to take shelter for the night, and Alexa nodded. She had a feeling that if he'd been out there alone, MacHeath would have kept on sailing, but she didn't point that out to him when he declared they were no longer safe in open water. She was not unhappy to take a break from the icy wind and the constant battle to keep the ship on course. Neither of them had slept in what felt like years, and the stress of the journey was finally taking its toll. She was exhausted and suspected, from the way the skin was stretched taut over his cheekbones, that MacHeath was also near the end of his reserves.

It also occurred to her that if they were no longer in a rocking, shifting boat, he might kiss her again. As tired as she was, she knew she'd gladly stay awake for MacHeath's kisses. And whatever might come after them. She conjectured on this as she minded the tiller—the delicious things a man might do to a woman in the dark, with his hands and his mouth and his lean, hard body—and felt herself begin to blush.

Nothing had ever felt as fine as being held by him. Except perhaps touching him back . . . sensing the restrained strength in his arms, and knowing she had the power to undermine that restraint. Feeling his muscles shift and tighten through the fabric of his coat and shirt, wondering all the while what his bare skin would feel like under her hands. She'd been so close to him, wrapped in his arms, drowning in his kisses and his heated, murmuring sighs, but she knew there was another, deeper closeness a man could offer a woman, one that beckoned to her even as it made her heart thud with apprehension.

She'd naively thought herself proof against such wanton desires—certainly no man before him had ever come close to breaching her defenses—but she'd discovered that all those carefully erected barriers had crumbled at MacHeath's first onslaught. He had only to look at her, through his tangled forelock, and her pulse raced. With a swift smile and a flash of his white teeth, he made her blood surge and her head spin. And when he caressed her, every vital organ vibrated. Sweet Lord, her entire body clenched and shivered all the way down to her toes.

And she knew he'd felt it, too, that incredible, insistent tug that made coming together seem like an inevitability. He was still her lodestone, as he'd been in her youth. But the most amazing realization was that she had now become his. Even though he hadn't touched her since he'd kissed her up against the mast, there was no denying the expression in his eyes whenever he looked at her—ardent . . . hungry . . . impatient.

It was nearing ten when they put in at a deserted, rocky cove somewhere between Weymouth and Lyme Aegis. There was enough of a shingle for MacHeath to beach the ketch. He set out the anchor just to be on the safe side, and then assisted Alexa from the boat. She craned her head around, observing the high cliffs that rose on three sides.

Following her gaze, he mused, "Do you think it's worth finding a path inland? There might be a tavern or a hostelry near here."

"No, we have the food from Nat, and we can light a fire to keep warm. I think we should stay by the boat . . . in case the wind dies down we can go back out."

"I'll get you home for Christmas, Alexa," he said as he

began to scout along the shore for driftwood. "Even if we leave in the morning, we'll be in Cudbright by late afternoon."

"I'll make the church service in St. Peter's, then." She looked puzzled when he turned to gawk at her.

"Why do I have a difficult time picturing you inside a church?"

"What? Do you think I'm such a hell-born babe that the roof would come tumbling down on me if I ever set foot in such a sanctified place?"

"Something like that."

"Well, it hasn't happened yet. And going to church on Christmas Eve is part of the ritual Papa and I share. We've never missed it."

He piled up the lengths of driftwood and the pieces of a crate that had been dashed on the shore, and proceeded to make a fire. Then he stretched out near the heat of the flames and leaned back on one elbow with a weary sigh. "So tell me about Christmas with the Prescotts. When I worked for your father, I seem to recall most of his men spent the holiday getting foxed in the waterfront taverns."

She tucked her knees up under her cloak and rested her chin on them. "On Christmas Eve the workmen and their families would come to our house and sing carols in the great hall. My mother and I served them punch from the wassail bowl, which we spent all afternoon preparing. Papa always said we came up from the kitchen smelling of cinnamon and nutmeg, like the finest sweetmeats."

"He was right. You still smell of spices and sweets." MacHeath just barely prevented himself from raising up her hand and tasting it with his mouth.

"After Mama died," she continued, "we kept up the same ritual. Church, and then the carolers. It became my duty to distribute the wassail punch to them. But I never saw you with the singers . . . I would have known it if you were there."

He looked away from her. "I never had much fondness for Christmas. I probably spent the holiday holed up in my lodgings with a book on navigation or a paper on hull design."

"At least you weren't off getting foxed at the Mermaid's Tail."

"A fellow can get just as foxed in the privacy of his own rooms, Alexa."

She suspected there was a telling glimpse of his own experience in those words. "And so did you?"

His gaze slid away from her. "In the beginning I did. I was new to Devon, and the other men who worked for your father didn't exactly welcome me. I had a Scots burr back then, if you will recall, and a hasty temper. I did not feel a part of things. So I ate my meals alone, I spent my free time alone. And when I felt the urge to take a drink, I did that alone, as well."

He leaned toward her and ran one finger along her arm. "And then the damnedest thing happened. This black-haired hoyden tumbled into the water right in front of me. I tried to rescue her and got a thump on my nose for my troubles. But after that, the girl's father took me under his wing. Doors opened to me . . . God, worlds opened to me. Suddenly I was part of the whole. I never got to thank you for that, Alexa, for putting me where someone could finally see my true mettle."

"I was always sorry I punched you. But it was very mortifying to stand there beside you all sopping wet and with my hair drooping down in elf locks."

He tsked gently as he began to dig into the sack for their supper. "Such vanity . . . you couldn't have been more than eleven at the time."

"Shows all you know. Do you think wanting to make a good impression on someone you admire is only the province of adults?"

"How could you admire me? I'd been there less than a month."

She took the biscuit and piece of dried beef he held out, and then cocked her head. "Why do you think I was walking along the pier? I was hoping to catch a glimpse of you. I'd seen you several times before from a distance; Quincy pointed you out to me once from our carriage—he made some rude comment about you being a shiftless Scot. I told him that the Scottish regiments were famous for their bravery and that anyone who had a brain knew it."

"Thank you, I think."

She looked down quickly. "I couldn't bear him making fun of you. You looked so . . . so different from all the others. Finer, somehow, not rough or unkempt." Her voice lowered to a whisper. "And you had such beautiful hair and the most remarkable eyes . . ."

MacHeath sat up then, setting the food sack to one side before he gathered both her hands together.

"Listen to me, Alexa. I know you had a childish infatuation with me. I used to wonder why you were always dogging me when you could barely utter a civil word when we were together. It took me a while to sort it out—that you grew tongue-tied or shrewish precisely because you did like me, and hadn't a clue how to express it. Am I right?"

"Yes," she said with a little sigh.

"But those days are far behind us. Who I was back then, what I was . . . they've ceased to exist."

"You think I don't know that? I don't understand why you even need to bring it up. What lies between us now is—"

"There is nothing between us," he said brusquely.

"But—"

"Nothing," he repeated for emphasis.

"You kissed me," she said, scrambling onto her knees. "Why would you kiss me if you felt nothing for me?"

"Men like to kiss women, Alexa, it's as simple as that. They enjoy it enormously, and they take every opportunity to do it." He rubbed his hand along the back of his head in frustration. "Christ, what did they teach you in school? Have you no common sense when it comes to men?"

She drew back, and her face darkened. "I refuse to believe you were merely dallying with me."

"You can think what you like. But I will not be fodder for your daydreams any longer. If you insist on mooning about over a man who barely gives you a thought—"

"You are such a wretched liar," she stormed at him. "If

you barely gave me a thought, you wouldn't have risked your life to rescue me on the bridge. You certainly wouldn't have stirred yourself out of the East End to carry me off."

"That was only because of a wager I made with myself."

"What!"

"I had a little money put by, and I bet myself that if I could increase it at cards in one night, I would ride off and intercept your coach. If I lost then . . ." He shrugged.

"You let my safety, my virtue, hang on the turn of a card?"

"And why not? You were a stranger to me, Alexa. A very old, very distant memory. A child I recalled with some fondness, it's true, but an adult I had no feelings for one way or the other." He coughed once and added gruffly, "I still don't."

She rose abruptly from the fireside, hauled up a blanket, and then stomped off in the direction of the ketch.

"Where are you going?"

"To sleep in the boat."

"You'll freeze."

She spun to him. "And why the devil should you care? You just told me that your feelings for me are nonexistent."

"I still have a duty to you . . . to see you are kept safe."

"Duty be damned," she growled, stalking back toward him. "Do you know what I think . . . I think you are afraid of me. Yes, afraid. Because I have higher expectations for you than you've had for yourself in ten years. I want to see you achieve something, create something. You had such talent, Simeon. Papa said it was a gift from God, the way you could make ships come to life on paper."

"Not any longer, I'm afraid." He raised his arm to display the false hand, and she kicked a gout of sand at him by way of comment.

"Oh, stow that," she muttered loudly. "I saw the drawing you made for the Gable boy. You've just as much skill with your left hand as you ever had with the right. The only place you're really lacking is in your heart. You've given up, Simeon. Nat said you weren't afraid of anything, and maybe that was true years ago, but now you are just a whimpering coward who starts at his own shadow."

When he made no response, she steeled herself and let her temper carry her onward. "Oh, you stand up to bullies well enough, waving your pistol about and acting brave. But do you know what is truly brave, what really takes courage? Looking inside yourself, facing up to life. Seeing the opportunities and reaching for them. It doesn't require two hands, it only requires determination. You've still got that, I've seen it in your eyes. Reach out, Simeon . . . and be part of the whole again." She drew a deep, ragged breath. "I got you back to sea, and I'll be damned if you won't let me finish the job and get you back to humanity. I won't let you go skulking off to the East End, Simeon. I won't."

She slipped to her knees, clutching her hands against her skirt, as she looked at him beseechingly. "I really won't."

He rose from the fire and went to her, leaning down to wrap his arms around her before he drew her to her feet.

"Are you finished now, hoyden?" he asked softly as he set her away from him, his hands on her shoulders.

She nodded, and then gulped.

"Good. First of all, I think your father would be very proud of you. That's the best tongue-lashing I've ever heard coming from a Prescott, and believe me, your father could part the waters with his voice when he was riled."

She gave him a weak grin.

"Secondly, I am not going to argue with you. Everything you said is totally true." He shook her gently. "But it's my life, Alexa. To win or lose, to strive or not. My life. It's gratifying that you care enough to berate me. And I thank you for that concern. Perhaps you are not old enough yet to have learned this, but sometimes we come up against things we cannot surmount, that confound us at every turn. You would, I think, batter yourself against such an obstacle until you were worn down. Admirable, maybe, but not very wise. I am different . . . I have stopped throwing myself against that wall, stopped fighting against my fate. I chose a life, I lived it, it has failed me. You have too much ahead of you to want to waste your time with a man who has no horizons left to him."

Her eyes brightened slightly. "Then, you do care for me."

His cheeks drew in and one side of his mouth curved up. "As you observed that first night, I am not a very good liar. Of course I care for you. Not the way you want me to, perhaps, but enough to keep away from you from now on."

She opened her mouth to protest, and he set his palm over it.

"Let it go, Lexie. Please. This isn't easy for me, either." He coaxed her down by the fire and then turned away from her.

"Now, where are *you* going?" she called out.

He swooped down and picked up the blanket she had dropped just prior to her tirade. "Where do you think?" he said without turning around. "To sleep in the blasted boat."

The next morning the sky overhead was a crisp, crystalline blue—several shades lighter than Alexa's eyes, MacHeath noted, but nearly as intense.

He made the boat ready before he roused her, and they shared a breakfast of biscuits and tea with little conversation. It was Christmas Eve, and he felt the lack of good cheer between them like a malediction. Even though he'd paid the Christmas season little mind during most of his life, he knew this was supposed to be a day filled with anticipation and excitement. His heart felt like a cinder blown up from a cold, dark hearth.

Alexa made idle small talk with him, like a lady at afternoon tea who had more pressing things on her mind. He sensed that she was drawing away from him at last, and his relief was coupled with a wrenching feeling of loss.

Can't have it both ways, old fellow, he reminded himself. By tonight he would have settled his business with her father and by tomorrow he would be heading back to Nat's in the ketch. Maybe he would spend some time with his former captain. The old man surely needed someone to look out for him.

Oh, there's MacHeath, rowing to the rescue again, he

thought ruefully. This white-knight business was strangely addictive. Still, he needed to think of something to fill his time after today. Alexa had been right about one thing—he could not return to the bowels of London. It was too bright, too clean, too invigorating here in the outside world for him to ever consider going back. And now he had the sea again, thanks to her.

He might never be the man she envisioned, with the confidence to overcome every obstacle, but neither would he fall back into that pit of despair and self-loathing that he had wallowed in for nearly two years. This adventure he'd shared with her had shaken him awake. His life was in his grasp once more. Not the life he desired, not the life that had been stolen from him ten years ago, but a far better circumstance than he'd had in London, dwelling on the fringes of Society like a whipped cur begging for scraps.

And, once again, he owed it to her.

His turning points, his crossroads . . . Alexa stood at all of them: his success at Prescott and his downfall there, as well. His recent decision to stir himself had been in her defense, and his new determination to return to the sea had been at her instigation. And finally she stood there at his side while he made the most difficult decision he'd ever been forced into—that of severing every bond between them.

Tonight, Christmas Eve, would be the last time he'd ever see her. It seemed fitting that he should give her something, offer her some gift to thank her for all she had done for him, whether intentionally or not. There were few coins left in his purse, and he possessed nothing that would be of any value to a wealthy young woman. That even a simple drawing would have meant the world to her did not occur to him. Those he handed out willy-nilly to children, but his Alexa required something more precious.

He pondered this as they continued across Lyme Bay. Yesterday's brisk, capricious wind was gone. In fact, the bay stood almost serene, and the single sail hung loose and flaccid at times.

Alexa grew fretful at these occasional delays. She paced from stern to mast and back again, but said nothing. Her face was drawn and pale, her eyes lackluster. The quick flashes of humor and spirit that he'd grown so accustomed to were absent.

Guilt racked him, but his resolve never wavered. She might pine over him for a time, but she was young and resilient. Recovery would be swift once he was no longer in her life, either as that phantom youth or as the adult MacHeath. It was he who would carry the lifelong regret, the sorry realization that not only had Darwin Quincy stolen away his good name and his position with Prescott, he had in truth stolen away his chance of any happiness.

Lord, he had not thought of Quincy for many hours. He wondered what the backstabbing mongrel was up to. With some distaste, he placed himself in Quincy's shoes. What would *he* do?

"Alexa," he said sharply, once he'd made a calculated guess. "I think Quincy might be awaiting us at your father's house."

She turned to him with troubled eyes. "I thought he was behind us on the road, waiting for his men to bring me to him."

"Maybe he was at first. But when we eluded them for so long, I suspect he might have given up that plan. The closer we got to Exeter, the less chance he could force himself on you. You are well-known in this district, Alexa, he couldn't risk that you might find an unexpected ally before he could carry out his seduction."

I already have found one, she wanted to shout back at him.

"Well, what is he doing, then?"

"Buttering up your father, I expect. And making a case for himself that he had nothing to do with any of this by steering clear of Finch and Connor. You've seen them both, but you've never seen them with him. I am the only one who can place the three of them together."

"And you are also the only one who has something to gain by lying about it. I mean, that is how Darwin will argue it."

She thought for a few minutes. "When we get to Papa's

house," she said at last, "I will go in first. I can reason with my father. If my cousin is there, I will get Papa alone. He knows I would never tell him an untruth."

"Unlike your cousin," he murmured. "A pity that sorry trait runs in part of your family."

"Only one very small part," she said with some spirit. "Anyway, I will tell Papa about the ugly customers, and how you risked your freedom to bring me back home. That should carry some weight with him." She bit her lip and then added hesitantly, "And I will make sure he is generous, Simeon. Generous in hearing you out properly, and generous in seeing that you do not leave Cudbright empty-handed."

MacHeath colored up. "It would be more noble, I suppose, to say I required no reward. But if I am to stay away from the East End as you asked, I must have a stake."

"You earned it," she said evenly. "And like you, I make sure I pay my debts."

Chapter 11

❧

They reached the mouth of the River Exe by three o'clock.
Cudbright was some two miles upstream. MacHeath steered
the ketch around the treacherous sandbanks that had formed
at low tide and then let Alexa take the helm once the river
evened out. She pointed out landmarks to him along the
banks, and then smiled to herself when she recalled that he
would know them nearly as well as she did.

Her father's shipyard was soon in sight, the tall masts of
the ships soaring up higher than the treetops. MacHeath immediately motioned for her to steer the boat toward the shore.

"We dare not berth at your father's wharf," he said.
"Quincy might have someone on the lookout for you there. It
will be safer if we skirt the village and approach your father's
home from the fields that lie behind it. Quincy wouldn't be
expecting that."

Alexa agreed at once. The longer it took them to get to
the house, the more time she would have alone with him.
Not that he was behaving in a manner calculated to reassure
her. He was still remote and aloof, his eyes guarded whenever he chanced to glance her way.

She'd spent the entire morning trying to put him out of
her thoughts, and decided she might just as well stop breathing. The shock of what he'd said last night had dulled
slightly into an inchoate ache, but every so often his words
of dismissal shifted inside her and cut like a blade.

She was too new at this game of hearts to understand how
a man could kiss a woman, as he'd kissed her, and then

merely walk away. Maybe other men could, the shallow, heartless ones. But for three years she'd seen the way passion had gripped Simeon Hastings, passion for his ships and his designs, so she knew that he was neither shallow nor heartless. She might never know why he had turned away from her . . . his argument that he was too beaten down by life held no sway with her, she'd seen the light of hope flash in his eyes there in Gable's barn, and any man who could still muster that emotion was far from defeated. Nevertheless, even if she had understood why he'd drawn back from her, it wouldn't have made the pain inside her any less acute.

After securing the ketch to an old piling, they hiked up from the river through a dense scrub of leafless bushes, and then scurried across the main road that led into the village. Beyond it lay open fields, fenced-in pastures, and the occasional small wood. If they kept parallel to the road, they would eventually come to her father's estate.

He had built his house on a hill overlooking the village; from its front windows, one could survey the whole of the riverfront, including his shipyard. To guarantee that view, he had chosen a secluded location. Their nearest neighbor was a quarter mile down the road, and the village was separated from the house by a terraced stretch of heavy woodland that fell away below the front gate.

As they tramped north, MacHeath handed her over stiles and guided her around tangled windfalls, but other than those brief courtesies, he barely paid her any notice. It was caution, she realized. He was totally focused on crossing this last stretch of ground that lay between them and the safety of her father's home.

They came to the edge of a beech wood, and she saw the house rising up in the distance. The sight of the smoking chimneys and the slate roof made her heart quicken. If the place held meaning to her before, it had now taken on the aspect of an El Dorado.

"Wait here," she said to him, "in the cover of the woods. Give me half an hour with Papa and then come around to the front gate."

Before he could answer, she broke from the trees and

began to run toward the high iron fence that surrounded the estate. MacHeath called her name, but she was too overset to heed him. She knew this would likely be the last time they were alone together, and she didn't have the fortitude to withstand any good-byes. She covered the open space swiftly, running from more than the threat of hired rogues.

There was a gate at the rear of the property, behind the stable block, and she breathed a sigh of relief when she reached it. When she heard a guttural noise off to her right, her head jerked up. A burly man was racing toward her along the fence. She rattled at the gate frantically and cursed when she realized it was locked. With a strangled gasp, she spun back toward the woods where MacHeath was waiting, but it was too late. Finch chased her only a short distance before he caught her around the middle, swinging her off her feet and muffling her cries with one enormous hand.

He set her down, one hand twisted in her hair, and placed his pistol hard against her throat. "You make a noise," he muttered, "and I blow you to kingdom come."

He marched her along the fence, forcing her in the opposite direction from the woods. *Fool, fool, blasted fool,* she chanted to herself in time with her footsteps. She prayed MacHeath was watching from the woods, that he'd not gone off somewhere to wait out his half hour. It was an idle hope that one of her father's servants would see her being trundled along like a fugitive and raise an alarm—the inside of the iron fence was lined by bushes, and furthermore, she knew most of the servants would be in the house preparing for the holiday.

Finch gave a short, sharp whistle once they reached a copse of alders, and two minutes later Connor appeared. His eyes widened in surprise when he saw Alexa. "This is a right piece of luck."

"Looks like MacHeath abandoned her in the end," Finch remarked.

Alexa began to protest and received a cuff on the side of the head for her troubles. "You'll keep quiet if you don't want me to slice your pretty neck."

He drew a cord from his pocket and tied her hands behind

her. She winced as he knotted a filthy handkerchief over her mouth.

"Now, walk along nice and ladylike."

They dragged her between them to another group of trees, where two horses were tied. Connor mounted and waited while Finch heaved Alexa up onto his own saddle. He climbed up behind her and set one beefy arm around her middle.

"A man once told me that Society ladies weren't worth the trouble," he said quietly against her ear as he slid his hand along the front of her coat. "I'm thinkin' he lied."

Alexa flung her head back sharply and butted him in the chin.

"Jee-zus!" he cried. "Alf, did you see that? She'll be lucky if I let her live long enough to have a taste of my—"

"Leave her be!" he exclaimed. "She isn't for the likes of you. You sully her, and our money goes out the window."

"Ain't gonna sully her," Finch said gruffly. "Just want to sample her a bit."

Connor sighed.

They trotted along above the village, keeping off the road, until they came to a small, tumbledown barn. Alexa knew the owners had moved away years ago and that the property had never been let. It was growing darker, the long winter twilight had begun, and she had despaired of MacHeath reaching her before Bully Finch did something unspeakable to her. Even if he'd seen her being marched off, he'd have no way of keeping up with two men on horseback.

Finch prodded her into the barn, while Connor went forward to light a single lantern. They had taken her to their hidey-hole, she noted numbly—there were bedrolls shoved into a corner, and a packing-crate table, with soiled dishes strewn upon it, was pushed against a wall.

Finch forced her down onto a rusted trunk and seated himself beside her.

"We got to send a note now," Connor insisted.

"Plenty of time for that," Finch countered. "Why don't you just take yourself off for a bit while I get acquainted with the lady."

"No."

Finch turned to his companion, his eyes puckered under his heavy brow. "Alf, we bin mates for a good long time. I would hate to have to put a pistol ball through your innards."

"He ain't gonna pay us if she is soiled. He warned you. . . . Damn it, Bully. When we get paid off, you can have any woman you want."

"I want this one. Got my appetite up chasin' after her. Anyway, I'll tell him that bastard MacHeath was the one who tupped her."

Alexa growled through her gag, and her eyes blazed.

"She's pretty when she's riled, ain't she?" He ran his hand down along her throat. "Smells good, too." He leaned his bulbous head into her hair. When he looked up, there was annoyance in his eyes. "You still here, Alf? Jehosephat, I never took you for a man who liked to watch."

Alf knew when he was beaten. There was no way he was going to challenge Bully and win. He slid the barn door open and sidled through it, while the visions of his windfall from Quincy disappeared. He couldn't imagine any man wanting Alexa Prescott, heiress or not, once Finch was finished with her.

As he wandered the perimeter of the clearing, he fumbled absently in his pocket for a peppermint. It popped out of his hand, and with a soft curse, he bent down to grope for it in the dry grass. He managed to locate it a few feet from his boots and was about to straighten up, when he realized he was looking at another pair of boots.

The length of wood hit him solidly on the side of the head, and he toppled forward like a clubbed ox.

"Sorry, Alf," MacHeath whispered as he stepped over his limp form.

He went immediately to the door of the barn and slid it open a few inches. Alexa was suffering Finch's attentions with icy disdain. Finch did not seem to be noticing, all his attention was fixed on the buttons of her coat.

MacHeath softly whistled a tune into the opening . . . *"Christmas is coming, the goose is getting fat."*

Alexa's gaze darted to the doorway, her eyes wide with shock.

"Alf!" Finch called out in a warning voice. "You get yourself away from there."

"But, Bully," MacHeath responded in Alf's whining tenor. "I heard somethin' in the bushes. You best come out here."

"It's like you to start at a bleedin' rabbit. Now, get away or you'll be the worse for it."

MacHeath swore silently. His ruse to get Finch out of the barn hadn't worked. It had, however, put some color back into Alexa's pale cheeks. He thought for a moment, and then hastily gathered up some oak leaves in the folds of his cape. On the side of the barn he found a place where several boards had fallen off, and he quickly piled the leaves under the opening. He scratched at his tinderbox until the leaves caught fire, and waited impatiently until they began sending up a thick haze of acrid smoke.

"Hang on, Alexa," he murmured as he used one of the fallen boards to fan the billows of smoke directly into the barn. He waited for a count of sixty, and then ran around to the entrance.

When Finch emerged, staggering and coughing, he had Alexa's wrist in one hand, in the other he held a raised pistol. MacHeath struck down hard with his false hand, knocking the gun away into the high grass as he tugged Alexa away.

Finch, still blinded by the smoke, bellowed, "Alf!" as he stumbled forward. His eyes narrowed when he recognized MacHeath through the hazy light that spilled out through the barn's door. "You're a dead man, Mackie!" he cried, coming forward again, his ham-like fists lashing the air.

MacHeath moved nimbly away from those fists. "And you, Bully . . . are about to be taught a lesson."

He ducked under the larger man's roundhouse swing and landed a punishing uppercut to the chin with his left hand before he again moved out of range. Finch roared in disbelief and launched himself forward like a missile. His head barreled into MacHeath's chest, and he lifted him right off his feet.

MacHeath clapped both hands smartly over Finch's ears and heard the man shriek—the wooden hand was turning out to be a surprisingly effective weapon. Finch dropped him and spun around the clearing with his hands fisted against his head. He finally stopped some ten feet from MacHeath, his eyes glowing red with rage in the dusky light.

"Dead!" he screamed. "You're dead now, ye bleedin' cripple."

He heaved himself across the space that separated them, with surprising agility for such a large man, but MacHeath sidestepped his onslaught and got in another satisfying blow. And then another.

Finch retreated with a loud hiss as he reached down into his boot. MacHeath saw the gleam of a knife in the failing light. He quickly pulled off his cape and wrapped it around his right arm. It occurred to him that he was still carrying a loaded pistol, but he had a score to settle with Bully Finch and merely blowing a hole in his midsection would have been distinctly unsatisfying. He wanted to see fear in the other man's eyes.

"Come on," Finch urged him, curling his forefinger tauntingly.

MacHeath smiled grimly. "It's hardly a fair match."

"Why, because I got my steel and you got none?"

"No," said MacHeath as he drew his own knife from a leather sheath at the back of his waistcoat. "Because there's not a landsman born who can beat a sailor in a knife fight."

"Sailor," the other man cawed. "That's a laugh."

But MacHeath was already advancing on him, holding his knife loosely, with the edge up. Finch feinted and MacHeath shifted back, and then retaliated swiftly with his own weapon. Finch grunted as the knife sliced into his forearm.

"First blood," MacHeath muttered. "Or second, rather, if you count my little gift on the bridge."

Finch cursed as he leaped forward, swinging his knife in a wide arc. It slashed through MacHeath's bundled cape. Before he could move back, MacHeath lashed out with one leg, catching him behind the knees. He tumbled down onto his back with a thud that shook several shingles loose from the barn's roof. MacHeath was on him in an instant, straddling his chest and leaning the edge of his blade against his throat. Finch's eyes widened as he felt the pressure on his windpipe.

"I should slice you from gullet to gizzard for laying your filthy hands on my lady," MacHeath growled softly.

Finch was making a gasping, whimpering noise deep in his throat.

"Still, I don't want your death on my conscience. But I will leave you with this small memento."

MacHeath tossed down his knife and quickly drew out his pistol. He raised it overhead and brought the butt down sharply on Finch's temple. The man's eyes rolled up, and the pitiful whimpering ceased.

MacHeath stood up slowly, willing himself to stop trembling. He wondered when he'd turned into such a cold-hearted bastard. Probably when he'd seen Finch stroking his hands over Alexa's body.

Alexa watched him, watched the blood lust slowly leach out of his face. She was leaning against the barn, trying to stay upright on legs that felt like jelly, trying to breathe through the noisome gag. She didn't know which was more disturbing—the liberties Finch had taken with her person, or the expression of icy, lethal rage she'd seen in MacHeath's eyes as he squared off against the big man. There hadn't been a shred of fear in his face, only stark, deadly purpose. She now understood what he meant when he said he'd been hardened by his life in the East End. Though hardened barely began to describe what she'd seen.

She'd forced herself to stay quiet during the fight, fearing to distract MacHeath. But she'd nearly cried out against the gag when she thought he was going to cut Finch's throat. That he had to fight to protect her, she understood, but she hated the thought of him becoming an executioner.

He crossed to her now and wrapped his arms around her. "I'm so sorry," he murmured hoarsely against her hair. "Thank God I got here in time." He tugged the front of her coat together, trying clumsily to do up the buttons. "When I saw him take you, sweetheart—"

She mumbled something against her gag, and he quickly untied it.

"I wasn't sure you even knew I'd been taken," she rasped, leaning into him to keep from falling down.

He set his hands on her waist. "Do you think I took my eyes off you for even one instant? I saw him catch you, but I was too far away to risk a shot. Fortunately, your father's gate has a lock a child could pick. I ran into the stable and stole a horse."

"You s-stole a h-horse?" she echoed shakily. "You stole a horse from my father's stable?" She was laughing and choking. "Oh, Simeon. Cut me loose . . . I want to hug you back."

He quickly sliced through the cord, and then massaged her wrists gently. "Better?"

"Mmm." She slid her arms around him and tipped her head back. The frightening, fierce expression in his eyes had completely disappeared, replaced by one of tender concern. "Take me home now, Simeon. Please."

"Not just yet," he said, brushing a lock of hair back from her cheek. "Quincy may have other men posted there. We need to get to your father when he's away from that house. Or send a message to him somehow."

"Church," she said. "He'll be going to church in the village tonight."

He looked skeptical. "Your father will be fretting over you, Alexa—you were due home yesterday, after all. And if Quincy's there, he has doubtless played on those fears. Do you think he'd really go off to church while he's worried about his daughter?"

She gave him a tolerant smile. "My dear MacHeath . . . that is precisely when people go to church. We can wait in the church's basement for the service to begin. There is a vault beneath the sanctuary, where they keep old pews and hymnals and such."

"It might serve," he said. "You'll be safer in a crowd of people."

He went into the barn and came out with a length of wire. Alexa helped him truss up the two men, and then they dragged them into the barn.

"Don't want to scare any stray passersby," he said when

she'd wondered aloud why the ugly customers couldn't just stay where they'd fallen.

They rode back to Cudbright on the horse he'd appropriated from her father. She hadn't protested when he'd boosted her up, then leaped up behind her, and settled her back against his chest. Truth was, she wanted to plead with him to keep on riding . . . past the village, past the city of Exeter, right on out of Devon.

Cornwall was a maritime county, a smuggler's paradise, in fact. They could live together, and she wouldn't care if he went back to his old ways. She'd be a smuggler's lady, waiting for her lover in the darkness, standing at the top of a high cliff with a shuttered lantern in her hand. Waiting for him to sail home from France. Home to her.

But MacHeath had a mission with her father. He wouldn't set foot out of Devon until that mission was accomplished. And then, she feared, he'd be gone forever.

Alexa guided him as they rode through the village, in a convoluted route that took them along the narrowest lanes and the darkest alleys, places no gently bred lady should have known about. MacHeath could imagine her as a child, slipping out of her father's house after dark to wander through these secret, shadowed byways. She wouldn't have felt any fear—she'd have known there was not a man or woman in Cudbright who would dare to harm Alexander Prescott's daughter.

Tonight there was no longer any surety of that.

Fortunately they passed few villagers during their circuitous journey. A few workmen in front of a grogshop goggled up at them, at the tall man and the slim young woman riding bareback upon a blooded horse, but they were too full of Christmas spirit—the smuggled French variety—to voice their amazement.

Eventually they came to the low stone wall that enclosed St. Peter's Church. Candlelight spilled out through the narrow, leaded windows, setting ghostly rectangles of bleached white on the dark, grassy surround. MacHeath halted the horse at the very back of the church grounds, behind a garden shed, before he dismounted and lifted Alexa down.

They crossed the yard swiftly, keeping to the shadows. The door to the vault at the rear of the church was locked, but Alexa quickly located the spare key under one of the flagstones on the path.

"I used to sneak in here as a child," she said as she pushed open the iron-bound door. "Whenever I'd done something to make my father cross."

"To repent your sins?"

She chuckled. "No, to wait for him to cool off. And to make up stories about pixies and hobgoblins. The vault is a rather fanciful place."

"I hope it's also a relatively untrafficked place. It won't do for the vicar to come stumbling down the stairs and find us holed up here."

"Maybe we should find *him,* Simeon." She turned to face him in the narrow entryway. "We can tell him about Quincy and the ugly customers. Mr. Featherbridge is a very understanding man—I promise he'll listen."

"No, I am not turning you over to anyone but your father. And whether or not the vicar is an understanding man, don't forget that I am still a fugitive."

He followed her down a short staircase into a stone chamber, where the diffused light spilling through the low cellar windows shone on a pair of dusty trunks, three rickety pews, and a tall, metal candlestick.

"No one's buried down here, are they?" he asked under his breath.

"Why?" She poked him in the ribs. "Are you afraid?"

He didn't answer her, but instead went to light one of the candles in the metal stand. Afterward he scouted the perimeter of the room, checking to make sure that the door that led up to the vestry was closed.

"This is a perfect place to store brandy casks," he observed as he settled beside her on one of the pews. It creaked ominously.

"In a church?"

He laughed softly and chucked her under the chin. "Your

education on smugglers has been sadly neglected. Church vaults are a prime place to keep smuggled goods until it's safe to carry them inland."

"And the vicars allow this?"

"The vicars, my little innocent, heartily endorse it. You see, a wise smuggler always leaves a cask behind for his host's pleasure."

Alexa frowned. "Papa vows Mr. Featherbridge has the best brandy in Devon." Her eyes widened. "Do you really think he has allowed—"

"Shssh." He held up one hand.

Above them the roof vibrated, and a deep throbbing sound penetrated the two feet of stone that separated them from the sanctuary.

"It's the church organ," she explained. "My father bought it for St. Peter's after Mama died. In her memory. I believe the choir has a last-minute practice on Christmas Eve, so the service should start within the hour."

The faintest sound of singing could be heard, but it was eclipsed by the heavier tones of the pipe organ.

"Christmas Eve," he said with a long sigh. "This is the first time I've been in a church for Christmas."

She appeared shocked. "Didn't your parents ever take you?"

He shook his head. "My mother died while I was very young. And my father . . . well, if he had a religion of any kind, it was probably something to do with the sea."

"How did he die, Simeon?"

He shifted slightly on the bench. "He fell off a ship he was working on and drowned before anyone could get to him."

She gasped and reached for his hand. "Oh, Sim, I am sorry. Now I understand why you were so afraid for me that day I fell into the water."

"The week after his funeral, I taught myself to swim. Went off to a lake outside Glasgow and walked into it, right up to my neck. It was March, and the water was like ice. But I got the hang of it eventually. I swam across that freezing lake and vowed that as much as I loved the sea, it would not be the death of me." He turned to her. "I remember your father telling me you'd learned in Barbados."

She clasped her hands between her knees and nodded. "I learned from some native children. Slave children, I expect. They seemed to be having a great deal of fun swimming in the waves, so I asked them to teach me. The water was lovely and warm, and so salty that it was almost impossible to sink. My mother was quite scandalized when I came home in my shift and as wet as an otter. But Papa said it was a good thing, since I was always hanging about the riverfront. He went out onto the beach and tried to give the children some money . . . but they were afraid, and they ran off." Her voice lowered. "I never saw them again."

He was quiet for a time. "He's doing it again, Lexie," he said at last. "Trying to buy you a proper husband in London. But *they* all ran off, as well. No wonder you chafe at his methods, they seem counterproductive, to say the least."

She bit at her lip. "I think *I* chased a few of them off. I've spent the last seven years surrounded by people I generally found intolerable, and I'm afraid I never tried to hide my feelings. It's not my nature to be conciliating."

"Did you form *any* friendships during that whole time?"

"I became friendly with a few married ladies who shared my interest in the Chelsea hospital. And there were several members of Parliament I was always pleased to converse with at parties."

"Hang your members of Parliament, Alex. I mean real friends, ones who would stand up for you, who would aid you without hesitation. The way Eb Gable and Nat Tarlton aided me."

She shook her head slowly, wondering how he would react if she told him he was the only person in her life who fit that description. If he knew he was her one true friend, that would be a bond between them. And he had voiced his determination to sever all bonds with her. He'd been keeping his distance from her since last night, as he vowed he would. And even though she'd had a brief hope that he might kiss her after he rescued her from Finch, she'd realized quickly enough that once again he'd merely been offering comfort.

"And what of beaus? Surely in all that time there were men who courted you."

"Only fortune hunters," she said with a sigh. "I had quite a flurry of them in the beginning, but my great-aunt was a formidable judge when it came to sorting out the wheat from the chaff. She soon sent them about their business."

"And what if one of them had taken your fancy? Would she have routed them?"

"None did, so I have no way of knowing if she'd have allowed me my foolishness. As for the other men in the *ton,* the wellborn lords and the wealthy landowners, they gave me a wide berth. I had something of a reputation as a shrew." She looked at him from beneath her lashes and was rewarded when he grinned. "And, of course, I was tainted by trade. Not that it ever stopped Darwin from pursuing me. He'd have married me if my father was a rag-and-bone man, providing I was to come into a nice fortune."

MacHeath merely growled softly.

"Now, tell me about how you came to meet Nat Tarlton," she said, hoping to distract him from his line of questioning.

"I met Nat at a tavern in Dover, where I'd gone after I escaped from Exeter jail. I figured it was far enough from Devon to be safe, and I hoped to find a berth on a merchant ship. Nat convinced me that smuggling was a fine life and took me on as part of his crew."

"And was it a fine life, being a smuggler?"

"It was never dull," he said. "The excise cutters were fast, and the men who captained them were a canny bunch. But my ship, the *Siren Song*—"

"That's a lovely name," she interjected.

"I had a *little* education, Miss Prescott, enough to know my Greek mythology. Anyway, I'd gotten her from old Nat when he retired from the trade. I changed her name after I'd made a few modifications on her keel. There was not another ship could touch the *Siren* when I was done with her."

"Papa always said you were a demon for a fast ship."

He grinned. "I understood the needs of commerce back

then. But smugglers need more than speed, they need cunning and luck. It was a hard, dangerous life, Alexa, but it made me feel so alive."

"At least you were doing something exciting back then. I was taking lessons in deportment and dancing." Her nose wrinkled. "It was dreadfully dull."

His fingers slid over her hand. "I would have liked to dance with you, Alexa." His voice was full of wistful longing. "To spin you around a ballroom until the lights blurred and you were breathless."

"That would not be dull at all," she said with a tiny gasp.

She sat lost in thought for a moment, and then slid off the bench and held out one hand. "Dance with me, Simeon. Just this once. A stolen moment, if you will."

His brow furrowed. "I don't think it's a—"

"For me . . . please. I know you're going away after you talk to my father. I won't hold you back, I promise I won't. But just give me this, a first dance . . ."—her voice lowered—"a last dance."

He rose hesitantly. "Very well, Miss Prescott."

She felt him shiver slightly as she set her hand on his shoulder. He placed his arm around her waist and drew her to the center of the chamber. Then he tightened his hold, and together they skimmed around the shadowed floor, swirling in time to the lilting tune he sang under his breath. As the dance progressed, he drew her even closer, until their bodies were nearly touching, though she had no mind to complain.

"You have a very pleasant singing voice," she remarked in her best Society drawl.

"What? You once said there was nothing pleasant about me."

She danced him back against the wall of the vault and then stood there looking up at him. "I was wrong," she whispered. "There are any number of remarkable things about you." She raised her hands to his face.

"No, don't," he said, pulling back from her. He should have known where this was heading. It was madness to have danced with her, to have held her in his arms. He tried to take another step back, but the stone wall blocked his retreat.

She continued on doggedly. "Your eyes are all the colors of the moor, gray and brown with flecks of silver and gold. And your hair . . ." Her fingers combed his forelock back from his brow. "There were days when I would sit on the dock and watch you working in the sun, and each time a spark of red appeared, I would smile to myself." Her fingers traced down over his lips, and he felt himself start to tremble. "And your mouth, my dear MacHeath. Shall I tell you that I dream of this mouth—"

He couldn't bear it another moment. He dragged her into his arms and set his mouth over hers, kissing her fiercely, raking her with lips and tongue and teeth, until she trembled in turn. His groans were echoed by her whimpering cries as her fingers clutched at him, digging into his back. She was arching against him as though she wanted to absorb every particle of his being. He nearly lost his sanity.

He spun her around and thrust her against the stone wall, raising her up so that they were mouth to mouth, breast to breast, and then he kissed her hard as he let her body slide— with divine, aching slowness—back down to the stone floor.

"Oh, God," she cried out as a shudder racked her.

Shaping his mouth around the curve of her throat, he laced burning kisses along her soft skin. She was rubbing the side of her jaw against his ear and panting raggedly. The staccato sound echoed the pounding, staggering rhythm of his blood as it surged through him. One hand drifted to her breast, molding it through the fabric of coat and gown. Her sharp gasp was instantly silenced by his demanding mouth.

He wanted her. The way a starving man craves sustenance. The way a dying man cries for absolution. He wanted to take her and possess her and hold her fast for all time. In blazing heat, in screaming passion . . . in mindless lust.

No, he realized in an instant of lucidity, there was much more than mere lust coursing through him at that moment. He twisted his head back, away from the temptation of her mouth, and drew his hand away from the soft warmth of her breast.

Sinking to his knees, he tugged her against him, shivering as he leaned the side of his head into the slight convexity of her stomach. After a moment he put his head back and looked up at her, knowing that every wild, soaring emotion he felt was shining in his eyes. She set her hands on his face, and gently flexed her fingers over his cheeks. That soft, whispery touch nearly broke him.

"I . . . I can't do this," he rasped. "Not here, not like this. And it's killing me."

She sank down, cradling him in her arms. "I know . . . it's killing me a little, too."

He shot her a rueful look. "I'm being paid back ten times over for taunting you in your room that night. God, I wish I'd taken you then."

She leaned her head against his chest. "I wish you had, MacHeath."

He tipped her face up to him. "So, I'm not Simeon any longer?"

She shook her head determinedly. "Simeon was a boy from my past . . . someone who lived in my daydreams. You"—she splayed her fingers over his chest and pressed down—"are very real."

He kissed her again, tenderly this time, letting himself savor her sweetness and her spice. She shifted slightly in his arms, canting her head back in her eagerness to reciprocate.

"I swore I wouldn't kiss you again," he groaned unevenly. "But sweet Jesus, Alexa, I can't help myself." His fingers tightened until they bit into the flesh of her arms. "But I cannot be with you. Nothing has changed. This . . . this is a stolen moment, as you said. The truth is, I sully you as much as that ruffian Finch did—"

"No!"

"I do. A man who takes advantage of a woman, when he has no intention of offering her his name—"

"Then, give me your name!" she cried. "I'll take Hastings or MacHeath. Oh, my love, I'll even take Broadbeam."

His inadvertent grin never reached his eyes. "Don't say that word, Alexa. I am not your love." Something in her face made him rephrase his objection. "Even if I were, sweetheart, I have no right to that privilege."

"Oh, stop spouting noble hogwash. I won't listen to it." She squared his shoulders. "Just look at me and tell me that you don't return my feelings. If you can do that, then I will stop badgering you with my attentions."

"It's not my feelings that are the problem, Alexa. It's my damned pride." He'd been looking away from her, but now he turned his head and held her gaze. "You are gently bred and a considerable heiress. I am the son of a shipwright and a naval captain's daughter, a man who is at present reduced to pawning women's jewelry for his bread. Even with all your grand notions of love, you've got to see what an unequal match we should make. I would resent you, and you would begin to find me a burden. No, don't leap in with your naive objections. Hear me out . . ." He ran one hand distractedly through his hair. "Love and desire are not the only requirements for marriage. It also requires that both people respect each other. You would not respect me, Alexa—furthermore, if I lived off your income, I could not respect myself."

He disengaged himself from her and climbed to his feet.

"You are being precipitate," she said, glaring at him. "If my father believes you, if he removes the charges against you, you can find respectable employment."

"What? Shall I sail off to India, then, and hope to discover a ruby mine? Because I won't come to you with nothing, Alexa. I will not be called a fortune hunter."

"As if I'd care a whit about that. I don't want a rich man. I would give up everything if that meant you would stay with me."

"And you would live in poverty, forsaking your fine clothes and your elegant carriages? You bristle when I call you naive, but it is there, coloring every word you utter."

She scrambled to her feet. "I think you'd best let me be the judge of what I am capable of forsaking. But I see now how easily you have forsaken me."

"I have not forsaken you, Alex," he said grimly. "I never promised myself to you."

He spun away from her and went to sit on the far end of one of the pews, his head bent, his hands curled in his lap. Alexa shifted onto one of the trunks, mindless of the layer of dust, and racked her brain for some way to make him understand.

She'd spent her whole adult life feeling at odds with

everyone around her. At the seminary for young ladies, she had been a rebellious, resentful student, never content to sit and sew or to practice for hours at the pianoforte like the other girls. Once she was out in the *ton*, she had made a point of speaking her mind on all topics and had adamantly refused to simper or flirt. And because of her disregard for the rules of Society, no one ever had come close enough to see inside her, or even cared to try.

Yet here was this incredible man who made her feel accepted and cherished, who found her combative tendencies amusing and engaging, who understood the wild part of her nature, and—wonder of wonders—who thought she was utterly desirable.

But now the thing that had been her only saving grace at school and in the *ton,* her great wealth, had become an obstacle. For once it was not her connection to trade that was the problem—MacHeath's parents were themselves of good common stock—but her connection to money.

She tried to place herself in his position, to understand that a man with so much pride that he wore a false hand to keep others from noticing his infirmity, would loathe being called a fortune hunter. But was that label worse than spending his life alone, without the woman he had come to desire?

She had no illusions that he loved her, as much as she might wish for such a thing. She suspected he was too damaged by life to hold much stock in romantic love. But she'd hoped that her feelings for him would win him over and that he would take the haven she offered—security, stability, a future where he could be anything, do anything. Instead he had tossed it all back in her face.

She groaned softly when she realized what she'd done. Just as her father had with the slave children in Barbados, she'd frightened him off by holding out a reward. Those children hadn't valued her father's coins, and he had been unable to offer them what they truly needed—their freedom. MacHeath didn't value her money, because it was not what he required. Wealth was relative . . . and if there was one thing she knew full well, it didn't guarantee freedom. Sometimes it was as much of a snare as poverty.

But what, then, did he need? And more to the point, was it something within her power to give him? The questions shifted through her head until her temples throbbed. What were the things a man needed to assure his place in the world?

Her father had acquired many valuable things over the years, in addition to money—a reputation for honesty, the respect of others, the certainty that he could protect his loved ones. And perhaps, most valuable of all, the conviction that he was meant to do great things.

MacHeath, she knew, believed he possessed none of those attributes. He viewed himself as a failure, a man without honor, without respect, who could barely look after himself, let alone those he cared for. And if he'd once had a youthful conviction that he was meant for great things, it had been flogged out of him by circumstance.

How could she convince him that he was wrong, that his every action proved his honorable nature? Was he blind to the fact that his friends respected and esteemed him? Didn't he know that he'd looked after her better than her own father could have? What would it take to assure him that his talents were still there, that his skill with a pen and his passion for designing ships were only lying dormant?

No answers came to her. She had a sinking notion that merely loving him could not undo ten years of deprivation and self-hatred.

A hand touched her briefly on the shoulder. "I think the service has started," he said quietly from behind her. "Perhaps we should go up now."

She rose at once.

"We can wait in the shadows in the back of the church. If your father is there, you can approach him as he is leaving. Even if your cousin is with him, I doubt Quincy will make a scene."

"What will you do? I mean, will you come with us to the house?"

He shook his head, and she saw that his expression was remote, as though he were going through an exercise that held little meaning for him.

"I'll duck out of the church once I've seen you with your

father. I want to scout around his house before I come inside, and that will give you a chance to talk to him."

She couldn't prevent herself from touching his sleeve. "You're sure you'll be all right? You've been keeping me safe for these past days, but once I'm with my father, I could guarantee *your* safety for a change."

His expression darkened, and his face grew even more remote. She nearly cried out in vexation at her poor choice of words. If she'd intentionally wanted to tread on his pride, she couldn't have done a better job of it.

She quickly patted his arm reassuringly. "No, I know you'll be fine. This waiting has just made me a bit edgy."

She followed him up the steps and out into the cold night air. There was no real wind, but the slight breeze coming up from the river was laden with a chilling dampness. For the hundredth time she wished she hadn't given her sable muffler to Reggie. *Poor Reggie,* she thought with a guilty twinge. She wondered if she was still in Reading or if she'd finally come here. Perhaps she'd gone back to London.

The sound of the choir was louder now, the blended voices pouring out through the glass windows and rising up over the church's slate roof.

Alexa felt a sudden, unexpected thrill bubble up in the pit of her stomach. What a glorious welcome this was . . . those heavenly voices singing out the joy of Christmas. Regardless of what her future held, she knew she would cherish every minute she'd spent with MacHeath; he'd awakened her to so much. Furthermore, she would never forget his single-minded determination to get her back to Cudbright.

Almost without thinking, she stopped him and set her palms on his cold cheeks.

"Thank you for bringing me home," she whispered. "I never thought I'd need a hero, but I'm so glad it turned out to be you."

He nodded once, his mouth taut with some emotion she could not read.

Chapter 12

They went up the shallow stone steps and into the vestibule. MacHeath eased open the door to the sanctuary, and they both slipped inside. He surveyed the interior of the small church, which was festooned with what seemed to be miles of holiday greenery, and then nodded toward a pillar on their left. From there they would be able to view most of the congregation. Her father, he knew, would be sitting in the Prescott family stall, somewhere at the front of the church. Alexa headed toward the spot he'd indicated, but he lingered a moment, letting his gaze roam over the sea of heads until he came to one that was blond and sleek.

Darwin Quincy was seated beside Alexander Prescott in an ornate wooden pew, leaning forward intently, his attention fixed on the man standing behind the raised lectern. MacHeath recalled teasing Alexa about the roof tumbling in if she ever set foot in a church. He wondered now how such a base villain as her cousin could sit there in patently devoted worship and not fear that a bolt of lightning would come crashing through the ceiling and pierce him in divine, sizzling retribution. He nearly grinned when it occurred to him that he might have earned a minor lightning strike or two himself.

"They're both here," he whispered to Alexa once he was at her side.

"I know. Look at Quincy," she hissed. "He looks like a blasted choirboy."

"Your father appears to be bearing up rather well."

"He never shows it when he's troubled. Soldiering on, he calls it. That way no one can ever guess that he is vulnerable. You should have seen him when Mama died—he never broke down in front of anyone, not even me."

MacHeath's heart tugged at the truth of her words. They soldiered on, those Prescotts, father and daughter, both. But how sad for a child of ten to lose her mother and not be able to share her grief with her remaining parent. When his own father died, he'd cried half the night with his father's mates. Hell, they had all cried. Maybe that was what came of being a volatile Scot. Still, Alexa was volatile enough in her own way . . . easy to show anger, but perhaps not so easy to show her grief.

The sexton had finished reading the biblical text recounting the birth of the Christ child, and now Mr. Featherbridge stepped up to the pulpit. The vicar was a rotund gentleman with a halo of graying brown hair surrounding a pale pink tonsure. A veritable Friar Tuck, MacHeath noted irreverently.

"Christmas," the vicar intoned in a deep, resonant baritone, "is not so much about birth, as it is about rebirth. It marks the beginning of Christ's time on earth, but it also foretells His rebirth after the baptism by John, which leads us inevitably to His death and resurrection."

He gripped the raised sides of the pulpit, and his bright eyes bore down on his congregation. "Without the baptism there could be no ministry. Without rebirth, there could be no resurrection. The Bible tells us little of the boy Jesus's early life. We see Him meeting with the elders in the temple, preaching to them. But, again, this is only a precursor to His adult ministry, when, as a man of thirty-three, He left behind the carpentry, the ordinary life, to follow a new vocation in the hills of Galilee . . ."

MacHeath heard only portions of the sermon after that. His mind was too busy assessing the implications of Mr. Featherbridge's words. Though his Bible learning was woefully thin, he did know that Jesus was well into adulthood before He began preaching. He'd never thought to question why, and he certainly hadn't known His exact age.

Thirty-three, the vicar had said.

He'd turned that same age in November—an occasion marked only by his winning five pounds from Alf Connor in a grogshop. It had held no significance to him at the time. But now he began to wonder if there was a portent in that turning. The money he'd won that night had been the debt that brought him into the Doxy's Choice. If Alf had paid up promptly, MacHeath would not have overheard Quincy, he wouldn't have found Alexa again or become fixated on the notion that he could clear his name. No, he'd still be moldering in the East End, doing menial labor for pennies, and losing himself in a gin bottle.

His world had shifted on its axis, merely at the turn of a card. And now that the changes had begun, he had no wish to stop them. For so long he'd thought all his options were past him. That, as he'd said to Alexa last night, he had no horizons left. What a stunning thing it was to consider that he was not too old to start over and make a better life. It was a sanctified course, if the Bible was anything to go on. Was it truly possible to shed one's old skin and shrug on a fresh mantle?

If he chose that path, Alexa would do everything she could to aid him. He was too proud to take her money, but he might not reject her support in other areas. Through her father, she had connections to important men in the shipping trade. It was not inconceivable that one of them might hire him, give him a chance to resume his old life. He barely dared to voice this possibility in his head, and yet, his heart swelled immediately at the notion.

Rebirth . . . it was such a tempting possibility the vicar had held out to him.

It was pointless to dwell on a bright future, however, until he spoke with Prescott. If the man refused to believe his story, then he would continue on as he was—a nonentity, a ne'er-do-well, a man truly without horizons. If fate was kind to him and he lost his fugitive status, then he could rejoin the ranks of humanity and, if that happened, he would be able to hold his head up for the first time in ten years.

He felt Alexa's hand slip into his. "The service is nearly over," she whispered.

"Go, then," he said, giving her a little shove. "To the back of the church. When your father walks out into the aisle, go to him. Kick Quincy in the shins to get past him if you need to, but get yourself safe under your father's wing."

She nodded and smiled swiftly. "I'll see you at the house, then."

"I'll be there, Alexa."

He watched her sidle along the dimly lit wall of the church. Her hair was hanging down in loose snarls, her cloak was thrown back over her shoulders to reveal the ill-fitting man's coat she had borrowed from Eb Gable. There was nothing of the proper young lady about her appearance except for the proud tilt of her chin and the assured determination in her eyes.

There ye go, me darlin'.

The apt words of an old Scots love song rose up in his head. Better than that blasted Christmas carol about the goose, he mused with a grin.

The vicar gave the benediction, and the congregation began to file out of their seats. The crowd parted in deference to Alexander Prescott, as the man and his nephew stepped into the aisle.

Alexa flew toward them, brushing past the parishioners, softly crying, "Papa! Papa!"

Quincy's face tightened, and he instantly stepped forward to intercept her, but his uncle thrust past him, holding out both hands.

"Lexie! Sweet mercies, it's my girl!" He caught her hands as she ran to him and tugged them to his chest. "Thank heaven, Alexa. Thank heaven you are safely come home."

Hug her! MacHeath urged silently from his hiding place. *For God's sake put your arms around her.*

But Prescott merely stood there beaming at her, the joy and relief that were evident in his face not translating themselves into a need to take her in his arms. MacHeath mut-

tered a curse, and then winced when he recalled where he
was.

He started moving toward the door, knowing that all eyes
were focused on the happy reunion that was transpiring near
the front of the church.

His hand was on the ornate brass latch, when a strident
voice called out, "There he is! Stop him! Someone stop that
man!"

As he flung the door open, two burly townsmen grabbed
him by the shoulders and spun him around.

"Not so fast there, my lad," one of them growled.

MacHeath easily twisted away from them, but another
man had barricaded the door with his body. He turned then,
with a stoic, shuttered expression, to confront his nemesis.

Quincy was striding down the aisle with uncharacteristic
speed; the watch fob and seals that ornamented his silk
waistcoat danced a jig against his lean belly. His eyes were
narrowed, his mouth twisted in anger, and MacHeath could
see a tiny froth of spittle on his lips as he closed the distance
between them.

"You'll answer to me for this, you filthy knave! Did you
think to just walk out of here?"

"I thought to bring Miss Prescott home," MacHeath said
softly. "Nothing more."

Quincy poked him sharply in the ribs with his walking
stick. "That's a fine sentiment coming from the man who
carried her off."

MacHeath slapped the stick away impatiently, his dark
eyes boring into the blond man's pale blue ones. "Sorry I stole
your intended bride, Quincy," he drawled softly. "It turns out
she has an aversion to poxy, debt-ridden scoundrels."

The color came up in Quincy's face, turning his fashionable pallor a bright cherry-red. He opened his mouth to utter
a scathing reply, but never got the words out.

Now that he was standing directly in front of his secret
adversary—and this was certainly the tall, weathered rogue
that Finch and Connor had described to him—he'd begun
noticing other things about him. The set of his shoulders, the

color of his hair, the damned probing eyes that never looked down in proper deference.

When the sudden, certain awareness of the man's identity filtered into his brain, his face blanched.

"No, it can't be," he murmured in a quaking voice. "He wouldn't dare come here . . . not after all this time."

"He did." MacHeath put his chin up. "I told you, I needed to get Alexa home."

Quincy staggered back slightly in shock, and then shook himself. "Here, you two," he ordered in a steadier voice, motioning the men behind MacHeath to come forward. "Hold him fast. I know this man . . . ten years ago he escaped from the jail in Exeter. We need to call in the constable."

"Indeed you do not!" It was Alexa, coming down the aisle, tugging her father along behind her. "Let him go, Quincy. He's done nothing wrong."

Quincy turned to her with a sneer. "Do you have any idea who this is?"

"Simeon Hastings." It was Prescott himself who uttered the name in a deep, disbelieving voice. He strode past his daughter and came right up to MacHeath. "By God, fellow, you've a nerve showing your nose in this town. And what had you to do with my daughter's disappearance?"

"This is the man who carried her off, Uncle. I had his description from Mrs. Reginald, right up to the fine gloves he wears." Quincy jabbed the head of his walking stick against MacHeath's right hand and seemed pleased when his victim did not even flinch.

Alexa grabbed the stick and wrestled it out of his hands. "Stop tormenting him, Darwin. Or I'll clout you on the hand and see how you like it."

"Perhaps," said MacHeath with amazing sangfroid, considering that half the population of Cudbright was now gawking at him, "we should take this discussion to a less public place."

"I have nothing to discuss with you," Prescott growled softly. "Except to say that I am amazed at your temerity." He turned back to the congregation and raised his voice. "I need someone to fetch a constable."

The entire crowd seemed mesmerized by what was happening by the door, and no one came forward to offer their services.

"No, Papa!" Alexa gripped his arm tightly. "I need to speak with you alone. There are things you must know before you judge him."

Quincy pulled his uncle aside. "She is turned about in her head," he whispered. "Look at how she defends Hastings—the man who dragged her from her coach. If I were you, I wouldn't pay any heed to what she says."

"Well, you are not him!" Alexa stormed. "He will listen to me. Please, Papa, promise me you will listen before you do anything rash."

Prescott's gaze swung from his daughter's face, brimming with entreaty, to Quincy's, which bore a taut combination of anger and malice. Simeon Hastings seemed the only one unaffected by this high melodrama; he stood calmly by, his face betraying nothing of what was in his thoughts.

"I can't promise anything," Prescott said. "There is still a warrant out on him. I'm sorry, Alexa, but you see it's out of my hands."

"That isn't true," she countered quickly. "You laid the charges against him . . . it would be a trifle to have them dismissed. But I am not asking for that. Just give him a fair hearing."

Quincy made a rude noise.

MacHeath's mouth tightened as he turned to him. "How the devil can I expect a fair hearing, when once again you have been beside Prescott, whispering your poisonous insinuations in his ear?"

"You damned, lying—"

"Enough!" Mr. Featherbridge, who had used all his considerable powers of persuasion to coax his reluctant congregation to begin exiting through the church's side door, now came hurrying toward them. "I won't have profanity in my church, gentlemen."

He stopped before Prescott. "Let's take this into the

vestry, Alexander. I'll come with you, if you need an ar-
biter." He took Alexa's hand. "Would that help, my dear?"

"I never meant for this to be a public spectacle," she murmured. "My cousin has made it so." She swung to
MacHeath. "Please, say something. Tell them what you told
me. Oh, how can you stand there so calmly?"

He hitched one shoulder. "Because I was a fool to expect
anything different. They didn't listen ten years ago, and
nothing has changed."

"*I'll* make them listen," she declared. She spun to her father. "He didn't drag me from my coach." She bit her lip.
"Well, he did in fact do that. But his intention was not to
harm me or hold me against my will. He was rescuing
me . . . from two ruffians that Quincy had hired to carry me
off."

Her cousin applauded softly. "Oh, that is rare, Alexa. I
give your rogue high marks for invention."

"Don't you mock me," she snarled. "MacHeath overheard you in a London tavern, giving orders to those two
men."

Quincy looked at MacHeath through his pale brows. "And
you saw me there, Hastings? You saw me face-to-face?"

MacHeath shook his head. "Only from the back, more's the
pity. But I *heard* you clearly enough. I think I have cause to remember your voice. Very good cause." He paused. "You'd be
surprised at all the things I remember about you, Quincy."

Quincy blanched slightly, but then recovered himself and
waved a hand in the air. "Pah! Half the men in the *ton* speak as
I do. It was no doubt some well-bred fortune hunter you overheard. My cousin has been prey to them since her come-out."

"You would know about that," MacHeath murmured.

"See!" Quincy hissed to Mr. Featherbridge. "See how he
baits me? A gentleman should not have to endure such
abuse. I cannot believe you would take the word of this ver-
min, this felon. Look at him, look at his tattered clothing. I
wouldn't give that coat he is wearing to a stable hand."

"This isn't a question of fashion, sir," the vicar reminded
him. "It is a matter of truth. A man's future hangs in the balance."

"So instead you impugn my word as a gentleman?" His gaze shifted to MacHeath. "You have no proof of anything."

"It was you. I swear it on my father's grave."

"Such melodrama," Quincy sniffed. "Well, Uncle. Has he convinced you?"

Prescott paused before he spoke, one fisted hand tapping his chin. "This has all taken me unawares . . . accusations flying left and right. I need time to think."

"Think on this, Father," Alexa said forthrightly. "Darwin is so deep in debt that to keep the moneylenders off his back, he lied to his friends, told them that he and I were betrothed." This pronouncement was met by silence all around. "So cousin," she said scornfully, "are you going to deny that, as well?"

Quincy cleared his throat several times, but when he spoke his voice was full of easy confidence. "A minor falsehood, and I admit that it was badly done. But I was feeling a momentary pinch and assumed Alexa would not mind my subterfuge. We are blood kin, after all." He laid one hand on Prescott's shoulder. "Dear Uncle, surely I would not have come here to support you, if I'd been involved in this business. Could you possibly imagine I could be so duplicitous?"

"*I* could," Alexa said hotly.

He disregarded her outburst. "This man is nothing more than a base opportunist. It's clear he took my cousin with hopes of redeeming her for a reward, and then made up some nonsense that cast me as the villain. The truth is, he sniffed money in the air and came after it like the cur he is."

MacHeath's eyes narrowed. "I risked my neck by coming here, Quincy. Would I do that for a few gold coins?"

Prescott stepped between them. "You betrayed me for a few gold coins, Hastings. I wouldn't put anything past a man who would ill-use someone who trusted him."

MacHeath heard the lingering pain in Prescott's words, like a wound that was still tender after many years. It gave him some faint hope.

"Sir," he said, holding Prescott's gaze. "I neither betrayed you nor ill-used you. Rather it was I who was betrayed—"

Quincy interjected with an impatient snarl, "This is a

waste of our time. I, for one, have better things to do of a Christmas Eve than listen to these pitiful, whining lies."

"Quincy's right. Come away, Alex. The carolers will be at the house anytime now. You must forget this man—"

"No!" She clutched at his arm, her fingers digging into it. "None of this has gone the way we intended. There are things I need to say to you in private . . . things MacHeath needs to say. And there *are* two evil men out there, in truth there are, Father. They carried me off from the gates of your house—"

Prescott set his hand over her mouth. "You are delirious, child."

"I fear Hastings has drugged her," Quincy remarked. "Look at her color, Uncle. Her cheeks are an unnatural red. . . ." His cool fingers drifted down over her face. "And her eyes are far too bright."

Alexa pushed roughly away from both of them. "That is because I am agitated beyond words, Father, by your sheer, blind stupidity."

"Alexandra!" Prescott's warning voice echoed out in the near empty church.

"How am I to behave when my own father has once again turned his back on me?" She dashed away her tears of frustration with one hand.

He regarded her, his mouth agape. "You expect me to side with this . . . this rogue? I begin to think your cousin has the right of it, you are turned about in your head."

"Look at this!" she cried, frantically pushing back the cuffs of her coat. "Look at these bruises on my wrists. Am I imagining them? Are they a phantasm?"

"Did this blackguard tie you up?" Quincy muttered.

"No, this was the handiwork of *your* men, cousin. After they dragged me from Papa's gate, they bound me with a cord. But MacHeath again came to my rescue."

Alexa laid her hands upon her father's broad chest. "Please, Papa, if you won't listen to MacHeath, at least let him leave in peace. I asked you once before, and you refused me. Don't refuse me now, I beg you."

"I do believe one thing you said, that he offered you no harm. And so, as it is Christmas Eve, I will not send for the constable. I don't want your visit sullied by such a sordid business. I will send him on his way—"

Quincy cried out, "No!"

Prescott shot him a look of reproof. "I have said that I will let him go. Alexa can consider it an early Christmas gift." He turned to MacHeath. "If you are wise, sir, you will not linger here."

Quincy gripped his uncle's arm. "How can you let him go without so much as a whipping? Are you totally lost to propriety? Your daughter is ruined, Prescott. Hastings might not have done bodily harm to her, but he has damaged her beyond repair as far as her reputation is concerned."

For the first time that evening, Prescott openly glared at his nephew. "If that information leaves this building, I will know who let it slip."

"What if *he* says something," he protested, pointing to MacHeath. "What if he brags to his friends about spending five days with my cousin?"

The vicar stepped forward. "I think that we are forgetting the main issue here—that Miss Alexa is returned. Now, you three go on home, there's no sense in agitating yourselves further." He then pointed to MacHeath. "You, sir, come along with me."

Alexa tried to catch MacHeath's eye as he sidled past her, but he refused to look in her direction. She had failed him, she knew. So much for being his advocate—her fearful temper had gotten the better of her, and she'd lost any power of persuasion. It was not all the fault of her temper, however. Her father's abrupt dismissal of her pleas on MacHeath's behalf had shaken her to the core; it still cut like a knife.

I am sorry, she moaned silently as he walked away from her without so much as a backward glance. *So terribly, terribly sorry.*

MacHeath leaned back in a padded chair in Mr. Featherbridge's cozy study and toyed with his glass. Dashed if Prescott hadn't been right—the vicar did serve an excellent brandy. And he set a fine table as well, which perhaps accounted for his substantial girth. Now well-fed and with his frustration and anger mellowed a bit by French spirits, he agreed to tell Mr. Featherbridge about his misadventure with Alexa.

"I never heard ill of you, young man," the vicar said, once MacHeath had completed his tale. "For the three years you worked for Prescott, nothing but praise came my way from the workmen and the shopkeepers. My own house-keeper swore you were wronged when we heard of the theft. She said you were more likely to be putting money into the safe than taking it out." He paused to cough softly. "And everyone in the village knew how Miss Alexa felt about you."

"Everyone but me," MacHeath said with a rueful grin. "It took me a few years to sort out why she was always around when she barely ever said a kind word to me."

"And now?"

"I don't wish to be rude, vicar, since you've wined and dined me, but I cannot speak of Alexa's feelings and will not speak of mine for her."

"So I take it you will not be bragging about her to your friends?" Featherbridge's eyes chided him gently.

"I'd like to rip out Quincy's black heart for even sug-gesting it," he muttered. "He truly did set those two men on her, they had her in their hands only three hours past. I left them trussed up in a barn on the old Kincaid property."

"So you rescued her once again, and got naught for your troubles."

"Prescott refuses to offer me anything, even his gratitude. Oh, he gave me my freedom, but that will last an hour or a day or as long as it takes the authorities to track me down. Quincy is doubtless banging on the constable's door this very minute."

"Then, there is risk in remaining here."

"I'm not running away this time," he declared. "If they take me, I will stand trial. And then the truth will come out. And if that does me no good . . . well, I'd rather hang than spend the rest of my life on the run."

"So you don't care what your death will do to Miss Alexa?"

He shifted toward the vicar and speared him with his gaze. "Miss Alexa might have a chance at a real life if I were to hang."

To his surprise, Featherbridge gave a loud chortle. "Ho, you are full to the brim with foolish nobility. If you think your death will free her from your spell, then you don't know the first thing about women. Nothing could guarantee a lifetime of pining like knowing the man she loved went to his death on her account."

MacHeath cursed softly.

"Yes, you are in a bit of a spot. If you don't mind listening to the advice of a country parson, I could make a recommendation or two. Before you can clear your name, you need to gain Prescott's ear. A good first step might be getting him to see that he nurtures a viper by encouraging Quincy."

MacHeath's brows shot up. "You believed me about Quincy?"

The vicar sighed and steepled his fingers against his round chin. "Darwin Quincy has been taking money out of the collection basket since he was in shirttails. He used up all his credit with the local shopkeepers while he was still at Oxford. Every gentleman's son in the district has been warned not to sit at cards with him, and my stable lad tells me that he's now reduced to playing at dice with the lowest men on the waterfront. In other words, Darwin Quincy is a loose screw."

MacHeath grinned, but then his face grew instantly sober. "He still means to have Alexa, Mr. Featherbridge. You could hear him angling for that very thing in the church. Pointing out to her father that she is ruined so that he can offer himself as husband to his sullied but incredibly wealthy cousin. I brought her to this, with my cork-brained plan. If I'd just warned her of his intentions—"

"Oh, there you go being noble again. It's a distressing tendency, Mr. Hastings—"

"MacHeath," he interjected curtly. "Simeon Hastings is no more."

"Very well, MacHeath it is. But as I was saying, you came here with a goal in mind. Now Prescott can be pigheaded when it comes to some things—especially regarding his daughter—but he is a fair man at the end of the day. You find some way to connect Quincy to those two rogues, and once you've discredited him, you've got a chance at gaining Prescott's trust. We might start by getting our hands on those fellows you left in Kincaid's barn."

He looked up in surprise. "*We*, Mr. Featherbridge?"

He rose from his seat with a wry smile. "I believe spending the night cleaning up the neighborhood is not a bad way to start off Christmas. I'll ring for my carriage."

The barn was empty. No bedrolls, no soiled dishes, and most disturbingly, no trussed-up ruffians. There were the remains of the wires MacHeath had twisted around both men's wrists and ankles, and that was all. He scouted in the clearing with a lantern and found the bloodied patch of grass where Finch's wounded arm had bled when he fell. Hardly enough evidence to convince the cleric that he was telling the truth. But Mr. Featherbridge did not appear at all skeptical, only disappointed.

"Quincy must have found them and set them free," the vicar said as they went back into the barn. "Though, how he managed to locate them in so short a time—"

"No, I don't think so," MacHeath interrupted him. He was crouched down beside a remnant of wire that lay beside a rusted jumble of farm implements. His fingers traced over the coil of metal while he pondered its location on the floor. "I left both men by the door. One of them must have rolled over here when he came to and loosened the wires against the edge of this old scythe."

"So you think they've left Cudbright?"

"I doubt it. Finch will want my blood, for one thing. And I believe Quincy still owes them money. Men like those two don't skulk off, not if there's a profit to be made. If they're still here, I will find them."

The vicar scratched behind one ear. "You can't go back into the village."

"That is exactly where I'm going."

"What about the constables? You won't do yourself much good if you are arrested the instant you set foot in town."

MacHeath gave him a sly smile. "I've rethought that. I don't think Quincy will bring the law into this. He's sailing too close to the wind right now . . . oh, sorry, I mean he's running the risk of being found out. He defended himself very neatly in the church, I will give him that, but he knows I recognized him in that tavern. He won't want me held here in Cudbright, where I might convince an enterprising lawyer to look into the matter."

"So we're back to finding those two men."

"Not *we,* this time, Vicar. I think I must do this alone."

Mr. Featherbridge nodded. "Then, I'll do what I can on the praying end of things."

They drove back to the rectory and went inside; the vicar watched from the kitchen doorway as MacHeath pilfered his cutlery drawer.

"A little insurance," he said as he tucked a long carving knife into his coat pocket. He then leaned back against the drawer and looked across at the man. "Why?" he asked. "Why did you help me?"

Mr. Featherbridge cocked his head. "For Alexa," he said simply. "The morning they carted you off to jail, I heard her crying in the church vault. I knew she sometimes hid down there, and usually left her alone. But that day her sobs alarmed me, and so I went down there to comfort her. It's the most difficult part of being a priest—consoling those who are grieving—and perhaps it's the thing that brings us closest to God. At any rate, she told me what had happened, that the night before you'd injured her cousin when he caught you stealing, and that when they searched your rooms, they found a cache of money."

"Yes, it was rather damning."

"She was never the same after they took you away. It was as though something bright inside of her was extinguished. I reasoned at the time that she had a father who doted on her, who would do everything to ease her grief. But she soon grew to womanhood, and I saw Prescott increasingly distance himself from her.

"He should have had a son, you know. He treated Alexa like a lad . . . well, you saw how she was, untamed and fearless. She had no graces, no manners. Her father realized too late that she would never make an advantageous marriage unless those tendencies were curbed. So he sent her away from here. The morning she was to leave, I again found her hiding in the vault. This time she was not crying, but striding about, railing at her father for his perfidy. It nearly broke my heart when she told me that the two men she esteemed above all others had betrayed her."

"She said something like that the night I carried her off. I had no idea she was referring to me, no idea my arrest affected her so deeply."

The vicar said softly, "Would you care to tell me what really happened that night?"

MacHeath's brow lowered. "I haven't spoken of it to a soul. I suppose I've been saving the truth for Prescott."

"Ten years is a long time to keep your own counsel, sir. And you could do a lot worse than telling me . . . the confidentiality of the confessional and all that."

MacHeath nodded slowly, and just as slowly began his tale, massaging the false hand with the real one while he spoke. When he was done, Mr. Featherbridge sat silent for a moment, his head bowed.

"Few men could have weathered the aftermath of such an injustice," he said when he looked up. "I congratulate you on surviving it. No, don't start to protest, sir. I see clearly that you have fallen on hard times, yet there's a core of goodness in you. Simeon Hastings may be gone, but something of his spirit burns on in MacHeath."

"You're starting to sound like Alexa," he muttered sourly.

"She's a wise young woman when she troubles herself to keep her temper in check." He grinned briefly. "You can make things right for her, Mr. MacHeath. I have a notion that if you can convince her father of your innocence, Alexa will begin to mend. It's got a nice symmetry. You make your peace with Prescott, and Alexa will make her peace with the world."

"I can't stay with her," he said quietly in response to the unspoken question in the vicar's eyes. "I've determined to go away as soon as I've settled things here."

"Why? Because you are poor? Or is it this?" He reached out and tapped MacHeath's right hand. "Don't appear so surprised. I watched you while you ate—you never removed your gloves and you never once used this hand."

"Alexa knows about this, it doesn't seem to trouble her. But I'm not going to spell out my reasons for leaving. Suffice to say, we should not suit."

"I think you would suit admirably. You don't require a simpering damsel, and she doesn't require a puffed-up popinjay, regardless of what her father believes on that score. But it's not my business, Mr. MacHeath. You will do as you choose." He followed MacHeath to the kitchen door. "You didn't by any chance arrive at the church in time to hear my sermon?"

"I was there."

The vicar grinned. "Interesting, isn't it, the possibilities the Bible holds out to us? All those new horizons, Mr. MacHeath."

Chapter 13

Alexa kept silent on the drive back from the church and went to her room the instant they arrived at the house. She needed time to compose herself before she again faced her father. Word of her return had been sent ahead; her maid had a bath waiting, and one of the dinner gowns she kept at the house was laid out on the bed. Obviously her luggage had not arrived, which meant that neither had Mrs. Reginald.

She stood gazing around the bedroom, blocking out her maid's excited prattle. She looked at the familiar lilac-papered walls, the elegant walnut bed, the books that were stacked on her writing desk, and tried to muster up some feeling of relief. Somehow this room, this house, had ceased to be her haven. Her eyes went to the drawing of a black-and-white spaniel, which hung over her desk in a gilded frame, and she felt an acute ache in her throat.

He was her haven now. The man who had given her that drawing, and all the others that were locked away in her dower chest, had completely supplanted home and family in her heart. Her only allegiance was to him.

Forsaking all others . . . The words from the marriage service whispered inside her head. A solitary tear coursed down her cheek.

Her maid roused her from her bittersweet revery—she tugged her out of her coat and began to undo the buttons on the rose-colored gown, muttering all the while that she'd make sure these ragged garments were tossed into the rubbish heap.

"No," said Alexa in alarm, clutching her hands to her chest. "You must not. They are all I have."

The maid gave her a look of bewildered incomprehension, but said nothing more.

The hot bath helped to restore some of Alexa's energy and a great deal of her resolve. She wouldn't be beaten down, she swore, not by her father, not by her cousin. She'd faced much bigger bullies in the past week and managed to keep a cool head. It was as MacHeath had told her . . . you must never let them know you are afraid.

But when she came downstairs again, now properly gowned and sleekily coiffed—and fully ready for battle—the carolers were just arriving. Alexa waited in the shadows of the great hall, well away from her cousin, and fretted at the delay. The program seemed endless, and for the first time, the bright songs did not cheer her.

There was no wassail bowl this year—no one in the kitchen had even given it a thought, distracted as they were by their concern for Prescott's missing daughter. But the carolers had known nothing of that, and had shown up at ten, as they always did, with smiling, ruddy faces, their young children, all gleaming eyes and mittened hands, held proudly before them. Her father made up for the lack of punch by handing out coins to each of them once they were finished singing.

Alexa then had to wait while her father closeted himself with her cousin. Somehow Quincy had stolen a march on her. He'd convinced her father that his need to be heard was greater than hers, and so both men had wished her a good night, her father placing a gentle kiss on her brow. She had tugged away from him and declared she would wait up. He'd merely shaken his head sadly, looking at her as he had when she was a child and had done something wicked or headstrong.

He was doubtless dreading his inevitable interview with her. She was sure her eyes promised nothing but trouble. She now paced up and down the hall, darting looks at the wall clock and, after a half hour had passed, she promised herself that if they did not emerge from the locked study in another five minutes, she was going to bash down the door with a fireplace poker.

Two minutes later the door opened, and both of them came out into the hall. Quincy bowed to her, his mouth drawn up in a smug smile, and then excused himself.

"I believe we've come up with a solution," her father said as he ushered her into the room, one hand on her upper arm. "I don't know why it never occurred to me before now. I suppose it was because I'd taken the lad in dislike early on. But your mother had a care for him . . . I should have been guided by her opinion."

Alexa stopped walking. "What on earth are you talking about, Papa?"

"Your cousin has offered to marry you," he said. "We've just been going over the—"

"Oh, no!" she cried, thrusting away from him. "I can't believe you would even consider such a thing. Did you hear nothing of what I said about him in the church?"

She bit back her anger instantly. It was imperative that she remain calm. But in spite of that resolve, this latest development had set her heart pounding; she felt as though she might swoon. She walked with shaking limbs to the sideboard and poured herself a glass of brandy, ignoring her father's muttered protest as she carried it to her mouth.

"I know you have an aversion to him," he said evenly. "But according to your aunt's letters, you have an aversion to most gentlemen. I've had a chance to reevaluate your cousin these past days, Alexa, and frankly he's surprised me. He's shown great concern over your disappearance, and concern for my distress, as well. He set several men to searching for you before he came here—"

"Not men," she interjected, "ruffians. From the worst part of London."

Her father waved away her protest. "Perhaps he felt it would take a ruffian to catch a ruffian. He also insisted we call in the Runners, but I feared there was little they could do so long after the fact. So he then suggested we advertise a substantial reward for information on your whereabouts, not mentioning your name, mind, only your description. My solicitor here in Cudbright was to field the replies."

"He was just lulling your suspicions with all these helpful suggestions," she pointed out. "Can't you see that?"

It wouldn't have surprised her if Darwin himself was angling for that reward. He'd get the brunt of it if his hirelings had been the ones who brought her home.

"All I can see is that you are determined to slander him," her father said with a scowl. "But he was here when I needed him. I'd never felt so thwarted in my life . . . I didn't know which way to turn. There was no sign of a ransom note, I had no way of knowing if you were even still alive. But Quincy stood beside me and tried to keep my hopes up." He shot her a look of reproach. "Why the devil didn't you write to me, Alexa, to let me know you were safe?"

She chewed on her lower lip. "I thought it better if you didn't know anything about it. I didn't want to worry you, and anyway, I'd hoped to be here yesterday, exactly when you expected me."

"And didn't you think that in the meantime someone else might have informed me that you'd been carried off? Mrs. Reginald or your cousin?"

"I wrote to Reggie at the White Hart and told her that I was not in any danger. I . . . I also asked her not to contact you—I didn't want you fretting."

"Well, I haven't heard a word from her. Though why you thought you needed to protect me—"

"I was worried about your health. You were walking with a cane last year at Christmas, if you will recall. And had no appetite to speak of."

"Those were passing ailments—"

"Well, since I never get to see you," she retorted, "how in blazes was I to know they were passing? How am I to know anything of what goes on in this house?"

"Don't start on that again," he said, holding out a warning hand. "God save me from single-minded women. You might let me enjoy the fact that you've come safely home, without instantly badgering me."

She paused a minute . . . something he'd said earlier was

now lashing around inside her head. The question formed itself slowly. "Then, tell me this . . . how exactly did my
cousin claim to know of my abduction?"

"He met up with Mrs. Reginald in Reading right after it
occurred. Said he was on his way here for the holidays."

Her eyes flew to his face. "He told me he was spending
Christmas in Shropshire. Why would he change his mind?
Unless he had business outside Reading, business with me.
According to MacHeath, the men my cousin hired were to
take me to a hedge tavern. Darwin was going to . . . well, do
whatever it is that men do to make sure women have to
marry them. And now you've played right into his plans,
handing me over to him without so much as a whimper of
protest." Her eyes narrowed as she added scornfully, "I hate
to think you're no better than those two hired bullies."

He was unperturbed by her harsh tone. "You start at
phantoms, child. Young gentlemen change their minds on
the merest caprice. I wager Quincy wanted to spend the holidays with his family, rather than among strangers."

Alexa was beginning to feel real sympathy for
MacHeath—she'd been just as pigheaded about believing
him when he's spun the same tale for her.

Her father came forward and took her hand. "I know the
idea of marrying your cousin comes as something of a shock.
But you brought this on yourself. It's clear that you didn't try
very hard to get away from Hastings. I doubt there's a man
could hold you, if you really wanted to get free. And no, I
don't believe he drugged you. He didn't need to . . . he's had
you in his thrall since you were a girl. The point is, regardless of why he took you, his actions guaranteed that your reputation was ruined. Quincy thinks Hastings might have
expected to marry you himself, the blasted upstart."

If only that were true, she lamented silently.

"But I think he merely wanted to ingratiate himself with
me. Use you to win my favor, maybe get me to drop the
charges against him."

"You're not far off, Papa," she said. "That is exactly why
he kept me with him. But it's not why he took me. He was
trying to protect me from Darwin's men. He's never stopped

protecting me." She eyed him darkly. "By the way, those two ruffians are tied up in Kincaid's barn . . . if you require more proof."

He ran one hand over the side of his face and then looked at her with impatience. "Has it occurred to you that those men are Hasting's own friends? Providing a bit of window dressing to convince you that you were truly in peril."

"Father!" she cried out, nearly overcome by frustration. "MacHeath shot one of them in the throat in Rumpley. Then tonight he slashed the same one with his knife." She glared at him from under her brows. "Is any of this getting through to you?"

He pondered her words a moment. "It's possible those two rogues were after you on their own behalf. I can believe that more readily than I could believe your cousin was behind it. He is . . . well, I hate to say the word indolent, but he's rarely shown much initiative over anything."

"And yet this creature you would ask me to marry?"

"He is a gentleman, the grandson of a baron. And face it, my dear, you are irretrievably ruined. By now, half of Cudbright has guessed that you were gallivanting across the countryside with Simeon Hastings. It won't take long for word to filter back to London. Quincy is your only hope."

"I'm not going back to London. So that hardly matters. I doubt anyone here in Cudbright would snub me." She met his eyes and said with a determined frown, "You forget that come the end of the week, I will be mistress of my own funds. You can't force me to marry anyone then."

"I will disinherit you," he growled. "You'll be out on the street without even your good name."

She nearly chuckled. MacHeath would have a hard time rejecting her then.

"You won't do that," she said. "Because in your own stubborn way you love me." Her eyes misted up suddenly, and her voice lowered to a choked whisper. "I am so sorry I didn't turn out the way you wanted, Papa. But you were the one who set me on this course; you encouraged me to be wild and headstrong. It amused you, having a daughter who spoke her mind and was full of sauce."

"You think I don't blame myself for that? All I wanted for you, once you were grown, was for you to take your place in Society. That is why I sent you away, child. So you could have the same advantages your mother had."

"I fear I take after my father," she said softly.

"Obstinate to a fault," he concurred, and she thought she saw a quick flash of admiration in his eyes.

"And loyal," she added. "To those who have earned my trust." She hesitated, and then said quickly, "Talk to MacHeath, Father. I know he looks ragged and worn, but he is still a decent man. Let him tell you his version of what happened that night."

"And what is that version? I gather he has told you."

"No, I didn't need to hear it. He risked his life for me, twice over . . . that's all the surety I need. But I'd say that puts you in his debt."

"Why because he defended a woman? Even a thief might have that much honor."

She thought furiously for some way to make him understand, and then took a bold gamble. "He lost his right hand at sea, you know."

His eyes flashed up in surprise. "Poor blighter. No wonder he's reduced to abducting women."

She forced herself to remain calm. "You mistake my point. I wanted you to see that in spite of his infirmity, he managed to save me from two professional thugs. He didn't have to help me, he didn't have to stir himself out of the East End, but he did. For whatever reason, for money or to gain a fair hearing from you, he brought me home safely. I promised that you would see him. Don't make me into a liar."

"It doesn't matter now. He's probably long gone from the village." He moved away from her to the sideboard and poured himself a glass of port. She heard him mutter under his breath, "Lost his right hand . . . what a damned, wicked shame."

She came up behind him. "He can use his left hand, Papa. I saw a drawing of a dog he made for a little boy. It was wonderful . . . so much life captured in just a few pencil lines. And he never left the sea, either . . . he worked as a smuggling captain."

When he turned to her, his brow was furrowed.

"Oh, I know you are going to object to that, say that it just proves he's a thief. But the brethren follow their own code of honor." She breathed a silent *thank you* to Mrs. Gable for those apt words.

"I wasn't going to object, I have no grievance against smugglers. There was my Uncle Patrick over in Cornwall, though perhaps the less said about him. . . ."

"What then?"

"I was surprised, is all. That Hastings would undertake something like that."

"And yet you thought him a sneaking thief."

"He wasn't a blasted thief, Alexa!" he bit out. "Not more than that one time, I'd swear it. The boy was as open and honest as a babe." His fingers gripped the side of his glass until they shone white at the knuckles. "Don't you think it destroyed *me* a little to watch him being carted off in chains? He was the best I've ever seen when it came to designing ships—full of bold, radical ideas. And all that promise was wiped out in one night's bad work."

"Then give him what you owe him, what he deserves."

"Will you marry Quincy if I speak with Hastings?"

"Oh, please," she cried in exasperation. "Don't even mention those two in the same sentence. As for marrying my cousin—a wise man once told me you need to respect the person you wed. You've worked your whole life long so that my idle fop of a cousin can spend his days following his amusing pursuits. What is there for me to respect in such a man?" He opened his mouth, and she put her hand up. "No, don't pretend you haven't been supporting him all these years. I know he's bled you—"

"Borrowed from me."

"Has he ever paid a penny of it back?"

"It will be payback enough if he is willing to marry you."

She gritted her teeth; this was beginning to feel like a bad dream. Every time she thought she'd made inroads at convincing her father to change his mind, he bolted back to the same old position.

"Very well," she said. "I won't badger you any longer.

But let me just say this—the whole time I was out there with MacHeath, all I could think of was coming home. To this village, to this house, to you, Father. To the place where I knew everything was fine and good, where I would be safe. But now . . ." Her voice quavered, and she quickly controlled it. "Now I find lies and deception everywhere I turn."

Prescott's mouth tightened. "I have not lied to you, Alexa."

"No, you are just another victim of them. Of Darwin's twisting of the truth."

"Go to bed," he said wearily. "This is not the homecoming either of us imagined."

"And what of Darwin?" Alexa asked. She couldn't leave the field with her future still hanging in the balance. "He needs to understand that I am not his for the taking."

"I don't want to shackle you to a man you claim to despise. If you can think of another way out of this coil, I wish you would tell me."

"I can't think of anything at the moment." She took a few steps toward the door, then stopped and turned to him. "He won't have me, Father, if that's what you are worried about. MacHeath, I mean. He wants nothing more to do with me, and that's the truth of it."

His gaze was probing as it roamed over her face. She tried to appear nonchalant as she added, "And I'm well over my infatuation with Simeon Hastings." She reasoned it was not precisely a lie. "I only want justice done where he was concerned."

"I will think about it," he said gruffly, and then added as an afterthought, "And I'll send some men in the morning to fetch those two ruffians from Kincaid's barn. We might get them to corroborate your story."

"We might," she said darkly. "Especially if you let *me* question them."

"You *are* an unnatural female," he responded with a sigh.

Once she was gone, Alexander Prescott refilled his glass, and then settled into the winged chair by the front window. He needed to give some serious thought to the accusations Alexa had leveled at Quincy. Was the man so reptilian, he wondered, that he could coolly plot her abduction—and subsequent deflowering—and then come forward, mouthing concern, to console her father?

If any part of it was true, he'd have the fellow horse-whipped through the town.

In all the years he'd known his nephew, he had never warmed to him. Well, not until these past few days. But he *had* trusted him. Darwin Quincy was a gentleman, after all. A man didn't look for betrayal from a member of the upper classes.

Not to mention, Quincy had no reason to cross him. He'd been supplying him with funds since his days at Eton, bailing him out of scrapes with shopkeepers, and making sure his gambling debts were paid. He accepted it as normal that some gentlemen in Society lived beyond their means—his own wife's late father had himself been deep in debt, which was why he'd allowed a wealthy upstart like Prescott to court her.

He also had to admit, it pleased him to keep Quincy around, to have a member of the gentry going in and out of his home at will. He'd even hoped that her cousin's polish would eventually rub off on Alexa.

No prayer of that happening, he thought with a grin. Not his wild rover.

Something about Alexa had changed, he realized. She was still as mulish and plainspoken as ever, but the quiet, simmering hostility he'd seen steadily growing in her over the past seven years had diminished. She was angry with him right now, he knew. And frustrated. But she'd faced him boldly, like the Alexa of old. There'd been none of the sniping comments, not a whisper of the creeping resentment he'd come to loathe.

She'd just now spoken of his love for her, but for the first time since she was seventeen, he had a notion she might possibly love him back.

He still recalled the day she'd gone off to the lady's academy, her face at the coach window, eyes dark and bitter, silently raking him for his betrayal. That forced departure had abruptly marked the end of their easy accord, an accord that had existed between them from the time she was a toddler, riding piggyback on his shoulders. Every night since, he'd prayed that his little Lexie, the openly affectionate child she'd been before he sent her off into the world, would come back to him.

Oh, she dutifully returned each Christmas, and they'd kept up the holiday traditions her mother had begun. Occasionally during her visits, he'd catch her eye and see her smile. But those had been his only glimpses of his Lexie. The aloof, hostile young woman who attended him over the holidays more often seemed a stranger.

It wasn't his fault he'd needed to send her away. He hadn't any notion of how to turn his reckless girl into a proper lady—the requirements for females entering Society were far beyond his ken. He'd never been able to make Alexa understand that.

It was a pity he had no sons—he knew about the molding of boys and young men, how to teach them and encourage them. He'd sometimes felt as though he had a son in Simeon Hastings—a bright, willing lad, full of ambition, and so damned talented. He'd have made any parent proud.

Prescott would never forget the way his heart twisted tonight, when he'd recognized the man Quincy was confronting at the back of the church. There was nothing of the gilded youth in that roughened fellow. Except that his eyes had not changed. They were still steady and intense and full of quiet intelligence. He'd looked into those eyes and known without a smidgen of doubt that Simeon Hastings had come back to Cudbright.

And that it was sure to mean nothing but trouble.

MacHeath walked through the village toward the Mermaid's Tail, mulling over the past week's events. Unsatisfactory seemed to be the watchword.

He rubbed the back of his neck in frustration, looking up at the heavens as though an answer lay there. The sky overhead was clear and laced with stars—he instantly thought back to that night in London, when he'd gazed up at Orion and the Dippers and mourned the loss of the sea. It felt like a lifetime ago. Since then, he'd regained the sea, he'd re-found Alexa, he'd met up with old friends, and tonight it appeared he'd made a new one. He was a sorry Robin Hood to have acquired such a fine Friar Tuck, he reflected with a grin.

Perhaps things were not so unsatisfactory, after all.

His embittered soul had begun to experience the occasional rush of joy, and his deep shame at the loss of his hand had started to fade. But mixed with these new blessings was a new, keenly felt ache. The deep stirrings of affection he felt for Alexa had to be crushed. He was not the proper man for her, and he would be wise to remind himself of that whenever he drifted into dreaming about a life with her. It was necessary to tamp down every longing, every desire, before he was overcome by them. He'd suffered the loss of his hand, and somehow had survived it. He wasn't sure he could endure the loss of his heart.

He was nearly at the tavern, passing along a familiar street, when two men came out of an alley and took him by the arms, one on either side of him. He knew instinctively it was not Finch and Connor, but had no clue as to their identity.

"This way, sir," the elder of the men said, as they steered him down a narrow lane that ended at the river. When they passed by a lit doorway, he craned his head around to look at the man who had spoken.

"William?" he said. "William Coachman?"

"So you do remember me, Mr. Hastings. It's been many long years since I've seen your face. This young fellow is my nephew Henry."

"It occurs to me that you and your nephew have been following me."

"No, sir. Truth is, we been following those other two rascals."

"The devil you have!"

"Since Reading," Henry piped in.

William motioned MacHeath to sit on the low wall that enclosed the grounds of the shipyard, and then settled beside him. Henry crouched down on the cobbles.

"After you stole Miss Alexa from the coach," William began, "me and Henry decided to follow after her. Henry's a clever lad—he was a game tracker off in Lincolnshire before I got him a place with Prescott. He recalled what you'd said about a message, and so we went off to the Lamb and Flag in Reading that same night. The landlord was more than happy to tell us about the arrogant gentleman that had been there before us. And about the drawing that gentleman carried away with him."

MacHeath smiled to himself. So, Quincy had found his little message after all.

"We went back to the White Hart to tell Mrs. Reggie that we were going after Alexa. She gave us the money that was in Miss Alexa's purse to use for expenses, and hired us two fine horses to ride."

"You didn't tell her about Quincy?"

"We talked it over, me and Henry, and decided we didn't have any proof against him. Just that drawing the landlord told us about. We figured who'd ever left it behind might be trying to incriminate him. So we set out toward Upavon, that being the next town of any size, and dashed if we didn't nearly stumble over two rough characters whispering in the stable of a little inn—"

"My friend Finch does have a carrying voice," MacHeath noted dryly.

"It was clear they were looking for a man and a woman. The big one was threatening what he was going to do to both of them, once he had them in his hands. But they never mentioned who they were taking their orders from."

"So you followed them?"

"Aye, we did. And they never caught on."

"Funny, ain't it," Henry observed, "how a hound on a trail never looks back to see if he's bein' followed."

"We were right behind them when they got to Dagshott, and then we followed them to a small village west of there. They doubled back and headed south to Rumpley. That's where I saw you, Simeon Hastings, and recognized you. After that skirmish on the bridge, it was."

"I wanted to rush in and tell Miss Alexa that we had come to take her home," Henry interjected.

"But I saw she was in good hands, sir. I saw you rescue her from the river."

"And it didn't bother you that I'd been accused of stealing from her father?"

"Pshaw . . . I never believed that trumped-up tale. You were a good lad back then. And I knew you would never do anything to harm Miss Alexa, thief or not."

Henry leaned forward. "We saw you and Miss Alexa go into the house beside the livery, so we hid under the bridge until it got dark, and then, sure enough, just like we suspected, those two rascals came sneaking back into town."

"We stole their horses while they were lying in wait for you," William said with a wide grin. "Figured it would give you some extra time to get away."

"Thank you," said MacHeath, "it did."

"Once those rascals were gone from the place, we had a word with the liveryman. Told him we worked for Miss Alexa's father. He explained everything, Mr. Hastings. How you'd rescued her from her cousin and his bully boys. He told us you were going to Bournemouth to find your old captain who would take you to Devon by boat. We headed down there, just to make sure you got away safe."

"Then it was you two who frightened Alexa at the cottage."

"Mmm. Didn't mean to do that. We weren't sure which cottage she was in and was just peeking in a few windows. After you sailed off, your Mr. Tarlton had one of the fishermen take us across Lyme Bay. We been here since noon, keeping watch for you at the wharf."

"We didn't come as far as the wharf," MacHeath said. "We put ashore downriver and walked up to the house."

"We was waiting to warn you that the same two men were watching the house."

"I discovered them myself. But why didn't you tell Prescott about them?"

William made a rude noise. "As soon as we got here we tried to see him, to tell him that Miss Alexa was safe. But

Mr. Darwin-Perishing-Quincy warned the butler that no one was to speak to the old man without he heard of it first. We were out by the stable, trying to think of a way to get a message to Prescott, when we saw those men creeping around outside the fence. That's when we went back to the waterfront to wait."

MacHeath leaned back on the bench and grinned. "The two of you are wasted as coachman. I believe Bow Street could benefit from your services."

Both men blushed, and William said, "It wasn't so difficult, what we did. It was just pure luck that we stumbled across those two rogues in the first place. The rest was just a game of cat and mouse."

"If the cat takes his ease, the rat takes the cheese," Henry quoted with a grin.

"What's to be done now?" William asked. "The old man didn't believe Miss Alexa in church, from what I hear in the servant's quarters. He all but called her a liar in front of half the parish."

"I don't blame him for resisting the truth—Quincy has swayed him. What I need now is to connect Quincy with his hirelings. Unfortunately, I am still the only one who's seen them together. But Quincy and I are not through with each other, and he's sure to have his bullies nearby."

"We'll scout the town, then."

"No," said MacHeath after a short pause. "I think it would be better if I played the cheese this time." One cheek drew in. "It was never a flattering role for Miss Alexa."

"You're going to use yourself as bait?" William muttered.

"Why not? If it brings Quincy to me with his men in tow, it will be worth the risk." He clasped each man's hand in turn. "Just stay close behind me, that's all I ask. Behind me, but out of sight."

"Gor," said Henry, with not unwarranted smugness. "We can do that with our eyes closed."

Chapter 14

MacHeath spent the night visiting every grogshop in Cudbright, which was a considerable number. He spilt more gin than he drank, knowing that he needed to keep a clear head, but by his listing walk and slurred speech, not a man in the village would have guessed he was still sober when three o'clock rolled around.

He was bellowing out an old smuggler's chantey, feeling his way along a dark alley, after being rousted from the Capstan, his last stop of the night, when the two men came up behind him.

He turned to face them, and then appeared to lose his balance. "Sorry," he said with a sloppy grin as he leaned into the brick wall. "Ever'thin's spinnin' aroun' and aroun'."

"Bleedin' sot," Finch said with a sneer. "Look at him . . . he's disgusting." He raised one tree-trunk leg and booted MacHeath in the belly. He went spinning in earnest and landed on his stomach in a puddle. He tried several times before he was able to raise himself up onto his elbows. "Alf!" he cried brightly when he saw the weedy little man beside Finch. "Lookee . . . iss m'old frien' Alf."

As Finch pulled out his pistol, MacHeath rolled onto his back, his arms wrapped around his middle. He gazed up at the man with a wide smile. "Teash you a lesson, Bully . . . gonna teash you . . ."

"You're not gonna shoot him, are you?" Connor asked worriedly, tugging at Finch's sleeve. "Remember our orders, what *he* told us, we are not to harm him. . . ."

Finch spat. "I recall it well enough. Our peacock wants that pleasure for himself, and he's paid well for the privilege." He fingered the fine gold snuffbox in his coat pocket. It was only a small inconvenience that the initials *A.C.P.* were inscribed on the lid. He knew a handy fellow in London who could alter those letters all out of recognition. "Anyway, we'll get to watch. Never seen the gentry at play . . . it might be entertainin'."

Between them they hoisted MacHeath onto his feet and half carried him out of the alley. MacHeath continued to sing lustily—in a surprisingly strong baritone—as they made their way up the cobbled street, but his captors were unconcerned. To any stray passerby, they would appear to be three harmless men returning from a night on the town, the two steadier ones, in time-honored tradition, helping their jugbit friend to stay upright. It was Christmas, after all, and celebratory excesses were likely to be overlooked.

They stopped at a boardinghouse on a street near the riverfront, and Connor pushed the door open. As they dragged MacHeath, now singing lyrically about the ladies of Spain, into the front hall, the door on their left cracked open an inch, and a bloodshot eye appeared in the opening.

When the door swung wide, Finch glared at the harridan in the dingy linen bed gown. Landladies and their ilk did not rank high on his list of tolerable people.

He forced himself to smile. "Sorry, Mrs. Cloyne. Our friend's got hisself the devil of a toothache. We called in the barber to have it out, but we figured to get him drunk first. He's turned a mite noisy."

She motioned to the stairwell with her chin. "Get him out of my hall, then. He's wailin' fit to wake the dead."

"Once the barber gets here and starts in to work on him, there's no tellin' how much of a squawk he'll make. So don't fret yourself if you hear him screamin' up there." Finch passed her a coin to make sure they would not be disturbed.

She bit into it with her few remaining teeth, and then nodded once before retiring back into her chamber.

It was tough work getting MacHeath up the narrow stairs. He'd gone limp on them by the second landing, still singing his lungs out as he lay sprawled on the planked floor. Finch muttered that he was of a mind to pitch him over the railing, and have done with it, but Connor managed to get him on his feet again.

He knew that Bully could have easily carried MacHeath unassisted, had it not been for the wound on his neck, the dog bite on his thigh, the gash on his forearm, and the injury to his temple, which was a swollen, stippled bruise of red and purple, quite like the inside of a pomegranate. The bruise on his own head was painful but fortunately less visible.

Connor recalled their recent interview with their employer. Old Quincy'd sure had his work cut out for him, convincing Finch not to kill MacHeath outright once they caught up with him. Alf had never seen his mate so riled. But Quincy had soothed him with promises of an even greater reward, and had made him swear on his mother's grave—an oath that held some meaning, even among the denizens of the East End—that he would bring MacHeath in alive.

They finally reached the top floor, where the room they'd rented earlier that evening, on Quincy's instructions, was situated. It had several things to recommend it—it possessed a fireplace, a luxury both men were looking forward to after their shivering sojourn in the abandoned barn, and it was the only chamber on that floor. No nosy neighbors, no squalling brats, no one to ask after the identity of the blond gentleman who would be arriving there as soon as they got word to him.

He helped waltz MacHeath into the room, and then shut and locked the door. MacHeath slumped onto the floor the instant Finch released him, and he only grunted slightly when Finch kicked him hard in the ribs.

"He's out," he pronounced, before he bent down and divested his captive of both pistol and knife, murmuring in admiration over the clever sheath that held the latter weapon behind the man's back. He'd have to get one like that . . . much handier than reaching down into your bleedin' boot.

Together they tugged off MacHeath's cape and greatcoat,

then they propped him up in a greasy upholstered chair and tied his wrists firmly to its arms.

"Go fetch him," Finch said to Connor as he sat down at the pine table and filled a mug from a bottle of stout. "No, stop looking at me like that. I promise I won't kill him." He eyed the knife that lay on the table beside the fine dueling pistol. "I'll maybe just have a little fun with him, once he comes to."

Connor was still shaking his head as he went down the four flights of stairs. Quincy better come along lively like if he wanted to have his chance at MacHeath.

MacHeath congratulated himself on ending up exactly where he wanted to be. Most men would consider being tied up and at the mercy of Bully Finch a less-than-heartening situation, but he still had a few aces up his sleeve. William and Henry, for starters. He'd seen the two dark shadows on the opposite side of the street just before Connor had shut the front door. His loud singing had made him and his two captors easy to follow. And, as he'd hoped, his drunken placidity had kept either of them from doing him any real harm. He'd been the very essence of benign nonresistance.

He shifted his head onto one shoulder and began to snore in loud, irregular bursts. Several times Finch came over and slapped at his face, and got nothing more than incoherent mumbling for his trouble.

"Bleedin' sot," he muttered.

After fifteen minutes had passed, Finch finally resorted to dousing MacHeath with the dank water from the pitcher on the washstand. He watched in satisfaction as his captive returned to sputtering consciousness.

"Hello, Mackie," he said with a grin.

"Zat you, Bully? M'eyes are all foggy. And what's wrong with my arms?" He twisted in the chair. He raised his head and saw the bottle of stout. "Lord, Bully, I need a drink. Just a little drink . . ."

Finch raised his mug and looked at MacHeath tauntingly over the rim as he took a long, deep swallow. Then leaned across the table and picked up MacHeath's knife.

"I got my own steel," he said, "but there's somethin' so satisfyin' about cuttin' a man with his own knife. Like a dog bitin' his own master."

He knelt down before the chair where MacHeath was trussed, and ran the razor edge of the knife along the bound man's jaw.

"Not a pretty face, Mackie, but I do hear the ladies admire it. Must be those strange eyes you got. Well, let's see if we can't get them to look somewhere else."

He was just raising the blade to his cheek, when MacHeath kicked out, putting all his back into the blow. The toe of his boot landed squarely on the Finch family jewels.

Finch collapsed instantly onto the floor, in a writhing ball of agony. MacHeath calmly sliced the cord on his right hand with Mr. Featherbridge's carving knife. He'd positioned it under the leather harness on his forearm, so that an inch of steel jutted out from his shirt cuff. While Finch rolled and bellowed before the hearth, he cut his left hand free and stood up. The big man put up little resistance as MacHeath trussed his wrists and ankles together, thinking to himself that he'd performed this task far too often tonight.

He then tucked his pistol into his waistcoat and sat down to await Quincy.

Alf Connor let himself in through the front gate of Prescott's house—which had been left unlocked as promised—and went immediately to stand below Quincy's bedroom window. He flicked a few pebbles against the glass, and eventually the window shifted open. Alf gave the high sign and watched him recede into the room. Five minutes later, Quincy came tiptoeing out the side door, his cloak over his arm.

"You best hurry," Connor whispered. "I don't know how long Finch can sit there without giving in to the urge to carve Mackie up into little pieces."

Quincy went quickly through the gate and headed for the brambly path that led down to the village. He was approaching the towering oak that marked its beginning, when he heard something rustling below him. He put his hand out to warn Connor, and together they waited in the darkness. Someone was coming up the hill—they could hear the ragged breathing over the sighing of the night wind.

Quincy caught the man from behind as he emerged into the road.

"Let me go," Henry cried. "Lord love us, Mr. Quincy, you know me. I work for Mr. Prescott."

"What are you doing out so late?"

"It's Christmas, sir," he exclaimed. "Been down to the Mermaid, I have."

Quincy released him slowly.

"What're *you* doing out so late, Mr. Quincy? If I can make so bold to ask."

"We're keeping watch on the house . . . in case that MacHeath comes back to bother Miss Alexa."

Henry pointed to Connor. "He helping you, an' all?"

"Yes, he's one of the men from Reading I told you about. Now, off you go."

"Aye." Henry gave him a wide grin as he turned toward the house, but Alf Connor stepped in front of him. "Wait a minute . . . I know you . . . I know your voice and I seen those gappy teeth before. You were in Rumpley—you were the lad who told us where to find the livery. Have you been following me, you damned—"

But Henry didn't wait to hear anymore. He darted around Alf and sprinted toward the house. The front gate was only yards away . . . all he had to do was get inside. Surely they wouldn't shoot him, not here, not right in front of the—

Connor's knife lodged high in his back. He fell forward, one hand still reaching for the gate, scrabbling in the gravel of the road. And then it stopped moving.

"Drag him into the bushes," Quincy ordered. "He might not have known anything, but I'm not taking any chances. Not now."

Quincy and Connor had no notion that anything was amiss at the boardinghouse until they reached the second landing. A white-haired man was passed out against a doorway—a Christmas reveler, no doubt, overcome by an excess consumption of spirits. They were about to brush past him, when Quincy happened to look down. Even though the man's face was tucked into his muffler and his head was canted against his shoulder, there was something familiar about him. Something too blasted familiar.

"Get up, William," he uttered as he prodded him with the toe of his boot. "We've already dispatched Henry, so don't look for him to aid you."

William climbed slowly to his feet, his eyes glaring bright in the dim light of the hall. "You festering worm," he hissed. "They'll stretch your neck for that."

"Phfff." Quincy shrugged. "And who's to lay charges against me? You won't be around to do it, I promise you that. Now, get up the stairs."

Connor was unlocking the door to the top-floor room, when he heard a muffled noise from beyond it. "Finch?" he called out. There was no reply.

Quincy instantly tugged William back against him, and set his pistol against the side of his head. "Go on." He motioned to Connor. "Open it."

The first thing he saw was Bully Finch, bound and gagged on the floor by the fireplace. When he beheld the tall man with a pistol in his hand, his guts clenched.

"Throw it down," he growled to MacHeath. "Or William will be the worse for it."

"Don't do it, lad!" the coachman cried. "I'm sorry they caught me . . . I should have stayed out in the street. There's no one to help you now . . . they already got to Henry, and I'm a dead man sure."

But MacHeath knew he had no choice. He hadn't counted on them getting their hands on his allies. He'd made no contingency for such a thing.

With a grim expression tightening his mouth, he tossed his pistol onto the table.

As weary as she was, Alexa could not sleep. She lay on her bed, the hours passing, and still sleep would not come. Her thoughts kept returning to MacHeath, and each time they did, something twisted painfully inside her. It was no use trying to curb her wayward brain—the need she felt was only partly the fault of that usually reliable organ. Most of the yearning came driving up from the pit of her stomach, where it meshed with the aching need in her heart.

Sweet Lord, she missed him . . . his voice, his touch. She missed his wry laugh and the way his dark eyes danced when he teased her. She longed for the comforting scent of him, which was the essence of everything she now craved— driftwood burning in a night fire, heather sprigs trapped in a folded blanket, sea spray sparkling on a cap of dark hair, the pungent smell of horses racing across a field, the heady aroma of claret poured for a newly wedded couple who would never have a wedding night.

She'd grown so accustomed to having him beside her, that his absence left her feeling incomplete and detached from everything. Her conduit to the world was gone . . . she was adrift and alone. She tried to convince herself that she would see him again, that he wouldn't leave without any word of farewell. It never once occurred to her that he might be gone already.

After five days with the man, she had come to know him as well as anyone she'd ever met. She understood the workings of his mind and the needs that drove him. Which was why she was sure he hadn't left Cudbright.

And as reassuring as it was to know he was still close by, it also made her fear for him. It was totally irrational, that fear. Quincy's men were trussed up in a barn, where they would remain until her father sent his men to release them. Quincy himself was under this very roof. It was possible it could have gone out during the time she was closeted with her father, but he was here now. She'd peeped into his bed-room on the way to her own chamber and had been reas-sured, by the sibilant sound of his light snores, that he was fast asleep. Dreaming of her vast fortune, no doubt.

For all she knew, MacHeath was still with Mr. Feather-bridge, drinking his fine brandy and watching him write out his sermon for Christmas morning. There was absolutely no reason for her to feel so troubled, and yet she couldn't shake off the premonition that he was in danger.

Finally succumbing to her unease, she pulled on a day gown and buttoned Mr. Gable's wool coat over it. If there was something wicked afoot tonight in Cudbright, she was not going to be blithely lying in her bed while it occurred. She brushed aside her own fears, she'd seen plenty of action this past week, and had become as seasoned as any recruit. Furthermore, it was not in her nature to sit back and wait while someone she loved was in danger, real or imagined. MacHeath had come to her rescue often enough, and maybe now she could return the favor.

She checked Quincy's room before she went downstairs. This time the bed was empty. A peek into his wardrobe revealed that his cloak was missing. Damn it! How long had he been gone? She felt his pillow with her palm . . . and thought it might still be warm. Not too long, she prayed.

She crept along the hall toward the front door and nearly screamed in alarm when her father stepped out of his study.

"Something's wrong, Papa," she whispered intently. "Quincy's not in his room."

"I was drowsing in my study . . . I thought I heard something out in the road."

They went out the front door and along to the gate, listening for any strange noises. It was Alexa who heard the groans coming from the bushes across the road.

Her father pushed aside the bare branches, and then knelt down. "It's Henry Wilkins, I think. Good Lord, the fellow's covered with blood."

Henry grabbed Prescott's arm. "Was comin' to warn you . . ." he groaned. "They have MacHeath. Boardinghouse on Fuller Lane, next to the farrier . . . top floor, I think . . . William's there waiting . . . please . . . go." He lapsed into unconsciousness.

Alexa ran back to the house to rouse the servants, and watched anxiously as Henry was carried inside. Her father meanwhile, had ordered two horses saddled.

"I've learned it's better not to leave you out of my sight," he said as he boosted her into the sidesaddle.

"I can look after myself," she declared, patting her coat pocket. "I found a primed pistol in Quincy's wardrobe."

Though the road to the village was more roundabout than the path, they made it into Cudbright in mere minutes, riding at a hard gallop. Alexa knew the boardinghouse Henry had spoken of. It was a rickety old firetrap that the city fathers had been threatening to condemn for years. But she was surprised when her father slowed his horse before the shipyard, reining in beneath the high iron gate.

"Wait here. I want to alert the night watchmen," he said. "I suspect we could use a few able-bodied men."

She watched him ride onto the grounds, and then turned her own mount toward the boardinghouse. The panicky feeling in her gut was inexorably drawing her there. She dismounted a block from the place, and tied her horse to a railing, before proceeding along the dark cobbled street. She kept on the lookout for William, but if he was anywhere nearby, he did not make himself known to her.

The only light showing on the facade of the boardinghouse was at the top window. It had to be where they'd taken MacHeath. Quincy was up there with him, she knew it in her bones, and her teeth showed white in a tiny snarl of fury.

She drifted back into the deep shadows on the opposite side of the lane and muttered a swift prayer that her father would hurry.

Then her head snapped up, and a tremor ran through her as a fearful, prolonged scream rent the still night air. It rose up and up, a sound of such indescribable agony that she had to cover her ears. No sane person could have made such a bestial noise. It was inconceivable.

But that scream had a human origin. Her whole body began to shake with sick fear, because she knew instinctively from whose throat it had emerged.

She had stumbled to the middle of the street, eyes intently focused on the top-floor window, before the last echo of that rending scream had died away.

She raised her pistol and aimed at the light.

Connor was already untying Finch when MacHeath relinquished his weapon. The big man came up off the floor and threw himself at MacHeath, forcing him back against the wall, grappling to get ahold of his lethal right hand.

"You're mine now, Mackie. I don't care what Quincy says . . ." He caught him by the throat with one huge hand and shook him like a lion savaging a gazelle.

"Steady, Finch," Quincy cautioned him. "I believe a little finesse is called for. And, no, I won't deprive you of your fun. I think you've earned it."

Finch grabbed a handful of MacHeath's shirt and flung him toward the chair. "Tie him up again, Alf," he ordered. "And the old man, too."

"No, wait on Hastings," Quincy said, stepping forward. He handed his pistol to Finch. "Here, keep this trained on him. There's something I've been longing to do."

MacHeath steeled himself for the blow, and was perplexed when Quincy merely reached out and took his right hand. "Very nice," he said as he pried off the tan glove and shaped his fingers around the wooden hand. "Ah, but what's this. He's got a knife up his sleeve. How very clever."

He removed the weapon, and then tapped it against MacHeath's chin. "I always win in the end, Hastings. You ought to have learned that by now."

"That's not what I hear back in London," he drawled. "Your bad luck at cards is legendary."

"That's of no matter now," he said with a delicate shrug. "I'm to marry my cousin . . . and will soon be rolling in the ready."

MacHeath's face darkened. "Prescott wouldn't give her to you . . . he can't be that bloody blind."

But Quincy made no reply. Instead he tightened his hold on the false hand and twisted it. MacHeath bit back his cry of pain as the leather harness dug into his arm.

"Look at you," Quincy snarled. "With your fine gloves and your fine sense of honor, pretending to be a gentleman." He twisted even harder. "But even with this, you're still a pitiful cripple. You're not fooling anyone, Hastings."

"Leave him alone!" William cried. "For the love of God—"

Connor smashed his pistol over the old coachman's head,

knocking him back against the fireplace, and then smiled up at the other men.

Finch was now fairly dancing with frustration. "When's it to be my turn?"

"Patience, my friend. I am only stoking the flames a bit for you." His gaze then drifted to the hearth, where a small fire crackled, and his eyes lit up.

He turned back to MacHeath. "You should never have crossed me. It was a mistake." And then he gripped the false hand tightly with both his own hands, and wrenched it right off MacHeath's arm. The leather straps bit wickedly into his flesh before they snapped, and he staggered almost to his knees.

"No!" he cried, reaching forward as Quincy flung the wooden hand into the fire. The next instant he was throttling Quincy, the fingers of his left hand digging deep into the skin of his throat.

"Kill me," he breathed against his ear. "I don't care anymore."

Finch pulled him off the blond man, and wrestled him down into the chair. "You'll be dead soon enough," he said. "Here, Alf. Give me that rope."

This time he not only tied MacHeath's arms to the chair, but his legs as well. And as a precautionary measure, he looped the remaining length of rope around his chest, affixing him to the chair back.

"You know," Quincy said, stepping back to observe him, "something occurs to me."

Finch spat. "What occurs to me is to carve him up till his own mother wouldn't recognize him."

"That's too predictable." His eyes drifted over MacHeath, the hatred in them like a living thing, coiled and vicious and eager to strike. He shifted his head and whispered to Finch. "What would a one-handed man fear losing the most?"

Finch's face broke into a wide grin of understanding. He reached down into his boot and drew out his knife. It was a heavier weapon than MacHeath's blade, made more for dirty work than splicing ships' lines.

MacHeath felt the sweat start to bead on his forehead. He knew they were going to kill him . . . he'd accepted that the moment he threw down his pistol. But how they were going to do it, and what they were going to do to him beforehand, was making his whole body quake. He wasn't sure how long his nerve would hold out, and the last thing he wanted was to give Quincy the satisfaction of seeing him squirm.

Finch knelt down beside the chair. He gripped MacHeath's left hand and laid the blade against the top of his wrist, pressing down hard enough to draw a thin line of blood. MacHeath's heart surged up into his throat and his insides went liquid, when he realized what Finch intended.

"Beg me," Finch crooned. "Beg me not to do it, Mackie."

He increased the pressure, and MacHeath felt the blade slice into his flesh. He shut his eyes and willed himself not to cry out. They'd be doing him a favor, he realized, if they killed him after this. He'd have no desire to live with both hands gone. It was too hellish to contemplate.

"You'll never touch her again," Quincy whispered silkily from beside him. "Never feel her skin beneath your fingers, never caress her face. Christ, do you think she'd even look at you after this, except to feel revulsion?"

The scream rose up from inside him and would not be denied. All the pain and all the loss he'd experienced in the past ten years came roaring out of him. Agony and loneliness and desolation all mingled together in that piercing sound. The two men beside him actually reeled back, and Connor fell against the hearth.

Quincy recovered first. "Do it!" he cried, his face twisted into a maniacal rictus.

Finch raised the knife in a hatcheting motion, his elbow cocked.

The next instant a pistol shot shattered the front window. Glass flew into the room as though it had exploded from a cannon. The three men who were not bound immediately ducked for cover, Connor beneath the table, and Quincy and Finch scrambling to get under the bed. They all cowered, unmoving, awaiting the next salvo.

MacHeath slewed the chair closer to the window. "Come quickly!" he shouted in his carrying, quarterdeck voice.

There was the sound of hurried footsteps on the stairs, and then the door cracked open. "On the table," MacHeath called out. Alexa flung the door wide, ran in, and snatched up the pistol he'd thrown down earlier. She kicked Connor square in the chest when he tried to grab at her skirts.

"Get up, all of you," she snarled. She was breathless and wild-eyed, and MacHeath thought that there wasn't a more beautiful woman on all seven continents.

"Well met, cousin," Quincy said as he climbed to his feet and brushed a legion of cobwebs from his coattails. "Still defending this rogue, I see."

"What I see," she said brusquely, "is something I've prayed to witness for five long days. And that is you with these ugly customers. You'll have a hard time explaining this to my father." Her gaze darted to Finch, who was sidling toward her.

"Get Quincy's gun," MacHeath said quickly. "And hold it on him. They won't touch you if you've got him."

She drew his weapon from his waistcoat, and then stepped behind him and set his own pistol against his ear, keeping the other one trained on Finch. She ordered Connor to untie MacHeath.

"You won't shoot your own cousin," Quincy said evenly.

"No, not if you tell me what really happened in my father's office ten years ago."

"I've told you what happened. I caught that scoundrel stealing, and he sliced my head open."

"I'll tell you Alexa," said MacHeath as Connor freed him. He stood up, and rolled his shoulders to get the feeling back into them. He then took the second pistol from Alexa and motioned Connor to join Finch on the other side of the room. "I've kept it from you long enough."

He spared a glance at the blond man. "Now you're the one who's sweating, Quincy. You see, I knew you would come after me tonight—I saw your face in the church when I said I'd remembered a great deal about you. The pity of it is, when it happened I didn't recall any of it until days later. Too late to keep me from Exeter jail."

"Go on," Alexa said. Her gaze drifted momentarily to something out in the hall, and her eyes brightened.

"I was working late, and I'd fallen asleep at my drawing table. The candle must have gone out, because when I awoke it was dark in the workroom. I thought I heard someone moving about in your father's office. When I went to investigate, I found Quincy in there, at the open safe. I'm not sure which of us was the more surprised, but he acted first. He leaped up and struck me on the head, with something from the desk I assume, a paperweight or a bottle. He hit me several times . . . there were at least three lumps on my head when I finally came to."

"This is utter nonsense," Quincy hissed. Alexa jabbed him with the gun and told him to keep quiet.

"The next I knew, I was being roused by the constables. They'd already bound my hands, and when they carted me away, I still had no idea what I'd done. I suppose I was in shock.

"I sorted it all out while I was in Exeter." He added ruefully, "You have a lot of free time when you are sitting in a prison cell. The thing was, Quincy knew I could identify him, and so he turned the tables and made me the scapegoat. But to do that, he had to strengthen the case against me. I would guess he went directly to my quarters at the shipyard and planted more money there, plus some things he'd taken from your father's desk. Then went back the office to rouse the watch."

"I was cut on the head," Quincy protested. "How do you explain that?"

"You tell me. What did you use?"

"What do you mean? You think I faked an injury to myself? No wonder you had to escape from Exeter . . . no judge would have believed that sorry tale."

"No, but I would have," Alexander Prescott said as he stepped into the room. Three men filed in behind him, each of them carrying a carbine.

"I was wondering when you were going to stop loitering out there on the landing," Alexa said.

"I had a mind to eavesdrop," Prescott responded. "And you looked to have everything well in hand." He gazed around him with distaste. "Though it looks like someone's been up to no good in here." Fishing out his handkerchief, he handed it to MacHeath. "You're bleeding, sir. And is that my good William there on the floor, all trussed up like the Christmas goose?" He motioned one of his men to untie him.

"Uncle!" Quincy cried, trying to push away from Alexa. "Thank goodness you are come here. Your daughter and that madman have been holding us here—"

"Us?" Prescott asked in a voice like ice. "Are you referring to these two ruffians? The ones you claimed you knew nothing about?"

"I . . . uh . . . that is . . . you've got to see that—"

When he approached Quincy, his blue eyes had gone black. "Somehow I doubt you can talk your way out of this, nephew. But if you are inclined to try . . . I suggest you do it to a magistrate."

"No!" Quincy cried, thrusting past his uncle and running to the door. "You don't understand . . . none of you understand . . . I didn't do anything wrong."

"You were caught stealing—"

"It wasn't stealing!" His fingers clutched the worn door frame. "I didn't break into the safe . . . I had taken the key off your watch chain . . . you'd fallen asleep in the library after dinner."

"So you stole the key, as well."

"I was planning to put the money back . . . it was just a loan." His eyes darted around the room, seeking one face that was not looking at him with harsh judgment in their eyes. Even his hirelings were gazing at him with scorn, though perhaps more for his loss of control than for his larceny.

Prescott shook his head sadly. "And for that you let an innocent man get sent to prison? I am ashamed that I ever offered you a crust of bread, Darwin Quincy, let alone years of charity."

"Charity!" Quincy snarled. "It wasn't charity, it was what you owed me. You were nothing compared to my family, just a self-inflated merchant." He pointed a shaking finger at Alexa. "*She* was nothing. No beauty, no breeding." His eyes nearly bulged out of his head as his gaze fell on MacHeath. "And *him*. A wretched, worthless Scot come begging at your door, who ended up gaining all your favor."

"Take him out of here," Prescott muttered. "I won't listen to his slander."

But before anyone could lay hands on him, Quincy ran up to Finch. "It's all your fault! You and that weasel Connor. Inept, dunderheaded fools. You brought me to this—"

"It's not my bleedin' fault, you poncy, clutch-fisted leech!" Finch cried, breaking away from the man who was guarding him.

He launched himself at Quincy, and together the two men careened out the door and onto the landing. As they slammed into the ancient railing, there was the sharp crack of wood breaking. Quincy's eyes widened with sudden awareness as he and Finch teetered there, and then Finch's weight sent them crashing through the damaged barrier and into the open core of the stairwell.

Their screams mingled as they tumbled the three stories to the hallway below.

Prescott instantly wrapped his arms around Alexa. "Sorry, sorry," he whispered raggedly into her hair. "I could have avoided this if I'd only listened to you."

"It wasn't anyone's fault, Papa," she said weakly. "Nobody's fault."

From over her father's shoulder, her eyes sought out MacHeath, but he would not look at her. His face was pale and drawn, his mouth a grim slash.

The men from the shipyard muttered their condolences before they went out, a bound, shaken Alf Connor in their midst. MacHeath started after them, assuring Prescott that he'd see to removing the bodies, and suggesting that perhaps he and Alexa should remain in the room until that grisly task was accomplished.

Prescott's voice stopped him at the door. "Hastings," he said slowly. "Words have little merit . . . but for now that's all I can offer you. I am very sorry."

MacHeath met his eyes, and then drew in a long breath. "So am I, sir. So am I."

William was sitting up now, holding the false hand in his lap. "I plucked it out of the fire," he said in a dazed, faraway voice. "It's only a bit scorched, though the leather is damaged. Pity they killed my Henry . . . the lad could have repaired it."

"Henry was still alive when we left the house," Prescott said. "They'd knifed him in the back, but I don't think it hit anything vital."

"Praise be," William murmured.

Alexa sank down into the greasy armchair, which was still wrapped about with rope. She had a fair idea, from the seeping wound on his wrist, what had made MacHeath scream. And knowing that, she could not find it in her heart to mourn her cousin. She certainly wasn't going to waste a second mourning Bully Finch.

There were footsteps out in the hall, and one of the watchmen came into the room. "He's still alive," he announced breathlessly. "Mr. Quincy, that is. He landed on that big rogue . . . most of broken his fall."

"Oh, blast," Prescott muttered.

"His back's all twisted, though. Don't know that he'll ever walk again."

Chapter 15

MacHeath slept until three that afternoon.

Someone had alerted Mr. Featherbridge to the tragic mishap down near the waterfront, and he'd appeared, just as dawn broke, to take over the arranging of things. "It's what vicars do, dear boy," he'd said to MacHeath. "You just get on back to the rectory and have my housekeeper put you to bed in the spare room. And have her take a look at that wound, as well."

So MacHeath had dragged himself to the vicar's house, where he immediately tumbled into bed. He'd only stirred slightly when the church bells tolled to announce the Christmas morning service, and he wondered if Mr. Featherbridge had returned from Fuller Lane in time to give another of his heartening sermons.

At three, the housekeeper came in with a tray and set it on the bed. "There's Miss Alexa waiting for you downstairs. She's been here since one o'clock, actually, but I told her you looked like you needed a week's worth of sleep."

"Thank her for her concern," he said gruffly as he ladled up a spoonful of hot soup. "But I am in no state for visitors."

She nodded and went off without argument. She privately agreed with his assessment—he cut a sorry figure, with his beard all coming out in bristles and his clothing dashed with mud and blood—though she had a notion he'd be something to behold once he was cleaned up proper. A youth who looked the way Simeon Hastings had, could not possibly age badly. Pity about that hand, though. She'd bandaged his wounded left wrist that morning, and had managed to get a peep at the severed stump while she was at it. Not as gruesome as she'd expected, but still a sorry shame.

MacHeath lay back, once he'd finished his Christmas lunch of invalid fare, and wondered what to do.

He *could* stay here in Cudbright, no doubt with the old man's blessing. For ten years he'd dreamed of that moment in the rooming house, of facing Prescott and receiving absolution. But now that it had finally happened, there was none of the joy or relieved elation he'd expected to feel. No victory, no sense of vindication . . . only a dull awareness of completion.

An icy shivering began deep inside him. It was too late, he realized. He was too broken to be mended by mere words. Or by any forthcoming offers of restitution. Ten years of his life, his prime years, had been wasted because of Quincy's falsehood, and there was nothing Prescott could offer him that would undo that.

And there was another thing gnawing at him now.

He'd thought during the church service last night that he could take on a new mantle. There, with Alexa standing beside him, he'd felt like he could do anything. But this morning, in that seedy rooming house, he'd been made humble. It was hard not to feel humbled when you'd screamed your heart out in front of other men.

The instant Finch set that knife against his wrist, any chances he might have at a new life had vanished. It hadn't taken a blade cutting through flesh and sinew, it only took the threat of it. The pride that had been his sole bulwark through all his deprivations—the thing that had kept him from sinking completely into despair, from taking on cutthroat work in the East End, or from succumbing to the lures of gin—was gone. He'd been humiliated, reduced to a whimpering, abject cur.

It didn't matter that he'd been saved in the end. The horror of that threat, coupled with his own horror at his reaction to it, had destroyed him. His honor with Prescott might have been restored, but the price of that restoration had been his soul.

Alexa also slept for a few hours that morning, though fretfully, hearing MacHeath's screams blended with those of her cousin and Finch, every time she started to doze off. Afterward, she rode off to Mr. Featherbridge's rectory to find MacHeath. The housekeeper had kept her cooling her heels for two hours, and then announced that although Mr. MacHeath had awakened, he was not feeling up to any visitors.

She'd come home in a funk, and had barely managed to choke down a bit of Christmas dinner. Both she and her father spent the meal conversing in hushed whispers. He told her that Quincy had been moved to the surgeon's house, which adjoined the shipyard. The prognosis had not been good—a broken back, and two broken arms, at least.

"He'll spend the rest of his life in a Bath chair," her father said wearily. "I'll have to find someone to look after him."

"You wouldn't bring him here?"

The expression on his face answered her well before he uttered a soft, final, "No."

"His family home is let," she said after some thought. "But we could find him a place somewhere near there, in Salisbury, perhaps."

"You are generous, Alexa. I didn't think you'd want anything to do with him."

She set down both fork and knife on either side of her plate, and leaned toward him. "He went a little mad, don't you think? I saw it in his eyes up there in that room. So I'm not sure he was totally sane any of the time. It's why he could lie and deceive, and still think himself a gentleman. He was all turned about in his head."

"Yes," he said, "what was it Mr. Shakespeare wrote? That 'a man might smile, and smile, be a villain.' "

"And meanwhile there was MacHeath, with all his scowls and bitter melancholies who ended up the hero."

Her father looked as though he was about to say something, and then thought better of it. He fidgeted with his napkin, then rose and excused himself from the table. "I'll be in my study, if you need me. We'll open our gifts tonight, if you don't mind."

It was nearing six o'clock when Mrs. Reginald arrived, unannounced and completely unexpected. Alexa greeted her with cries of relief, and then sat with her in her bedroom and patted her hand while the lady tried to weather the shock of Quincy's tragedy. Alexa insisted she nap, and promised that later that night she would fill her in on everything that had happened.

Well, she thought as she went down the stairs, *we're all here now. All together for Christmas. Just like old times.*

Yet the pall that hung over the house, reminded her of Christmas the year her mother had died—the whispered conversations, the servants tiptoeing about. No laughter or gaiety, only a somber determination to acknowledge the holy day.

A footman approached her. "There is a gentleman here to speak with Mr. Prescott. Your father asked me to put him in the drawing room until he was free, and he suggested you might want to entertain his visitor in the meantime."

Alexa slid open the double doors, wondering who would intrude on her father at a time of family crisis.

MacHeath rose from the sofa and bowed once as she stepped into the room.

"Oh," she said in a small, flustered voice.

"I didn't expect to see you," he said bluntly. "I have business with your father."

"Yes," she said with a bit of her usual spirit. "I've heard that before."

Without asking her permission, he sat down again and began to study the ceiling, his arms folded over his chest. She noticed that he was not wearing gloves; there was a bandage on his left wrist, and the cuff of his shirt was pinned up under his right-hand coat sleeve. It jarred her a bit, seeing that unnatural truncation, and then she shrugged it off. She'd get used to it soon enough . . . well, if she was ever given the chance.

He'd also managed to find a razor—his chin was clean shaven—and someone had removed most of the road grime from his greatcoat. He looked a lot less piratical now, almost civilized. But no less attractive.

"Did my father send for you?" she asked as she settled on the far end of the sofa.

"No. As I said, I have—"

"—some business with him," she finished. "Is this business anything to do with me? Because if it is, I think you ought to tell me first."

MacHeath shot her a look of rebuke. "It's not *that* kind of business, Alexa."

She decided to overlook this unsatisfactory disclosure. "So what will you do now?"

He shrugged. "Go back to Nat's, I expect. See if I can't scrape up a ship somewhere."

She shifted closer to him on the cushions, fighting the urge to take him by the shoulders and declare herself. It was nearly impossible to hold back. Her heart *would* be heard. "Why wouldn't you see me at the rectory? I waited there for hours."

"I wasn't in the mood for visitors," he said in a flat, distant voice.

"What's wrong with you?" she cried softly. "Why won't you look at me? You are talking to me as though I were a stranger. Is it this house? Is it being in here, sitting in this drawing room for the first time, that has struck you dumb?"

His eyes flashed at her, the first sign of animation she'd seen in him since she came through the door. But his voice was icy and remote when he answered her. "I haven't very much to say, I suppose."

She flew off the sofa and faced him, her hands clenched. "You hate us now, don't you . . . not just Quincy, but me and my father. Because we wronged you horribly, and then stood by while you were humiliated and imprisoned. And it happened again last night . . . no one believing in you, no one listening to you. No one there to aid you when that fiend laid his knife on your good hand—"

"Alexa!" He stood up, and his face was quite white.

"I heard you scream, MacHeath," she hissed at him. "All the way down in the street I heard it. My whole life long I will never forget the horror of that sound."

"Please go," he said between his teeth. "While I still have some command of my temper."

"No," she said. "I . . . I am not saying this to anger you or embarrass you . . . God, not that. I only wanted you to know that I would have torn those men to pieces if I had known what they'd done to you. I . . . I only sorted it out afterward." She forced her hands to relax; her nails were carving half-moons into her palms. "Still, I don't blame you if you despise me. We all failed you, in one way or another. I saw your face before you left us this morning . . . it was so sad, so weary." She reached toward him, but he drew back. "But the thing is, I tried. I really tried. To help you, to be your advocate." Her voice started to break, but she kept on regardless. "So please don't hate me, MacHeath. I was the only one who never stopped believing in you."

He finally met her eyes. His own were a dull black, and there were smudged shadows on the skin beneath the filigreed lashes. "I know that, Alexa. And I don't hate you, or your father. The truth is, I don't feel much of anything right now, good or bad."

She paced away toward the windows, needing to work off her anxiety. In the Chelsea Hospital she'd tended men sent home from the war, some whose mental wounds were far greater than the ones their bodies had suffered. She'd seen in their eyes the same dead expression that now dwelled in MacHeath's eyes. Shock, despair, hopelessness. As if the foundation of their every belief had been shaken.

She wanted to rail at him, challenge him, do something to stir him from this frightening malaise. But she feared throwing her anger at him would just make him retreat farther.

It was like that time in Gable's barn, when he'd hidden in the shadows rather than have his shame revealed to her. But what was his shame this time, what did he have to hide from her? She'd seen him without the false hand before, surely that was not it.

What made men ashamed? What drove them to punish themselves and, therefore, those who loved them? The answer formed itself, once she thought back to that fearful scream.

Cowardice.

One of the worst slanders one man could level at another, and possibly the worst a man could level at himself. She'd have to go delicately with him for a change. No foot stomping, no fierce lectures, no flashing eyes.

"Come," she said, taking his good hand and drawing him down to the sofa again. He went unresisting.

"Remember the night you told me that you'd chosen your life, and it had failed you? It occurs to me that you were wrong on both counts . . . you didn't choose it. It was forced on you. But I believe you always made the best of it, when you could. William told me something Nat Tarlton said to him, that three years ago you'd stopped smuggling brandy and started smuggling English spies into France." She added with a gentle drawl, "Of course, you would never tell me of this . . . it might reflect well on you. Eb Gable told me you'd more than once rescued one of your crewmen when they were in danger. I'm sure there are any number of admirable things you've done that you've never told anyone."

"I'm a bleeding saint," he muttered.

"Well, an unlikely one," she said, pleased by his small show of ire. "Still, you perform these noble, even selfless acts, and then dismiss them. As if you don't deserve any credit for your deeds. As though MacHeath is always in the minus column, no matter what he accomplishes or withstands."

"I wish you would get to the point," he said, keeping his face averted from her.

"I just said *withstands* . . . think on that word. I believe if someone asked me to describe you, I would say, 'He withstands a great deal.' Scorn and loss and pain. Betrayal and deceit." She shifted onto her knees before him, still clasping his hand. "Perhaps courage is not always measured by going out and fighting battles. Sometimes it means tolerating that which is intolerable, sustaining your honor when there is no honor around you . . . putting yourself at risk so that another will be safe. Withstanding, MacHeath . . . enduring their blows, even if you cry out, even if you scream out, but not letting them break you."

"They did break me!" he breathed raggedly, pushing away from her and leaping to his feet. "Don't you understand that? They snapped me like a piece of kindling. Good God, Alexa, you said yourself that you heard me scream. I shouldn't wonder if they heard me in Exeter."

"You don't sound very broken to me," she observed from her position on the floor. Her eyes danced wickedly up at him. "Maybe they just bent you a bit."

He reached down and dragged her to her feet, his good hand clamped hard on her shoulder while he shook her.

"You dare laugh at me?" he stormed. "You dare laugh in my face?"

"It's better than crying," she said evenly. "Stop lamenting, MacHeath. Life is too short." Her hands slid up to cradle his face, and she said gently, "We all have moments we'd like to erase. But think how many more there are that we want to cherish and preserve."

Unable to weather the stark uncertainty in his eyes, she tugged his head down to her shoulder and held it there, her fingers stroking soothingly over his hair.

"You used to be naive and full of foolish pronouncements," he murmured into her throat.

"And now?"

"Now you make sense a great deal of the time. It's unnerving."

She chuckled. "Shall I tell you about the thing I would like to erase from my past?"

"You mean Smelly Ned?"

"No," she chided him. "Something I did that I would wish undone."

"Tell me," he said, pulling back a little so that he could see her face.

"Well, first you must understand that money became my curse once I got to London. I saw there that Alexa Prescott was of less value to the world than her purse, and so I began to wither on the inside. I became sour and discontented with life . . . a grumbler of the first water. I wasted seven years of my life refusing to see the good around me, and only ever saw things that displeased me."

"We are a pretty pair," he muttered. "The cripple and the malcontent."

"We are neither of those things now, Simeon. That's the beauty of what's happened between us. We both found the spark that was missing. You have gotten past your fears and your loss, and I have found something to make me smile again."

"Being home?"

"Being with you."

"Oh." He was just starting to smile himself when the footman came into the room.

"Mr. Prescott will see you now, sir."

For an instant her eyes closed tight in frustration. This was dreadfully bad timing.

"Thank you for that, Alexa," MacHeath whispered as he set her away from him. He went to the doorway, where he lingered a moment. "Maybe someday I'll return the favor and give you the answers that you require."

"I don't recall asking for answers," she responded gently.

But she knew the questions were in her eyes, all of them beseeching him, and she knew, further, he was not unaware of them. He started to say something, but curbed himself.

And then he pushed roughly away from the door; he recrossed the room in a heartbeat and dragged her into his arms. She moaned softly when he kissed her, a brief but surprisingly thorough kiss.

"Such a spark, Alexa," he said hoarsely, up against her ear.

And then he went striding out, right past the astonished footman.

*   *   *

Alexander Prescott greeted his entry with a nod. And then went back to sorting through the papers on his desk. It was not rudeness, MacHeath realized—the man was nervous as a cat on a griddle. His fingers shook enough to be detectable, and his gaze never once crossed the desk to where MacHeath sat after that first, curt acknowledgment.

"So?" MacHeath asked at last, feeling an edgy gnawing begin in the pit of his own stomach. He wanted to say his piece quickly, and then get away. That brief, heady taste of Alexa had shaken him, and the longer he sat here, the harder it would be to resist the urge to taste her again.

"So," Prescott echoed as he set down his papers. "If you've come to hear a formal apology, consider it spoken, and from the heart, I might add. However, there are other things I could offer you, to make restitution—"

"You don't owe me more than an apology," he stated flatly. "It was all I came back for, originally. But now I find I still have some unfinished business with you. There is the matter of Alexa."

"I see you still don't shilly-shally. I always liked that about you, Hastings . . . er, MacHeath." He shot him a look of apology. "My girl tells me you prefer that name. So out with it, then. What about Alexa?"

The old man wore a smug expression, as though he knew beforehand what MacHeath's business was.

"She needs to be here, with you, sir. Not off in London wasting herself on idle people and pointless occupations."

Prescott's brow knotted, and one hand began to tap on the surface of his desk. "Forgive my confusion . . . I suspected you wanted to speak to me of her future, but this is hardly what I envisioned."

MacHeath slid forward in his chair. "Her future is here, at Prescott Shipyard. It was her life for seventeen years, it's where she belongs now. And don't hand me some trumped-up objection because she is female. We both know she could run this place better than any man . . . it's in her blood. You're a fool if you don't see the potential in her. You raised her to be your heir, so why not let her take her place, then, as is fitting?"

Prescott made no comment at first. He rose and went to the sideboard, where he poured them each a glass of wine.

"Well, you don't mince words, do you?" he said once he'd resumed his seat behind the desk. "I've a mind to call you an interfering jackanapes, but I don't fancy a bout of fisticuffs. I will think on what you've said . . . Lord knows the girl's been bringing it up time out of mind. But what of your own future, MacHeath? What will you do, now that you are a free man again?"

"That's not the issue here."

"Then, you have made no plans? Well, I'm not surprised . . . only yesterday you were a fugitive from justice. But now the world has turned about for you. Would it be rash for me to offer you a job here at Prescott? Something, say, with a bit more responsibility than your previous position. I could use a good right-hand man."

MacHeath's eyes flashed up at him, and then he shook his head. "I want no favors . . . for myself. All I ask is that you keep Alexa here."

"Still got that proud, stubborn Scottish streak, eh? It's a wonder you and Alexa didn't butt heads constantly during your journey here."

MacHeath's face relaxed for an instant, and he almost smiled. "There were . . . um, occasional moments of conflict."

Prescott did smile, a wry crooked smile. "Ho, there speaks a diplomatic man."

"She set my coat on fire at one point, actually."

And then both of them were chuckling, MacHeath shaking his head in amused recollection, Prescott grinning back at him.

"Stay, lad," he said with sudden intensity, the humor in his eyes now replaced by earnest appeal. "I have need of you. We both have need of you. Stay here in Cudbright." He hesitated, and then added in a gruff whisper, "Please."

Well, that's it, MacHeath thought. *Full circle.* He'd been carted away in disgrace, deprived of everything he held dear, only to return a hero . . . with old Prescott himself begging him to stay on.

"I had a feeling this was how the wind was blowing," he said at last. "And I am not ungrateful. But I cannot accept your offer. I cannot stay here. Cudbright, the shipyard"—he'd almost added Alexa—"they remind me too keenly of all I lost."

"What was lost can sometimes be regained," Prescott pronounced. He rose from behind his desk, leaning his splayed hands on the gleaming surface. "I've made you an honest offer, not out of guilt, but out of my own need. I value you, lad. Damn it, I'd have taken you back the instant you were cleared of those charges—"

"Ah, but what if I hadn't been cleared? Would you have stood by me, found me a clever lawyer, kept me from the noose? Or would you have washed your hands of that proud, stubborn Scot? Good God, Prescott, you never even came to see me in Exeter. Never came to ask me my side of the story. I was a condemned man the instant Quincy pointed a finger at me. I saw then what it truly meant to have nothing . . . no friends, no allies, no one who believes in you."

"Alexa believed in you . . ." Prescott injected. "But she was a child of fourteen, I did not heed her. I was too shaken, my feelings over your betrayal were too raw. Perhaps if my admiration for you had not been so great, my shock and disappointment would not have been so extreme. For a time those feelings blinded me to any possibility of your innocence. Then, when you escaped, I saw it as proof positive that you were guilty. I see now how naive I was to think that."

"Another trait that runs in your family," MacHeath said under his breath.

"Still, why would I have doubted Quincy, standing there with his head all bloodied, swearing to your guilt? He practically grew up in this house, MacHeath, I never thought he would steal from me."

"No, it was easier to think that I would."

"Devil take you! What else was I to believe?"

MacHeath cast him a long, potent look before he murmured intently, "You might have sided with one of your own, Alexander." He rose from his chair. "But it's water over the dam, as my old captain used to say. I didn't come here to fight with you or to make you feel remorse. My only issue was Alexa."

"Well, then, what of my girl?" he asked as he came around the desk. "You going to run off from her yet again? She's kept you in her heart all these years, but I should warn you, even obstinate Prescotts weary of the chase eventually."

"She'll find another man if you allow her to stay here," he said. "I suspect she was like a falcon in a cage in London, fretful and unhappy. But once she can spread her wings, once she's back in her own patch of sky, she'll soar again. You'll see, she'll have suitors lined up from here to Penzance."

"And that notion doesn't bother you?"

"Why should it?" MacHeath spoke the untruth with bold-faced calm. "I desire her happiness as much as you do."

Prescott shook his head. "You're a fool, MacHeath. And a dashed poor liar. But it's not my job to make you see the right of things. I suppose I could argue that you ruined the chit, haring over half the country with her. But the last thing I want for Lexie is an unwilling husband."

"When she meets the right man, it won't matter to him whether she's ruined or not. Not if he cares for her." He paused to take a steadying breath. "I'm going now. Tell her . . . tell her that—" He winced slightly, and a small tick throbbed twice in his cheek. He drew an oblong package from the pocket of his greatcoat and laid it on the desk. "Well, just give her this."

"You're not going to say good-bye to her?"

"We've said everything that needs to be said."

He crossed the room, and then turned at the door. "Please remember what I told you about your daughter, Prescott. She needs that patch of sky . . . we all do."

And then with a swift nod of farewell, he went out.

Chapter 16

Alexa sat in the drawing room, trying to remain calm. Talking sense into MacHeath was always equal parts draining and agitating. She vowed that this was the very last time she would be forced into this waiting business, this matter of sitting by, inert and fretful, while men made up their minds about her future. No, never again. Regardless of what transpired between her father and MacHeath, she made a solemn oath that she would never sit and wait, not for any man.

When an hour had passed and there was still no sign of MacHeath, she went down the long hall to the study and tried the door. Her father was alone, sitting behind his desk with his hands clasped before him, his gaze focused on those entwined fingers.

"He's gone," he said without looking up at her.

Alexa sank into one of the chairs and willed her heart to keep beating.

"I did not try to stop him. He seemed determined to follow his own course."

"What was it he wanted to discuss with you?" she asked, somehow forming the words in spite of the dry, constricting pain that was sealing her throat.

"Your future, Alexa. Your future here in Cudbright."

She nearly groaned. A week ago that would have been cause for celebration. Now she didn't care where she lived. Without MacHeath, life held nothing to tempt her.

"He was rather vocal on several points. He pinned my ears back, in fact. Told me you were wasted in London, that

I was a damned fool for not letting you come back here and help me. I nearly called him an interfering jackanapes and several other unflattering names, as well. Instead, we had a glass of claret together. I offered him his old job back, Alexa. I told him he could be my right hand—a poor choice of words, I now realize—but he turned me down. He said there was nothing for him here but bad memories. Which surprised me."

"I am not surprised," she said with a sigh. "He warned me that he wouldn't be fodder for my daydreams any longer." She managed to give him a tight smile.

"Here," he said, pointing to the package on the desk. "He left this for you."

She rose and, with fingers benumbed by shock, undid the paper wrapping.

It was MacHeath's spyglass. The copper casing had been polished to a bright sheen that was achingly reminiscent of the hidden, fiery streaks in his hair. There was a note among the discarded paper. She picked it up and read the words with a quaking heart. The message was but a single line. *So the sea will never again be out of view.*

He hadn't even signed it.

Oh, and which name would he have used? she asked herself wretchedly. He'd acquired so many names . . . Simeon Hastings, Madman MacHeath, Mackie the Cripple, even Mr. Broadbeam. He'd lived so many lives, and she didn't care about any of them, only the life that he now ultimately refused to share with her.

With awful care she set the glass down on the desk, and then began to gather up the wrapping paper.

"Well, my girl, you're taking this like a fine little soldier. I thought it would be all tears and swooning and calling for the smelling salts."

She looked at him and shrugged. "You know me, Father. I never cry."

Then her face crumpled, and she let out a long, shivery sob. "Oh, Papa . . ."

Prescott moved from behind his desk like a shot. He held

Alexa in his arms in the next instant. "There, my sweetheart.
I know . . ."

"He was so . . . I was . . ."

"I know," he murmured. "Why the devil do you think I
offered him a place? I could see it in your face, Lexie. The
same look I saw in your mama's dear face for thirty years,
whenever she looked at me. But you can't force a man into
anything. He's changed a great deal from the willing lad he
once was. . . . Not that I was disappointed in him, mind. He
never backed down from me an inch, and you know I always
admire that kind of grit."

Alexa tried to rally herself while he delivered this dis-
jointed, rambling speech. For all she knew, that was exactly
why he was doing it. Finally, she managed to stifle the last
of her sobs. She blotted her eyes with her father's substantial handkerchief and rubbed her chin on his shoulder.

"Thank you, Papa. I've missed being cosseted, and I've
especially missed being hugged."

He tightened his hold on her and set a firm kiss on her
forehead. "So have I, Lexie. Indeed I have."

Her birthday dawned to bleak skies. The air was laden
with moisture, and a dense fog hovered over the river, sending exploratory fingers up into the village. Prescott came
home from the shipyard for his luncheon and seemed determined to inject some humor into the meal. Alexa smiled
wanly at his sallies as she picked at her salmon.

"I'd like you to come down to the shipyard with me after
lunch," he said at one point. "No time like the present to get
you started."

Her gaze darted up from her plate. "But you never
said . . . you never agreed—"

"Indeed I did. I promised MacHeath I would find you
something worthwhile to occupy your time besides wither-
ing on the vine in London. I thought you understood."

"Papa . . . how is it that for seven years you disregarded
my pleas to come home, and then in one short session
MacHeath managed to convince you?"

He shrugged. "The man's a dashed fine advocate, Lex."

His voice softened. "And he told me how bitterly unhappy you were . . . like a falcon in a cage, he said. I am ashamed to say that I never took your requests seriously. I couldn't imagine that you weren't having a splendid time in London. I thought you only brought up coming home to bedevil me, because there's nothing you like as much as a good brangle."

"You thought I was just being contrary? Oh, Papa, I was never more earnest in my life."

"So I comprehend." He rose and held out his hand. "And now we'd better get to work. I've just gotten a commission for a sailing yacht from the Earl of Stovings—"

"But you don't build yachts—"

"I will be building them now. In fact, I'm thinking of putting together a special team of designers."

As Alexa and her father walked beneath the wrought-iron arch that led to the shipyard, she couldn't help but notice a workman on a ladder. He was applying a coat of dark blue paint to the metal sign that hung above their heads. Her father made no comment, so she swallowed her curiosity and followed him into the brick building where his offices were situated. He settled her at a desk in a small room on the ground floor.

"There are some invoices I'd like to go over with you, so you can get an idea of who supplies us with materials." He patted his coat pockets and muttered, "Drat, I seem to have left my reading glasses upstairs in the workroom."

"I'll fetch them," she said.

"Yes, you do that."

As she went up to the first floor, the sound of the creaking stairs was music to her ears. She had been up and down them so many times, she knew exactly where the loose boards lay and which of the risers had been chipped along their edges. She recognized the seagull-shaped stain from the time she had dropped a bottle of India ink and used her pinafore to blot it up. These small things had not changed in seven years, and every one of them welcomed her back.

The designers' workroom held drafting tables for six men

set up at even intervals. It was usually a bustling place, but it was empty now; she assumed the men were off having lunch at the Mermaid. Her father's glasses were not on any of the worktables, and as she started toward his office, she realized there was something different about the room beside it. As far back as she could remember, it had been used as a storage space. But now it was furnished like the workroom, with a drafting table and a bank of flat files. Upright stands of drawing pens and pots of brushes lined the window ledge. A man she did not recognize was bent over the table, his upper body set in dark profile before the large window.

He looked up as she stepped into the room. "My father believes he left his—"

It took her several seconds to be sure of his identity, and another several seconds for her to remember to close her mouth.

He was attired in a coat of claret-colored Melton over a waistcoat of striped silk. Below this he wore black broadcloth breeches and a fine pair of boots. His neck cloth was snowy white, and his hair had been trimmed into stylish disarray. There was nothing of MacHeath here, nothing except the deep-brown hair and the silvery-brown eyes. And the fold of a shirtsleeve pinned neatly up at the end of his right arm.

"I'm sorry to surprise you like this," he said with a grimace. "But your father would have his little jest. I see what you mean about him being hard to withstand once he sets his mind on something."

"What are you doing here?" she asked in a parched voice.

"Working?"

"But he said you'd refused his offer. He said you'd gone away."

"Mmm. I sailed off to Nat's right enough."

"But apparently something has changed your mind. Were my father's terms too tempting to refuse? Is that why you came back?"

He growled softly, tugging at his crisp neck cloth while

his eyes reproached her. "You're going to be difficult, aren't you?"

"Why should I make things easy? You hurt me, you and your damned pride."

"Ah, yes . . . my damned pride." He shifted his gaze to the window, where a gray mass of clouds hovered close over the village. This was nothing more than he deserved—her anger, her scorn.

"But I'm all past that now," she added. "I am done with waiting for you." She gave a little toss of her head, to cement her lack of concern.

"It's only been five days, Alexa."

She sketched one hand in the air. "What does it matter, ten years . . . five days. The point is, I am finally over you."

"The devil you are!"

"It's true," she said. "If you wouldn't stay with me after I poured out my soul that day in the drawing room, if that wasn't enough to convince you that we belonged together, then there is no help for you. I say go on back to Nat Tarlton and good riddance."

"Nat doesn't want me," he said with a frown. "He all but parted my skull with a belaying pin for leaving you here."

"Good for him," she murmured.

He reached his hand toward her. "Don't turn me away without a fair hearing, Alexa. Not a second time."

"Then, tell me this . . . why did you leave? How could you just sail away?"

He looked down, and then shot her a wry glance through his brows. "Because I'm a boneheaded clot?"

"There is that," she said starchily, schooling herself not to smile. Her catechism was not yet finished. "But it's hardly an excuse."

"This is all new to me, Alex," he said haltingly. "Two weeks ago I couldn't imagine having these feelings, I barely felt anything at all. And now I am completely at the mercy of them, tossed like a ship in a gale. To use your own words, please spare me a little consideration."

"Go on . . ."

"After I left, I kept thinking about what you'd said. About

not having chosen my life. About cherishing the good things. And I thought about my stubborn pride. I'd always believed it was a good thing, being proud." He leaned toward her. "But I've since realized there are two kinds of pride . . . the kind that makes you stay on the right side of things, that helps you keep your head up. But *my* pride was a coiled snare that trapped me, that kept me from ever reaching out, from ever asking for anything or taking anything that was mine by right."

He paused and glanced at her, seeking some sign of weakening. Her chin was up, canted in judgment, but her eyes were focused on him, bright blue and unwavering.

"I felt such terror when I thought Finch was going to lop off my hand, it . . . it humbled me. All my false pride just shattered. And there was Quincy, baiting me, reminding me that I would never, ever get to touch you again. Something broke loose inside me then, Alexa." His words came faster now. "The thought of losing you for all time . . . God, there were so many things I wanted from you that I'd never dared ask for, because I felt so unworthy. But I saw in that moment that I could be as worthy as any man—if you were beside me. But then it was all being wrenched away. Whether Finch maimed me or killed me, I could never be with you."

He drew a breath and looked up, his eyes wide and earnest. "And that is why I screamed. From the agony of that loss . . . that the instant I realized what I wanted, beyond everything, all my options were gone."

"Then, I ask you again," she said in a low voice, "why did you sail away?"

"When I left here I thought I was doing the right thing. I still believed Finch had broken me. It wasn't until I got to Nat's that I realized the truth, that he'd really freed me." He fidgeted with a stick of charcoal. "I . . . I . . . Damn it, Alexa, I was barely out of the harbor when I started to call myself a blasted fool for leaving. But I kept on sailing. I had that, you see. I thought the sea would be enough. But heading back to Nat alone . . . it felt empty and pointless. I wanted you there with me, minding the tiller, trimming the sail."

She leaned back against the opened door. "You can always find someone else to go sailing with you, Simeon."

He flung the charcoal across the room, and then followed in its wake until he was standing before her. "Is that what you want? For me to go off and find some other infuriating hoyden to fall in love with, because I just might do—"

Alexa threw herself at him, tugging his mouth down, kissing him for all she was worth. Which was considerable. He caught her around the waist, pulling her right up against him until their bodies meshed. There was hunger in his kisses and in the unleashed strength of his arms. She arched into him, savoring his taste and his scent, the things she had missed so keenly and thought never to have again.

He was all smoky heat, as he coaxed her mouth open and let his tongue dance against hers. She responded with a drawn-out moan, feeling her insides clench as he pressed her into the door and probed her mouth even more deeply. Her fingers clutched at his shoulders, the rippling muscles shifting urgently under her palms as he drew her even harder against him.

Eventually he pulled back from her with a breathless groan. "I'd sail through hell for that, sweetheart," he murmured raggedly, "let alone across Lyme Bay."

This is the MacHeath I know, she sighed to herself. The old, dearly loved MacHeath, with mischief lurking in the wry twist of his cheek and heat simmering in his eyes.

Her own eyes flashed up at him. "Ah, but will you sail away again once you've had your fill of me?"

He gave her a swift grin. "I've only gone away but once, Alexa. The first time was not by choice, if you recall."

"Then, you're here to stay?"

His eyes narrowed. "I do have a few stipulations."

"Oh, here it comes . . . you don't want my money, you don't want my—"

"Hang your money," he growled softly, tightening his hold on her waist. "You are welcome to keep it. Though I might even help myself to a bit of it every now and then. Ned needs a cottage in Cornwall where the air is warm. And

I'd like to send something to Eb and his wife for helping us."

"And what about you . . . don't you want anything for yourself?"

"I want a ship, Alexa. But I'll earn that in time. I'm to be in charge of your father's new venture, designing sailing yachts for the gentry."

"So you'll have another *Siren Song*."

He shook his head. "No, I was thinking of calling this one the *Infuriating Hoyden*."

She laughed out loud. She'd missed his teasing as much as anything about him. Once she'd managed to contain her chuckles, she reminded him that he still hadn't told her his stipulations for staying.

He tipped her head back until their gazes met, and then set one finger on her mouth. "I want no more stolen interludes, no more stolen kisses. What I want from you I will take openly. Agreed?"

"Yes," she said as a little thrill shuddered through her. "So am I to be your kept woman?"

"You are." He lowered his head and angled his mouth over hers. "Kept in my heart," he murmured against her lips. "For all time."

She relaxed against him, savoring the slow, sweet kisses that he lavished on her like warm honey.

He raised his head and whispered gruffly, "Will ye have me, Alexa?"

She looked up at him, her eyes bright with joy. "Oh, Simeon," she murmured with a tiny throb in her voice, "you *finally* asked me. I've only been waiting thirteen years. Time was, I thought I'd have to have to clout you over the head and force you to marry me."

He shook his head in wonder at her bemused, awestruck tone. "*That* was infatuation," he reminded her.

"Oh, not anymore," she proclaimed boldly as she twisted her hands in his hair and tugged his head down, leaning up on tiptoes for better access to his mouth. He didn't require much coaxing, setting his mouth over hers, kissing her, caressing her, until she was nearly scalded by the fierce heat that radiated from his lean body.

When at last he shifted her back over his arm, his breathing was ragged, his eyes the color of jet. His dark gaze swept her, telling her without words what he felt. There was ardent need in that look and tenderness and something very much like relief.

He traced a fluttery kiss over her cheek. "This is for you, Alexa," he murmured silkily. She clung to him, waiting eagerly for him to once again claim her mouth.

Instead, he gave a low chuckle and slipped a small pouch into her hand.

She pushed back from him abruptly. "If that isn't the dirtiest trick, MacHeath! And to play it on me twice in one lifetime."

"Open it," he said with a puckish grin.

She rolled her eyes as she emptied the pouch into her hands. The jewelry he'd pawned for her, the ear bobs and her rings, lay scattered in her palm.

"I took the mail coach to Dagshott before I came here. Nat loaned me the money to redeem them."

She put the ear bobs into her pocket and slipped on her two rings. A third ring lay in her palm, a single, stunning sapphire set in gold. Her eyes widened.

He took it from her hand and held it up. "You still haven't said yes, Alexa," he teased, twirling it under her elegant nose. "I would appreciate it if for once in your life you gave in without an argument."

"But—"

"See," he said, as if to a heavenly jury. "It's never an easy road with this one."

She clutched the lapels of his fine coat and shook him. "Yes," she said. "Yes. Yes. Yes."

"You'll have me to husband, then, one-handed, beknighted fellow that I am?"

"Put the ring on my finger, Simeon," she muttered softly. "Before I change my mind."

He slipped it on, and then entwined his fingers with hers,

holding her fast. He was startled when a teardrop fell onto the back of his hand.

"Are you crying?"

"No," she said, swiping her sleeve across her cheek. "I never cry." She gave a little, hiccuping sob. "Never. But I'm so . . . It's so . . ."

"Come here, my shrew," he said gently as he tucked her against his side and raised up the hand that now bore his ring. "Do you like it? I wanted to match your eyes—I told the jeweler the stone had to be the color of the sea at dawn. He probably thought I was a bit daft."

"It's perfect," she said with what she hoped was her last sniffle. "I just can't believe Nat loaned you enough money for *this*."

"It wasn't Nat. And I didn't take to the High Toby, either, in case that's what you're thinking. I came by the money honestly enough—I sold my pistols in Exeter. They were a matched pair of Mantons and fairly valuable. I . . . I imagined I wouldn't be needing them any longer."

Her eyes grew instantly wistful. "Now you'll be the falcon in a cage, Simeon. This life will be so tame compared to what you had before."

"No, Alexa. Not at all. This is the life I want, it's what I was always meant to do."

"Are you sure, really sure?"

He turned her around and pointed to the drawing he'd been working on. "Look at this . . . it's a sketch for the first of my new ships. They'll be sleek and up-to-date, Lexie, and fast. Your father's looking into the new steam-powered ships, but I want no part of them. I'm a sailing man, you know. I can't give up the wind and the canvas." There was no arguing the enthusiasm in his voice. "I'll have her on the water by spring."

"I expect you will need another person to help you sail her," she remarked idly.

He hitched one shoulder. "As you said, I can always hire someone."

"The devil you will," she said with a grin as she set her

hands on his chest. "If I'm to be your mate, sir, it will be in *all* your endeavors."

He swung her around, so that she was bent back over the drafting table, and then he leaned into her, elbows propped on the wooden surface.

"Ah, no, it's not going to be tame," he said, his eyes bright with anticipation. "Not with you, Alexa. Promise me you won't ever stop beating against those walls. It's what I live for, watching you plunge in and take life by the throat."

She slid her arms around his neck. "And I live for that look in your eyes."

He cocked his head. "Which look is that?"

"The one that's there now." She nuzzled his cheek and sighed. "I love you, Simeon MacHeath Hastings . . . Broadbeam."

"And I love you, Alexandra Prescott," he said softly. "More than I ever thought possible." He traced his thumb gently over her cheek. "Though, speaking of names, there is something I ought to tell you."

He leaned down and whispered into her ear.

"No?" she said with a wide, delighted smile when he was finished. "You'd do that?"

"I already have," he said with a grin. "Come and see."

William and Henry stood under the iron archway, heads canted back as they watched the painter obscure the sign overhead with a new coat of blue enamel. Henry now carried his left arm in a sling, but his expression was merry. Out of gratitude for their devoted service, Prescott had relieved him and his uncle from their duties as coachmen and put them in charge of security at the shipyard. Not Bow Street, exactly, but close enough.

Prescott himself came out of the building and walked up beside them.

"Change is in the wind, my friends," he said. He squinted back at the window of MacHeath's new office, and hoped his eyes were not playing tricks on him. His wayward daughter and her champion appeared to be waving at him through the glass.

Sweet Lord, he hoped they'd make a match of it. Let MacHeath have the ordering of her for a change. She was a handful for any man, let alone one who was nearing seventy. But MacHeath had always been able to keep her distracted, and once there were babies on the way. . . .

Prescott grinned to himself. Maybe he'd have better luck handling *their* children—provided they were all boys.

"So what is the new sign going to say?" Henry asked, interrupting his pleasant musings.

"Prescott, Prescott and Prescott," he replied.

"Three of them?" William and Henry said in unison.

The sign painter looked down at the sheet of paper tacked to his ladder and read aloud, "Alexander Charles Prescott, Alexandra Prescott and Simeon MacHeath Prescott."

"He's taking your name, sir?" William exclaimed, puzzlement creasing his ruddy face. "I always thought MacHeath was too proud to take a groat from his granny."

Prescott shrugged. "He says it's an old Scots custom—that when a man marries into a more powerful clan than his own, he takes their name as a sign of respect. He told me that next to Alexa's hand, my family name was the best gift I could bestow on him."

William digested this, and then turned to Henry with a broad wink and whispered, "Guess no one ever told the lad about Smelly Ned the cockle monger."